Mary J's
COMMUNITY

LIVING OUT YOUR DREAM

SECOND EDITION

CLYDE EDMOND FISHER

Publisher: Clyde Edmond Fisher
Email: clydefisher53@yahoo.com /clydefisher53@gmail.com
ISBN: 978-1-952182-22-8
eISBN: 978-1-952182-23-5

CONTENTS

CHARACTERS

- Mary J: Main character
- Pap Fisher: Mary J's husband
- Alma Tucker: Pap's sister—One Mary J closest friend
- Fred Fisher: Pap's brother
- Pap's nephews and niece: Phillip, Samuel, Henderson, Della Jane
- Solomon and Susan Lennie: Pap's Grandparents
- Grandma Mag: Mary J's Grandmother—Raised Mary J and her siblings after Parent's death
- Mag Children: Charlie; John Wesley; Annie
- Mary J's Aunt Annie three children: James miller, Annie May, and Clarence
- Mary J's Siblings: Showalter, Ella, James Westley, Lucy Gray, Alvin, Margret Ann, Willie Welt, Lorraine
- Salland—Mag's sister
- Zack—Salland son in law—Mary J first cousin on her Mother side
- Ovine: Zack's wife—Mary J's first cousin on her father side
- Ada—Mary J Mother
- John Westley—Mary J's Dad
- Showalter—Mary J's oldest brother
- Ella—Oldest living sister
- James Westley—Mary J's brother
- Lucy Gray—Mary J's sister
- Alvin: Mary J's brother
- Margret Ann—Mary J's sister
- Alvin—Mary J's brother
- Willie—Mary J's Brother

- Larraine—Mary J's youngest sister
- Luke: Community Businessman
- Eunice Carter: Luke's wife
- Walter Dennis: Luke's son
- Ovine—Zack Wife and Salland's daughter
- Chloe: Charlie's wife
- Bertha Ray—Zack and Ovine Daughter
- Odessa: Pap's outside child
- Elise May: Pap and Mary J's Oldest daughter
- Dora Lee: Pap and Mary J's daughter next to Elsie
- Buddy: Pap and Mary J's oldest son
- Pastor White: Mary J's childhood Pastor
- Plump: Friend from the community
- Eli: Friend from the community
- Oscar: Owner of a funeral home

STORYLINE

Although some scenes and characters have been fictionalized for dramatic purposes, this book is based on a true story. Mary J was a woman that grew up during the Great Depression years. She refused to be just another echo or imitator of someone else wondering in the wilderness of life. She had an intense desire to reach her God-given potential as an entrepreneur. By eleven years old, she had already decided to be a store owner. She felt this was her birthright as an American citizen. She did more than just entertained the thought; she acted upon it by the use of creative visualizations and affirmations. Although losing both parents during her childhood in the 1930s, she went on to be part of a thriving business community. Because of the bewildering impacts from the Great Depression years upon her community, she used her grocery store to help friends and neighbors fight their personal battles for survivor.

Chapter
1

MARY J'S CHILDHOOD

Mary J lived in a two-story house with a large front porch. The landscape incorporated two large oak trees, flower beds, fruit trees and a garden. Mary J's family included her Grandma Mag, Mother Ada, Daddy John Westley, along with eight sisters and brothers. Their birth order from the oldest to the youngest: Showalter, Ella, James Wesley, Mary J, Lucy Gray, Alvin, Margret Ann, Willie Welt, and Lorraine. Mary J's family lived upstairs—her Grandma Mag's room was downstairs—Showalter had already moved out to start his own family.

Before sunrise, Ada had awakened as usual to fix breakfast and her husband's lunchbox. She arose out of bed quietly as she noticed that her baby was sound asleep. Using a rotating schedule, it was Ella turn to be her assistant, Ada walked downstairs to the kitchen while Ella followed several minutes later. Ella was now nearly fifteen years old.

"Ella", said her mother, Ada, "We need to hurry this morning because your father will be coming down any minute. His lunch needs to be ready. Grab a jar of fruit out of the pantry for his desert."

"Yes, Mama," said Ella, "do you think apples or pears will be the best?"

"Ella, my little darling," said Ada, "don't worry—, just grab one."

Ada knew that her daughter Ella was always overly concerned about making mistakes. She supposed that it had begun to affect her self-confidence.

"Ok, Mama, I am on top of everything this morning," said Ella, beaming with her usual glorious smile.

Ada didn't want to overwhelm her daughter Ella with negative messages. She laid down her knife and then began focusing her attention on Ella—wanting to say something to boost her confidence. "Today Ella, I decided what you are going to be."

"Again?" said Ella, grinning at her mother.

"You need to become a nurse."

Ella giggled like a little girl. "Why, Mama? What made you think of a nurse? You got to be kidding me; I don't even like the sight of blood."

"That's useful work, my dear. You would be helping sick people."

Ella lowered her lashes to hide the delight in her eyes. "But that takes years of training and cost a great deal of money. All of your children want to be gospel singers, just like you. You sing in front of hundreds of people nearly every Sunday."

"Yes," said Ada, "but the freedom to plan your life doesn't mean that everything will be easy for you. Our community itself is a living laboratory to gain experience and education. The best equipment for education is that which encourages participation in one's local community. Your sister Mary J has a dream; maybe you should have your own dream."

"You mean like Mary J?"

"Yes," said Ada, "be controlled by an unrest that urges you to rise above your circumstances. Progress doesn't mean there can never be any setbacks. A self-motivated person is one who has learned to use their God-given potential."

"You right, Mama, the preacher said that God has filled the heavens with stars without number."

"Now let's finish up our work, before one of my headaches hit me."

Snappishly awakened from the noise coming out of the kitchen, Mag gradually got out of bed. She strolled onto the side porch with a pan in her hand for bathwater. After missing her apron, she placed the container near the water pump. She then walked through the side door that led into the kitchen. She found a fresh apron hanging on a nail right at the kitchen entrance. Mag always had two aprons—one for wearing around the house and another for going out to visit.

Ella stuck her head through the kitchen entrance. "Good morning Grandma, could I do something for you?"

"No, my little sweetheart, you just be a respectable young lady and help out your mother, just like you are doing right now."

"Oh, Now, Mother Mag," said Ada, "You don't need to be concerned about me, just tell Ella to pump that water for you, so that you can wash up for breakfast."

"Ada, I know what to do, let's Mary J come down here to help, she is big enough." Mag moved closer to the staircase then hollered out, "Mary J," please come downstairs to help us."

Ada neither frowned nor smiled but harmonized her voice with Mag into one strong command. "Mary J, you need to come downstairs right now."

Mary J walked out towards the edge of the staircase, still in her nightclothes. She reached for the stair rail, "I am only eleven years old; what can I do?"

"Here we go again," Mag said, halting. "We will show you, young lady. Since you always like to boss all the other children around, it's best that you know more about things. We will show you how to be a good worker, just like your sister."

Mary J shouted, "Yes, ma'am." She quickly ran downstairs towards the side door that led to the kitchen. "I have two mamas, which means I should be smarter than the rest of these little brats. Look… at all the children we have running around here! Mamma Ada, you have nine children; Uncle Charlie next door, he has eleven children; Mr. Zack and Ovine have three children. Maybe if we look hard enough, we might find eight to ten more children around here. Who can keep up with this gang? I tell you, Mama, someone needs to keep these children on the right path, just like Daddy teaches us in Sunday school."

Ada shook her head. "Before you can teach others, you must learn what to do. You are going to work with me in the garden. Ella can help Mag in the house."

Mag swallowed hard. Keeping her face blank, "Mary J! You heard your Mama, so come eat some hot fruit, biscuits, and molasses before going into the garden."

"Yes, Ma'am," said Mary J, "I know Mama needs help because it is going to be hot out there today. But don't forget, Daddy built me a playhouse—Rosie lee is going to play the storekeeper's game with me today. Also, Mama, please take me to Aunt Loretta's store this week, so that I can help her in a real store. Someday, I know the Lord is going to bless me to own a great big family store. All of my children and husband will work together in our own little business."

"Mary J," said Mag, "that's the spirit young lady, you are going to be a credit to the human race someday with that attitude."

John Wesley came rushing downstairs to get his lunchbox.

"Good morning Daddy," screamed Mary J and Ella as they were eating their breakfast.

"Good morning, everyone," said John Westley as he pinched Ella on her cheeks, then picked up Mary J and gave her a little kiss on the right cheek.

"Mary J," said her Daddy, "I have finished your little playhouse outside, so be good and help out, then you can play with Rosie Lee in the back yard."

Mary J set her hands on her hips, then glared up at him. "You don't have to worry about the playhouse, you put the right person in charge, me! We are going to get some leaves so we can make Zack and Ovine some collard greens and clay dumplings. Then maybe, we will also stew them a chicken!"

For a moment, John Wesley stopped, looking at her with strange glitter in his eyes. "Please don't play with those yard chickens and provoke that old red rooster, he may attack you. Although you intend no harm, you must understand that in his eyes, you are a big threat. He may decide to bite you." Then, he tickles Mary J; she giggled over and over. He gave her another big hug.

"Daddy," said Mary J, "I am not scared of that ugly red rooster. I will deal with him by grabbing his head. After that, he will know who the boss."

John Wesley laughed at Mary J's comments, then said goodbye to everybody. He picked up his lunch bucket, then headed towards the door. Ada walked her husband outside to discuss some needed items for the family veggie garden and her flower beds. John Wesley gave Ada a big hug and assured her that he would try to get those items. Ada would be 38 on her next birthday; John Westley being two years her senior, was now

40 years old. The year was 1930, and times were tight for everyone. Ada needed to maintain the garden and fruit trees for survival reasons.

Unexpectedly, the children began waking up, running all over the place, Mag was forced to put order back into the house. The baby, Lorraine, was also now waking up. She was upstairs in the crib. Mary J wanted to go upstairs and pick her up—Ada wouldn't allow it, thinking that she might hurt her. Mary J loved little Lorraine and figured that she was the best one to look after her. Everyone knew that Lorraine was a good baby. She would always sleep through the night. After going upstairs, Ada brought baby Lorraine downstairs, then allowed Mary J to hold her.

"Oh, Mama Ada," said Mary J, "she's just as sweet as sugar."

Ada mouth twisted into a little smile. "Mary J, please be quiet so she can go back to sleep; then we are going to work for a while in the garden and flower beds."

Lorraine closed her tiny eyes and pressed her fingers over her eyelids. She went immediately back to sleep after receiving her milk.

Ada said, "Lorraine is sleeping. Now Ella, please take her back upstairs for me—come on Mary J, let's go to work in the flower beds and veggie garden."

Mary J whispered to her mother very slowly, "ok, but maybe we can bring some of the other children."

Ada stared confidently at her with a half-smile. "Get dressed; you're coming with me."

Chapter

2

GARDENING WITH MOTHER ADA

da took Mary J by the hand. They went outside to start working in the veggie garden and flower beds. "Mary J," said Ada, "there are some things you need to know about taking care of plants, flowers, and fruit trees. You must develop your mind's eye to see hidden things that are interacting together in different ways. Common sense is your most valuable guide in watering plants."

Mary J was leaning against a massive oak. "What's that, Mama?"

"Ada leaped to answer it. "Plants have roots, stems, and leaves. They are mostly concerned with getting and storing food. A growing plant absorbs large quantities of water from the earth. This process allows leaves to begin their development in the plant's buds. But remember, dry soil is a good indicator that watering is necessary. You don't want to wash away the dirt; you must apply the water gradually so it can penetrate the soil. On the other hand, roots standing in waterlogged soil is likely to rot and kill your plants. Just take a quick walk around your plants; you will see many opportunities to make improvements."

Mary J stared at her Mother Ada, somewhat surprised that plants were so important to her. The why behind the how didn't interest her too much. "But mama," Mary J swallowed nervously. "I got it. Plants need water."

Ada smiled and said, "Well, well, well. You are a smart young lady."

Mary J continued to express her point of view. "You don't have to worry. Just look at these pears; they are meltingly soft, sweet, and juicy straight from our trees. I picked these pears at the perfect moment. I also know how to keep a watchful eye out for insects and hunting birds. They will make our plants sick—Look, Mama, I am going to pick these blackberries for our pie tonight. We have no time for laziness."

Mary J was in motion, flying over here and over there, with an innocent playfulness. She was continually imitating her Mother by singing to herself—softer and softer, especially when she moved around in a somewhat circular motion. Mary J was creating her own intellectual experiences and challenges as if she was enjoying her time and memories in self-discovery.

Ada raised her eyebrows and tightened her lips. "Well, Mary J, I am counting on you helping me have a good garden this year. The drive for success has its cost: hard work!"

Mary J stared directly into her mother's eyes as her enchanting smile flickered. She began speaking in a deep tone of voice, tiptoeing slowly towards her. "Sure! But there are still some people like Grandma that don't feel they're doing right by their plants, unless they're doing something to them. Mama, I thought to myself, what a strange person my Grandma is."

Ada stood there for a moment with dropped jaws—hands on her hips, somewhat undecided on whether or not to correct her. To Ada's way of thinking, trust was essential for a relationship to grow and develop. She felt that Mary J needed to know more about her Grandma's past to appreciate the reality of her.

Ada placed both hands on Mary J's shoulders. "Now listen… come on, let's sit down on the garden-swing and rest, while I tell you somethings about your Grandma's life journey. She was born in 1863 during the American Civil War. This war was a bloody battle that tore our country apart for four miserable years. A horrible war that twisted brother against brother, killing thousands of people. Additionally, families were witnessing the destruction of their homes and landholdings. People became so weak that they could scarcely make their way around. Poverty prevented them from doing normal activities.

"After the Civil War, Davis Island was lost by the Davis family, so Mag's parents, Benjamin and Sarah Davis, along with their seven children moved into Davis Shore. Mag, as a little girl like you, could observe the battleground between the sea and the land. From studying the interactions between the sea and land, she learned how to be reliable—to see possibilities when others saw none—seized opportunity when others hesitated—keep at it when others gave up.

"Your Grandma Mag was married to John Kit in 1881; to this union, there were three children: Annie May, Charlie Edward, and your daddy John Westley. "After a major hurricane that packed powerful winds... most people, including your grandma and grandpa, moved away from Davis Shore. They moved here and built this house. As you know already about your grandma, she is a little short fussy woman—just like you. You should be very proud of her. So, whenever you feel down and out—find life hard to bear—just think about her past struggles.

"Despite the dark times in my life, your grandma always inspires me to sing around here with energy and joyousness. She used to tell me about her Baptist church on Davis shore; wherein, both the blacks and whites attended together. Most of the people had to walk two or three miles through heat, marsh, and mosquitoes to attend their services. The Black people were called upon to sing every Sunday evening. If you didn't get there early, you wouldn't find a seat. She makes me see the many possibilities for my singing. She makes me feel like the whole world loves my singing."

Mary J thought over and over; when suddenly she notices plants with delightful green and white leaves. "Grandma is like these plants—strong with self-confidence."

"That's a girl," said Ada. "We must always stand on a hilltop looking down on times gone by. You will soon forget your family, if you don't understand their past struggles of life. This little story of your grandma will help you love and appreciate her."

"As I look from the hilltop," said Mary J, "I can see people of vision and energy discovering amazing possibilities and opportunities—just like Grandma and her family."

"Well!" said Ada, "now that's right; just let your grandma do things her way."

Mary J giggled: "Okay, Mama, but I do think we ought to plant a row of watermelons. They would be mighty nice to eat, especially while we are lying down on the grass during the summer."

Both laughed. "All right," Ada said. "We'll plant us a row of watermelons; so now, let's get back and help your Grandma. Remember, we need to wash our fruits and vegetables…shell some fresh peas as well as pick pin-feathers out of a chicken for our dinner."

Mary J answered quickly; she had been waiting for an opportunity to play. "Okay, Mama, just let me walk around the yard for a few minutes."

Unconsciously, Ada pressed her hand against her face and along her tightened throat. She was a little unsure what Mary J was planning to do in the yard, yet she permitted it just the same. "You go right ahead while I get everything set up properly."

Everyone could hear Ada singing as she went around the house for a bucket of water to clean the fruits and vegetables. Her voice was deep and rich…moving beyond her home, spreading throughout the pond basin and up the hill. A person could quickly get the impression that her voice circled the entire community. Her husband's brother, Charlie, came out on his front porch and shouted out teasingly: "Cut out that noise."

Ada had begun to demonstrate her feelings by utilizing many gestures— by the tone of her voice, a turning down of the lips, a contemptuous flick of the hand, a half closing of the eyes. Like always, she just kept right on singing without ever missing a note.

Mary J skipped swiftly down the yard path that was lined with flowers, down the sagging steps. She leaped from the wooden walk and crouched right over a ditch. Nothing was moving along the dusty road, but the wind shaking the grass and trees. Something pressed against the ball of her foot. She shifted backward and glanced down at the offending pebble.

Mary J spotted her brother James Westley. He was sitting on the edge of the ditch, waiting for his Cousin Monroe. Unexpectedly, some ants crawled from their nest and began biting his ankles. He started rubbing his feet along the ground; the dust made a satisfying surface to tackle the itch.

Monroe came out of his house with a puffy hat sitting upon his head. He had on high-buttoned shoes darting from under his pant legs. Monroe and James Westley loved beautiful clothes, especially when hunting girls. They climbed the ditch bank and went into the backyard, near the big iron pot propped on stones. They sat down on the old hickory chairs leaning against the house, under a thin line of shade that the mounting sun ate away. Monroe whispered something to James Westley that caused his mouth to be pressed together like a wild fox.

Mary J looked and looked and looked at them with her fast-moving eyes, as though there wasn't enough time. She dashed over to them. "Monroe, don't get my brother James Westley into any trouble. I will certainly tell Uncle Charlie, your daddy, the whole truth."

Monroe glanced up, startled, he then spoke up in his usual soft voice. "You better go into the house with Granny and your mother. You need to learn to keep your opinions to yourself."

James Westley, squeezing out one of his funny laughs, "Mary J, you need to quit minding everybody else business. Granny and Mamma are just spoiling you."

"For God's sake," Mary J said. "What difference does it make? Do you really Care?

James Westley was clenching his teeth. "Yes! Yes! You need to wash your mouth out with soap...do not like the sound of it myself." He gave Monroe a high five and let out another squeezing laugh.

Mary J put her hands to her head in a dramatic gesture of despair. "You need help, my brother! Monroe is going to trick you out of all your stuff. He has an evil spirit in him."

Monroe began winking his eyes wickedly at James Westley. "Yes, I believe in the spirit of thunder that causes lightning. If you keep messing with me, that spirit is going to get you. When you see lightning traveling from one part of a cloud to another, then from the cloud to the air, you better be aware of evil spirits lurking near your house."

James Westley coughed to mask his laughter. Then he cleared his throat. "Now, Monroe, do not frighten my little sister. She will be scare of thundering and lightning the rest of her life."

Mary J raised her eyebrows and tightened her lips. "Do you see what I mean, Brother? Monroe, with his easy-going ways and soft voice, always sounding like an angel of light in dark places. But in reality, he works for the devil. You are going to end up just like him. Just running from woman to woman with no loving family around you. I am just a child and got more sense than both of all of you put together."

James Westley's heart soared into his throat. "Great balls of fire! Now, little sister, you do not need to be so mean."

Monroe rocked back and forth, laughing with delight. "Listen to me; Mary J. We can work this out. These are troublesome times. When you get rich with your little play store, give me some of your food and money."

"Wait! Have you gone out of your senses? What is the matter with you, you—big—big—idiot," said Mary J with a quarreling voice. "You aren't going to sweet talk me like you do, James Westley. He is your fool, not me."

"Yes-mam," Monroe uttered with a startled, doubtful laugh. "I was hoping that you and I could get along little cousin. Only if you would just quit meddling in our business—stop trying to control everybody's life. You aren't the boss of everything around here."

Mary J started laughing. "All-right, now mister big shot; here comes your daddy."

As Charlie slowly approaches the boys, his heart sank even lower, seeing them sitting around doing nothing. "What's the devil going on around here? You boys need to be working at something to make money."

Mary J clapped her hands with delight: "Oh, my Uncle Charlie! Oh, my... what a good idea! Please get these bums and hobos out of here. Who in the world needs lazy men hanging around the house?"

"Mary J," said Charlie, "you get on up to your house before I call your mother out here."

Mary J flashed her tongue out with hands waving from each ear in the direction of Monroe. Then, she ran toward the house, screaming for her mother and grandma with her throat clog with tears. "Monroe said the spirit of thundering and lightning is going to get me!"

Her Mother and grandma stopped everything they were doing and sat down to talk with her. Ada said. "We don't need to waste any more time with this; you have been raised in the church and should know better than to believe Monroe's lies."

At the same time, Mag became very upset. "I am going to tie Monroe up to my bedpost if he keeps telling you this type of foolishness."

"You just wait till your Daddy comes home tonight," said Ada. "He is going to talk to your Uncle Charlie about his son Monroe trying to frighten my little girl. Come on over here and give mama a great big hug!"

Mag voice was as quiet and peaceful as winter rain dripping over a bedroom window. Her softness was like an angel of light. But in times of trouble, she spoke like a true lady. "Remember Mary J," said Mag, "you must not dry up your compassion for your Uncle Charlie's children. All of you are my grandchildren. We must have a neighborly spirit with each other. It's difficult sometimes to be kindhearted to those who are being mean to you. Especially with your cousin Monroe, his shady ways of working out deals may be misleading in spirit and truth. On the other hand, we must never have the attitude of crossing over to the other side of the road with family."

For Mary J, this sounded too easy and simple. In her mind, things didn't always turn out so good when it came to Monroe and James Westley. She shook her head, then shook it again. "But Grandma, Cousin Monroe always cheats James Westley out of his things, including his little bit of money. Always telling him, grinning with a soft voice: 'We are going to work it out'"

Ada turned to Mary J, smiling, placing both hands on her shoulders. She looked directly into her eyes: "Where is your proof?"

Mary J glimpsed up at her mother, somewhat shocked by her compromising question. "Our Cousin Monroe is strange. I tell you; I don't know what's going to become of him. But now your son James Westley, he has a different problem. He's just plain headstrong and won't listen to reason."

"Now young lady," said Mag. "We must not harden our hearts and distance ourselves from our family. We cannot do these things and receive God's blessings."

"Your Grandma is right," said Ada. "God can change your Cousin Monroe's tricky behavior."

Mag straightened her shoulders and lifted her chin. "My little Mary J, the best way to survive and enjoy life is to put things into a proper perspective. The greatest show on earth is the starry night sky. Throughout the day, you cannot see the stars, but they are still there. Don't listen to

Monroe; there is no evil spirit coming out of the clouds to attack you during a thunderstorm."

Ada patted Mary J's head, "Monroe is just full of hocus-pocus. You don't need to worry about cunning people and ghost stories. James Westley and Monroe are always together. They will find a way to help each other. You must pray for them."

There was a moment of silence, then a voice spoke from the far end of the house. James Westley flung open the door. "What going on here?"

Unconsciously, Ada pressed her hand against her face and along her tightened throat. She hid her smile. "Mary J thinks it's unfair the way Monroe tricks you out of your stuff."

James Westley slowly removed his cap. He held it in his hands, then looked at his mother and said, "It hurt me so bad that my little sister would talk about our cousin Monroe with such disrespect. She needs to mind her own business."

Mary J jumped up into James Westley's face, then put her hands on her hips and rocked back and forth. Suddenly, she began grinning and shaking her head elaborately—with a finger in his face. "Monroe is too clever for you, my big brother. There's a deceitful streak running clear through him. By the way, your name is not Pretty boy, but Pretty stupid."

James Westley stood before them, expressionless, waiting to hedge a little from all the laughter in the room. He could think of nothing else to say. The whole thing didn't make any sense to him. He knew there was no way to win this argument. Reluctant to question the finger-pointing, he hurried back outside.

Monroe was waiting for him as he walked on the porch. "Come on, let's go down the street and have some fun."

Suddenly, James Westley had a flutter at the pit of his stomach and a sour taste at the root of his tongue. His heart sank even lower after seeing a grin on Monroe's face. "I don't feel like it today. Mary J makes us look bad."

"Look now, Cousin," said Monroe. "It hurts me so bad when you are sad. We always do everything together. I remember us drawing pictures together before you could walk and talk. I have your back; we are going to party tonight, yeah!"

"How?" said James Westley.

"Cousin, you got any money?"

"Just a small change."

"Well," said Monroe, "that's all we need. I can arrange the rest for us. Just Maybe, we can make a little money over at Tom Bell."

"Are you crazy, going down to the whiskey house? Both Mama and Grandma would have a fit. Then, they will say that Mary J is right about us."

Monroe patted his hand... being somewhat suspicious. "Now James Westley, this is different, Mary J is just a little girl with a big imagination. Why don't you look at this through her mind's eye? She goes over to Loretta's place, thinking that someday she is going to own a big store and house. Who cares? She is just a daydreamer. Who knows the right course or outcome of any dream? Come on now, if you got your little bit of money in your pocket, let's get out of here. Maybe something good will happen to perk you up."

"Okay, cousin, you're right as usual."

James Westley went back into the house, then upstairs and got his money. On his way out, Mary J shouted at him. When he didn't answer, she followed him out of the door onto the porch. Suddenly, she saw Monroe there waiting for him.

Mary J hollered out to Monroe. "Hey, Money, who's the trick on today?" She paused for a few seconds, "My stupid and dumb brother?"

Monroe looked into Mary J's steady eyes for a few seconds. Then quickly, he and James Westley walked fast towards a small path that led through a wooded area behind the house.

Expressing faith in Mary J, James Westley stuck his chest out with a sense of pride. "You must say, my little sister is pretty smart for her age. When she grows up. I am going to let her take care of all my money."

Monroe drew in a deep breath, and his face changed. Unexpectedly, he saw the real James Westley, the one who wasn't acting. Monroe quickly said: "Okay, I got it; that's the only way you'll probably have anything. Anyway, that doesn't matter now, let's go to Tom Bell and have some fun."

Chapter

3

FAMILY SINGING TOGETHER

everal weeks later, on a Friday morning, a heavyweight played upon Mary J's mind as she worked in the garden with her Mother. The rudderless rainstorm that had swept the region several days before had now blown itself out. The weather had improved considerably—the sun even going so far as to put on a half-hearted appearance—Mary J's community laid bathing in yellow sunlight once again.

Mary J made a suggestion, "Mama after, supper, let's bring the whole family together so we can sing songs. It's Friday! Let's have a good time. We can hear Showalter play the piano and his guitar. You can sing, and the rest of us may act like your choir. Your singing is mind-boggling."

Ada started breathing a humorless laugh when she suddenly thought of the various possibilities. She embraced her daughter. "Oh, for heaven's sake, it's a great idea; you can be the organizer."

Mary J turned towards her Mother and screamed without a sound. Her mind jolted into action; it began swirling up, up to real possibilities. Mary J was determined to be warm and inviting to everyone as the organizer. She refused to manage this program by her narrow self-interest. She wanted everybody to participate in singing activities. Her Grandmother told her that she could always: 'catch more flies with honey than with vinegar.'

"Now, Mama," said Mary J, "I want you to sing like a songbird as you do at church. Our neighbors will come to hear you sing, just pretend you are washing clothes or taking care of our garden. These people will come out onto their front porches, just to hear your beautiful voice. Don't worry, Mama, you'll be surrounded by friends that will provide you a sense of community."

Ada smoothed her soiled apron over her lap, thinking about creating a meeting of the minds so that they could share the same mental picture. "Now Mary J, every game has its rules. Unless there are rules for guidance, there will be confusion and chaos. You simply cannot go in any direction you wish without regard for another person, so be open-minded when dealing with someone else. People usually mirror your treatment of them. If you are warm, you will receive warmth in return. People respond eagerly to warmth, which enables you to get more of what you want from life, because they are more willing to help you. We must have an innate instinct to treat others with courtesy and respect; there is no greater protection against the storms of life. Success, after all, seldom comes easily and is rarely accomplished on the first try."

Mary J was grinning and shaking her head elaborately. She doubted those predictions but had a stealthy hope that there might be some truth. "Mama, that like going outside in the rain without an umbrella."

"Yes, my sweetheart, but when it rains, you can think of no better gift than the unappreciated umbrella."

"All right; oh yes, I see. Don't worry, Mama: Sweet, Friendly, and Thoughtful consideration will be my best helpers today."

With her Mother's encouragement, she set out to have an elaborate and spectacular entertainment show. She believed that her nearby neighbors would undoubtedly join in to help make this a special community event. She arranged to get the word out to everybody, especially to her Uncle Charlie's children next door. Her Aunt Annie, three children: James miller, Annie May, and Clarence were already sitting on the pouch. Mary J asked everybody to organize something unique to perform at the evening family gathering. All of her brothers and sisters would be there.

Mary J ran down to the far end of the field to tell Showalter. "Hey, Brother! Mama said we could organize a musical program for this afternoon. So, get your guitar ready; I am going to tell James Westley, Alvin, and Monroe to put your piano on the front porch."

"Little sister," said Showalter smiling with amusement, "You are on the ball. I'm counting on you—just let me finish chopping these two rows of corn."

Fuel by her passion, Mary J's special event spread quickly throughout the community. She wanted to start as soon as possible. She had her mother to plan a few songs and to organize a back-up choir. She also insisted that somebody perform a dramatic scene. Mary J imagined that her Uncle Charlie's children would put together a gospel quartet with Monroe, James Miller, James Westley, and Alvin. Her sisters Lucy Gray, Ella, and Margaret Ann could form another little singing group.

Mary J thought—"holy smokes—there ought to be two thousand seats. My duet with Annie May will blow the people away; I will also schedule myself to perform as a soloist. Showalter will play all the back-up music, using his various instruments."

Mary J felt that Showalter was an extremely talented musician who could make others take notice. She was proud that he was a self-taught musician, inspired by the old piano in the living room. Mary J nearly wept out of pure joy. She knew that Neighbors, friends, family, and even strangers would be amazed at Showalter's ability to create music. In her opinion, his gift was a thing of beauty. Now, she was confident that everything was going to be all right.

Mary J said to herself. "Showalter can make pots and pans blend as one prearranged beat. He can reproduce almost any music he has heard without having witnessed another musician playing it. Showalter can hear musical sounds mentally in his head, along with the rhythms and pitches. Also, he can sit down with his piano or guitar to reproduce it. Wow, what a great brother!"

What caught Mary J's eyes were the large crowd gathering around the porch; they had begun pouring over into the yard. Mary J was pulling herself over the edge of a fence when she saw how the various groups were organizing themselves. She began thinking within herself, as Showalter sat at the piano: "Golly, this is beautiful!"

17

Showalter called curtain time by playing music on the piano. Everybody began to gather around the big house porch. The weather seemed to be perfect for this outdoor family event. As the people started to hear Showalter's music, they came together near the front porch. He was playing a gospel song. Some of the performers who gather near the front porch to participated were: soloists, the family choir, quartets, duets, and other community members waiting to be recognized by him. Chairs were placed all over the front yard so people could sit down.

The first person that Showalter introduced was his Mother. He said with an enthusiastic voice: "This woman maybe my Mother, but her voice is from heaven, because she sings like an angel, come on—let's receive her now."

As Ada started to approach the front porch stage, Showalter commenced to play a musical selection that became mildly infectious and mesmerizing. The music represented the background for a song called: *We'll understand it better by and by.* Ada reflected an energetic and emotional style of revival singing, similar to Mahalia Jackson. She had the ability to embellish a performance with melodious beautification and creativeness. She expressed in music and words an extremely spiritual experience. Ada could bring on sanctifying moans, wails, cries and shouts with gliding pitches. She served as an inspiration for her entire family. Ada continued to lead the entertainment by singing several more selections, which included "Amazing Grace." She embellished the melody of these songs by lending heart and soul to a highly emotional performance.

Mary J was truly proud of her Mother singing and Showalter musical abilities. Ada never tried to duplicate another performance. She always enjoyed herself with the melody of the song, by adding a lot of trimming and accent. Ada voice could switch from soprano to alto when appropriate for inspiration. From the onlookers' point of view, Ada and her son Showalter were indeed an impressive musical team—producing foundational stones for authentic music.

Showalter next introduced the family choir, which had a highly specialized singing style. Showalter said in his introduction: "We have a combination of songs to be performed in various styles by our choir groups that include my brothers, sisters, and cousins. They have been under the melodramatic supervision of my Mother. So, let's hear them sing!"

The family choir began by singing several musical selections— interacting together in ways that created a biological response among the audience. Alvin, James Westley, Ella, Lucy Gray, and Margret Ann performed both as groups and individuals. The music was being tossed back and forth between the choir, soloists, and various groups. The people hollered, go, James Westley, go on, Lucy Gray, you got it, Alvin, look at Margret Ann sing! You can do it, Ella."

All of the onlookers were on their feet, clapping their hands and singing with them. They were having a good time. These onlookers were impressed with the fact that these were children: Ella (eighteen), James Westley (fifteen), Mary J (eleven), Lucy (eight), Alvin (seven), Margret Ann (five), and Showalter (twenty-three) playing all those musical instruments.

"One thing for sure," said the onlookers to each other, "these children are full of energy and inspired by Ada and Showalter."

Showalter continues hosting this live musical show with words of admiration: "This next group has style and elegance. They are simply untouchable with their rhythmic movements. They have a compelling beat and musical style. Their voices range from sweet tenor to rich baritone. Now give it up for the Soul Searchers."

Finally, Showalter introduced Mary J. She began singing her favorite song.

"O' Lord, I'm your child, I will go into thy vineyard, and
I will work there until you come...........................
Stand by me Lord, stand by me,—I will go into thy vineyard
and wait there until you come."

The crowd said, "go ahead, little Miss Mary J." Everybody began singing along with her as they became part of the music. After Mary J finished her song, the onlookers gave all of the performers a standing ovation for their extraordinary performances.

As darkness surrounded the house, all the joy went out of the celebration. There was just one little crisis, the nonsense chatter from

Mary J's Uncle Charlie after a few drinks. Mary J quickly felt a stab of terror when she observed that her Uncle Charlie was under the influence of alcohol. She could see people frowning from the stink of filthy roadhouse whiskey on his breath. He was like a fish out of water, or even an owl out of air. Charlie started to whine vigorously and piped a tune on a tin whistle. Next, he tried to celebrate the singing by pouring and passing around his whiskey.

Mary J shook her head; her spirit began to rise. She felt a tightening in her throat, but later after thinking about it, she chuckled joyously about his actions. According to her way of thinking, everyone knew of his good deeds outside of drinking too much whiskey. She realized that conflicts would arise no matter how much people care about each other, no matter how often they provide opportunities to increase their closeness. She now understood her Daddy's old saying that 'only when its dark enough can we see the stars.'

THE CHURCH SERVICE

Another Sunday meant another word from the preacher. Mary J's entire family was getting ready for their Sunday morning services. Not only was John Westley a deacon and Headmaster for the Sunday school, but he also had the responsibility for opening the church doors. John Westley had on his best dark-blue suit. He carried the church's keys in one hand and the Bible in the other.

"John Westley," shouted Ada to her husband, "don't take the children with you this morning; I will bring them to Sunday school. "Ada called out again with a loud voice because there was no response. "Hey John Westley, you know that you heard me, please answer me!"

"Woman! I heard you," said John Westley. "I will be searching for my family at Sunday school. We don't want to raise ungodly children. No, no, no! They must have good character and not be part of a shambling loose community with shiftless ways. By the way, my sweet darling wife, are you ready to sing that new song? You have been practicing all week with Showalter. All of us want to hear you sing: *The Storm is Passing Over.*"

"Mr. John Westley! I am ready," said Ada, "you just make sure your Mother Mag is getting ready for church as well… we need only to make one trip."

John Westley looked pleased: "How about our preacher, Reverend White?"

"You don't have to worry about him because one of the deacons will be picking him up for the morning service. He will not be attending Sunday school."

John Westley chuckled at her response. "Ok! Let me go so the Lord's sheep can get into the church."

John Westley looked around, not wanting to go without his family, and yet not daring to question his wife's plans. He rushed out to unlock the church doors for the early comers: teachers, deacons, and helpers. His eyes grew soft with responsive emotion as he stood at the church door entrance, welcoming members, regular attendees, and guests with consuming passion.

When the time came to start the Sunday school program, John Westley opened with the following remarks: "Good morning, my dear friends and spiritual family, the Lord our God desires to give us wisdom and to declare His purpose in our lives. Let us prepare our hearts to receive His teaching through the Holy Spirit. The Bible says that the 'fear of the Lord is the beginning of wisdom.' So now, let's seek Him accordingly to His Word. We are a God Centered Church; therefore, may His will be made known within our hearts. Through the grace of Christ, each of us should be comforted by the shade of his or her conscience. Please join me in prayer: O' Lord, please give us wisdom, knowledge, and understanding of your Holy Word and Spirit; so that we may receive a more intimate relationship with you. O' Lord, allow your Spirit to rest upon each of our Bible teacher this morning; so, we can improve our spiritual awareness, in the name of Christ Jesus we pray, Amen."

John Westley commenced teaching his class: "One of the first great truths concerning God's salvation is found in our Sunday school text this morning at John 6: 44. Jesus says, 'No one can come to me unless the Father who sent me draws him.' Jesus knew that God, the Father, must be active in drawing people to himself before they could ever know the joy of salvation. How significant is this statement concerning your life?" Various people in the audience began to raise their hands; this question launched several exchanges of thoughts.

John Westley continued, "God has called you into a loving relationship with Himself and one another in the community through Christ Jesus. In other words, you are special! You are the object of God's calling. You didn't choose him; He chose you. You can count on it; your salvation must begin in the heart of God. The only true foundation for faith and life is God's Word." The class smiled and agreed with every word, and there was plenty of participation and many thoughtful questions.

John Westley closed Sunday school with a prayer: "O' Father God, our Lord and Creator, according to your divine plan of salvation… help each of us to enter into, a healthy and loving relationship with you and one another. We ask this according to your wonderful grace through Christ Jesus. Amen."

John Westley, immediately after his prayer, saw Mary J moving around in church. He called her over and said: "You need to stick with your Grandma Mag because your Mother is singing with the choir. She may need your assistance with the other children." He gave her a little pat on the shoulder, then told her to use this meeting to deepen her spiritual life.

Mary J straightened her shoulders and lifted her chin. She went straight over to her Grandma and sat down on a wooden bench next to her. Mary J's head sunk between her hunched shoulders; there were all sorts of confusion and bewilderment within her mind. Questions rushed through her mind like an unseen wind. As the preacher positioned himself to start the morning service, she caught her breath with a stab of pain.

After Pastor White opened- up the Sunday morning service with a prayer and a song, Ada came marching down the center aisle. She was leading the choir in her pure and heavenly featured voice. Ada was singing a beautiful song: *The Storm is Passing Over*. After the choir was in place, she led another song called: *'We'll Understand it Better By and By.'* This full-packed church of several hundred people, suddenly jumped to their feet in a spirit of gratitude.

Mary J was clapping her hands harder than anyone, shouting, "that's my Mama!" She jumped to her feet, glanced up at her Grandma, and then sat down again. Mag grabbed at her with compassionate eyes. But still, she allowed Mary J to capture the memory of her Mother's most beautiful moment.

Reverend White's sermon, along with a closing Hymn, had begun to complete the church service. There were several statements by various members, then finally prayer. After the ceremony, John Westley led a small team of church members to visit homes in their local community. They wanted to celebrate God's goodness with their neighbors, friends, and family. They went from house to house in loving fellowship.

After the community visit, the church team returned home for their Sunday dinner. John Westley was walking into his home when none other than little Miss Mary J met him. She was very concerned about her uncle Charlie.

"Daddy," she said, "we have to do something about your brother Charlie."

"What are you talking about, my little busybody?"

"Well! You know. He is drinking whiskey again! This time on Sunday morning instead of going to church. Grandma Mag is not very happy with him. She is upstairs praying for him right now."

John Westley answered her frankness with revelations equally frank. "Mary J, come on with me, let's go talk to him."

Mary J and her Daddy walked into the house. Charlie was sitting in a corner area, laughing his head off. One could easily smell liquor on his stinky alcoholic breath.

John Westley unconsciously softened his homely voice. "Good evening my brother, why are you so happy?"

"Well," Charlie smiled, "Because I am in love with life, I am planning to live it to the fullest."

"Mary J, your little niece, is worried that you might fall and hurt yourself."

Charlie raised his head and stared at him with somewhat surprise turbulent and shame raging within himself. "Now, my brother, you should be very proud of that young gal because she loves and respects everybody. Mary J is a little boss at times; nevertheless, she tries to teach a good lesson to others in her fussy ways. If I do stop drinking, it will be for the children. But to be fair, my brother, I work hard during the week and only drinks on the weekends, so my family should give me a break."

Sadness developed in John Westley's voice as he answered, "well, brother Charlie, we love you and want you to be safe. I want you to know that not only does your family loves you; but also, the Lord Jesus loves you."

Charlie face became more serious: "By the way, there is nothing wrong with a small drink now and then"

John Westley said, in a kind voice, "Alcohol should never devour all of your time on your short weekends, you are setting a bad example for your children and my boys. Showalter, James Westley, Alvin and little Willie Welt love you too death. I am afraid you might influence them to drink."

Charlie's tone was thoughtful. "Oh! No, if I catch any of our children drinking, a switch will be ready for them. I love my family; someday, I may stop but not now, but maybe someday soon. Here is some advice for my little Mary J; Please, do not ever marry a drunkard because you will be along on the weekends."

As John Westley sensed his change of mood and the troubling uncertainty of his thoughts, he remarked: "Brother Charlie, since you didn't attend church today, we could read a verse of Scripture together, and then we can have dinner."

Charlie desperately wished to cover his awkwardness. "I believe that religion is pure nonsense, but for Mary J's sake, ok... that sounds good to me."

As a moment passed, John Westley thought with sudden hopelessness that pressed against him like a heavy hand. He smiled and went on with a question in one word, "why?"

The reason is simple; nature is never mistaken, whereas people often are wrong. People are just hungry for immortality. Of course, there might be a God who governs the order in heaven and earth, but he doesn't grant immortality. Plus, science continues to find no evidence for the existence of God or an afterlife. Now, we can easily see why most scientists are atheists. In the future, I believe that most ordinary people will follow the views of science. So come on, my brother, let's eat, drink and be merry."

"My brother," said John Westley, just as a child is born into a physical family, it is the same when a person is born again into a spiritual family. The Bible tells us: *But to all who did receive Him, He gave them the right* to be children of God, to those who believe in His name, who were born, not of blood, or the will of the flesh, or the will of man, but God.' "(John 1:12-13, ESV.)

"Here's my point," said Charlie. "People are thinkers, so they must consider the world from a sensible point of view. In the long term, we must realize that reason will win. Yet, people must find a way of life that will help them face the reality of death. Now just in case, there is a God, I don't want to go to the lake of fire that's reserve for the devil and his angels, so let's finish your sermon."

John Westley looked at him and clicked his tongue with a deprecating sound. "Here's the point, my brother, our failure to comprehend God fully shouldn't strike us as strange. Scientists cannot see God in a telescope or a test tube. On the other hand, it's a terrible mistake to think of God as apart from our everyday world. We live surrounded by mysteries that we cannot fully clarify through our sight. Now consider, there are invisible things like the air, gravity, love, time, or even our emotions. Doctors can observe the brain, but its thoughts are intangible to us. We can't even see those things responsible for keeping us alive.

Mary J laughed aloud as if she had said something exceptionally witty. "Oh, my goodness, Uncle Charlie, the Bible, intends to teach us how to get to heaven."

Charlie was frowning with disagreement. "Mary J, when you get as old as your Grandma Mag, you will find science, not the Bible, telling people how to get to heaven. You just mark my words, there will be a scientific rebellion changing the way our society views the very nature of religion. It won't bring utopia, but there will be new dawn that helps to solve some of this world's problems through science instead of the Bible. A man named Einstein has already come up with a theory that explains how the earth began—there was no magic wand!"

John Westley was too exasperated to debate the broad heading of science verse God. He thought about how Darwin's evolutionary theory had begun to erode the Christian faith. Therefore, Charlie was doing what was right according to his values instead of seeking Biblical Principles.

John Westley finally broke the silence. "Come now, Brother Charlie, let's go and have some dinner."

Mary J grabbed her Uncle Charlie's hand on one side and her Daddy on the other side. Altogether, they walked towards the kitchen table. Little Mary J felt very proud of her daddy and mother. She wanted to feel the same way about her Uncle Charlie. As she looked at him, she thought, My God, please help him. He is not only a drunkard, but also an atheists. His soul will definitely be thrown into the lake of fire. We might as well let him drink and be merry while here on earth.

Chapter

5

AUNT LORETTA'S STORE

The following Saturday morning felt somewhat drowsy but peaceful, as smoke rose over the Wood Burning Stove. There was no echo of footsteps—talking, or laughter that usually humanized the family environment. The wind carried scents of burned, wet wood and cooked meat. The grass had been newly cut, it smelt sweet and creamy, just like spring; sunlight was shining through the front windows. The house's interior landscape was surrounded by propagating plants that had been cultivated in containers.

As Ada was dressing to take Mary J to visit her sister's store, a million questions rushed through her mind concerning her children. Ada paused and thought vaguely about how selfish and self-centered she might have been without them. She could easily recall all the times that she spent providing insights for them into the mind and heart of God. Yet internally, she was somewhat frightened that her many agonizing headaches might be a life-threatening condition. She felt confused, discouraged, and guilt from the pressure of an uncaring world. She couldn't help remembering that five of her nine children had not reached their twelfth birthday. She knew that her helpless little ones wanted her always. They needed to learn how to walk, talk, and take care of themselves before she left this world.

Ada made a small movement. Her face was thoughtful—hands swept up in gestures. Beautifying herself, she turned to face the mirror. She gazed for a long moment at the reflection of her deepening beauty. She twisted and leaned back while letting her eyes scrutinize the perceived image. Observing, asking questions, accumulating answers in this manner, she was acquiring knowledge of herself.

Unexpectedly, she noticed her husband standing in the doorway—slowly but surely, walking towards her. Ada asked inattentively, "What's the matter?"

There was distress in his tone. "Ada, please come along, we have promised our daughter a visit to your sister Loretta's store. As you know, Loretta allows Mary J to pretend that she owns the store."

Ada dashed her fingers through her hair, dislodging some of it from clips. There was a bit of laughter, then Ada said, "Oh, for goodness' sake! You're going to spoil that child. Mary J is going to grow up thinking that she will own a family's store. As you know, her determination is like a steel wall."

John Westley's voice was firm with pitying eyes, patient, and understanding. "Ah, yes, you're probably right, but there's more than one way to understand my heart. Sadly, too many of our children today live and die with their dreams, never becoming a reality. We need to support Mary J's dream of becoming a store owner. Remember, I am the one that built your sister's store and added on to this house. Only if the Lord let me live to see, Mary J becomes an adult. She is a good girl that goes to Sunday school and church with us all the time. I pray that the Lord give her a chance."

Ada grinned so infectiously that her husband had to smile back. "Now John Westley, I know why I married you. With the flowing of time, you have become more and more a friendly man, extraordinarily gentle, and a peacemaker. Your tender and gentle heart will inspire little Mary J, who will only, maybe, grow up to be somewhere around 5 feet tall and weigh no more than maybe 99 pounds." Ada laughed—slipping into her shoes. "I sure hope she has a muscular husband to defend her."

After several heartfelt laughs with his wife, John Westley said: "You know, it's only a pipe dream that someday Mary J might finish High school—only if she could at least get through the eighth grade. But now, according to farmer George Ball, he told me personally that any education for children beyond the rudiments of literacy and figuring would only be a waste of time and money."

"Well," said Ada, "you are right John Westley, a decent education for Mary J would help her in running a store. But as you know, only a few children stay in school beyond their primary grades. Children have suffered a lot during these Great Depression years. Many children lack food; some are still suffering from hunger and diseases."

John Westley's eyes grew soft, inspired by a kindly tone. "You're right. There are a lot of obstacles facing our children, who are thirsting for education. Just look how hard it is to get good teachers—like Miss Caroline. It's good for Mary J to pretend, even if it doesn't happen in real life. Our children need hopes and dreams!"

Ada drew a deep breath of reasoning; she shook her head. "All right, wait a minute." She looked at him directly in his eyes. "Mary J's school is just a neglected building that's half-way standing in a rocky field, along with dust-covered weeds growing through a damp and disgusting floor. People can see broken benches that are jam-packed several times their normal capability. If lucky, you may find a few shabby books. Farmer George Ball makes a good point. Sometimes I feel that the children might as well be in the fields."

John Westley paused, and in the silence, his eyes were focused upon his wife. He cleared his throat, rubbed his hand across the stubble on his jaws. "You are correct, sweetheart. Teachers are greeting people in a depressed voice that's noticeable in their speech. There are usually four grades packed into one open space. One may observe a worn-out teacher proceeding with her daily instructions. She will go to the blackboard and write out an assignment for the first two grades to complete while conducting spelling and word drills for the third and fourth grades. These are the type of assignments: Write your name five times; draw a dog, or a cat, or a rat. Now you tell me, how in the name of God's good earth, can Mary J run a business off this junk education?"

Ada sniffed loudly and looked worried, wiping her hand across her nose. She spoke slowly with words that were groping for guidance. "You don't have to worry, my sister Loretta will teach her how to run a business.

Mary J is only eleven years old, so we have time to help her. Now, let's take her over to my sister's store."

Loretta's store was located just about one mile away. The store was freestanding and capped by a pitched roof. Its appearance was a simple structure with a decorated façade, with an architectural style that was rural in formation. As people entered the store's interior, they would have noticed the following items: plank counters, wooden legs tables, a meat grocery scale and wood shelving lined with goods. Loretta sold essential items: rice, sugar, coffee beans, lima beans, canned goods, and dry goods for sewing cloth. She would often extend store credit even at her husband's opposition.

They arrived at her store during the midmorning hours. Loretta peeped through her store window to see if any customers were outside. She was surprised to see her sister, Ada, with her husband John Westley, walking up the path. She noticed that Mary J was skipping and running right behind them. All of a sudden, Mary J couldn't help herself. She dashed around her parents—rushed into the store to greet her Aunt Loretta—shouting with a thrill of joy.

Loretta's heart melted with compassion. She hugged Mary J, then chuckled at her strong feelings about her store. "Oh, my dear, why are you so full of energy this morning? Let me guess; you're planning to help me run the store."

Mary J wanted to leap over the sales counter. "Oh yes, you just stay here and talk to my mommy and daddy, I will handle the customers this morning."

Right at this very moment, several customers came into the store. Mary J ran behind the counter switching from one side to another. "Now, what can I do for you folks today?"

One of the customers said, "Please give me: one box of rice, a bag of sugar, and two packs of lima bean."

Mary J ran and got those items. She waited for her Aunt Loretta to come and collect the money. After each customer's transactions, she would always say with a big smile, "Thank you, and please come again." Then, she went to the next customer, using the same process, always waiting for her Aunt Loretta to collect the money. This process went on and on until Loretta gave Mary J another assignment of organizing the shelves.

Loretta turned her head to look directly at her brother-in-law. "You and my sister must get Mary J her store."

John Westley said. "Behold our dreamer! She has already made me sign the papers to build a store on her twenty-first birthday." He was laughing like crazy, along with his wife. Everyone in the store started to laugh, including the customers; Mary J just kept on working at cleaning, organizing and helping even more customers.

Ada's face twisted slightly in the shadows, grinning. "Our daughter has made up her mind to be a store owner. So, we are going to help her. Her Dad will build the store. I will supply her fresh produce from my garden. The rest of the family can help with the cleaning and re-stocking the shelves. We have nothing much more than our bare hands in saving. Although her dream looks impossible, I still applause her determination."

Loretta turned slowly around, leaned over and patted her sister's hand. "Well, to begin with, I'd believe that you folks got the right idea. Mary J simply refuses to fit into a checkbox. She wants to make the rules instead of following them. She despises being told what to do because she values freedom. She wants to live life on her terms. We must find a way to stop our world from destroying her entrepreneurial spirit."

As the shadow of Mary J came between them, Ada laughed in response. "Come along, Mary J, let's get ready to go home. We have been here for several hours. It's time now for your Aunt Loretta to get ready for her evening customers."

"Yes, mama, I just want to wait on one more customer! She saw a customer approaching the screen door. She quickly ran behind the counter. "Mr. Frank, what are you looking for today?"

"Loretta," Mr. Frank said with a big smile on his face. "I see you have hired a little helper."

Loretta chuckled cheerfully at him. "Frank, you are right. I mean, a good one!"

Frank smiled and nodded politely. "Well, little Miss Mary J, please give me a pound of fatback meat."

Mary J drew a deep breath of delight: "Coming right up!"

There was an outburst of giggles throughout the store. Frank's hands flew over his belly. His laughter tore at his throat. "One thing for sure, she is efficient, which is a good thing—businesspeople certainly come in all sizes. You folks have stirred up a business spirit in this child that's comparable to an inexhaustible flame. She is certainly a sight to behold, and a treasure to appreciate."

Loretta quickly came around the counter and took control of the purchase. She felt a sudden surge of admiration for her niece. "I believe that every mother, father, aunt or uncle holds in their hands the ability to inspire an entrepreneurial spirit in a child. As you know, we control our children's ultimate destiny—not the teachers, employers, or anyone else. The making of a child's spirit starts at home nowhere else. But we have to remember that from the day a child is born, the outside world will be desperately trying to defeat every semblance of a risk-taking spirit."

Loretta's words made her sister Ada's heart melt. Ada said with delight in her voice. "We are leaving before you steal our daughter."

Loretta walked closer to Mary J and then leaned forward with a smile. She gave Mary J a bag full of candy. "I just want to thank you so much for helping me today."

Mary J gave Loretta a big hug and kiss, and then sadly left with her parents. She and her family went back home through a trail located behind the store. It led through a wooded area that went across a field, which carried them to the rear of their home.

After arriving near the backyard, Mary J saw Rosie Lee and her siblings out near her playhouse. Mary J began hollering out as she ran towards them. "Now listen to me," as she stood there, tense, rigid, facing them, staring at them. "Please listen, because I don't intend to repeat this again. I hope everyone knows who owns this playhouse; my Daddy built it for me with his own hands. Now get out of here! She shooed them away like backyard chickens."

They looked up at Mary J with concealed curiosity, mumbling together over her fussy attitude. "If she wants to become a store owner, she better learn to respect her customers. We are her customers, don't' she knows that…? " All of a sudden, they started laughing extremely loud, as if their heads might come off.

Rosie Lee, her best friend, and constant playmate stayed around after the others departed into several directions. "Mary J, why are you running away, my brothers and sisters?"

Mary J lapsed into a silence of resentful acceptance. She looked at her sympathetically—leaning over towards her in a whispering voice. "Except for you, Dolly Gray and Clyde Edmond, your brothers and sisters are out of control. For example, Ralph is outright mean—Willard is a little sneaky—Monroe is always trying to work out a deal—and poor Sterling wants to fight. If your Daddy would stop drinking 150 proof whiskey every weekend, he could then go to church on Sundays with his children. The church is probably the best thing for your family."

"Well, Mary J," said Rosie Lee, "you need to get your head out of the clouds. Otherwise, we aren't going to have any customers. So, why don't you go and call them back? We can then play your little, silly store game!"

"Ok," said Mary J. She then waved her hand, telling everyone to come back to play the store game. She performed the role of owner, using her experience at Loretta's store as an example to follow. Rosie Lee played the part of the helper. Mary J treated her the same way that she had been treated by her Aunt Loretta a few hours earlier. The remaining participants played various roles as customers.

While playing the store game, a tiny cloud appeared and began to grow. It seemed to explode—the sky darkens from a slated-gray to a greenish-black—trees bent under a blast of winds. Rosie Lee lashed out, "lookout for the downpour. We better make a run for home!"

Mary J thought about Monroe. He had told her that the lightning was going to get her for being so mean to him. Mary J's fears—crashed on her like a tidal wave. She began to develop an irrational fear of thunderstorms. Perhaps, she thought, they must be some type of perplexing mysteries—full of black magic.

Unexpectedly, a big tree was struck by lightning and crash to the ground with its roots extended outward. In the yard, the thieving jays, sparrows, and squirrels all ran to find safety. Birds flew up, then dived for shelter while the sky was blazing with lightning and roaring with thunder. Flight birds showed their feathers forming a smooth surface that curved to an angle in midair on a descending stroke; other birds were expanding their wings like slats on a venetian blind, soaring into the darkening sky.

When the full energy of the storm hit, everybody went home and slammed their doors behind them. As soon as they were inside, a cluster of lightning lit up the area with high winds. One could hear the rain hammering on the roof that produced sounds like hail. Mother Ada made the whole family sit in the living room with their Grandma. Crash after crash sounds of thunder—lightning was zigging here—zagging there, never striking in a straight line but on all sides. Mary J became very much afraid. She then began laying her head upon Mag's shoulder. The storm continued for at least one hour under darker and darker clouds that raced across the sky—letting down sheets of rain.

After John Westley said a sincere prayer, the rooftop on Charlie's house slowly stopped struggling with the wind. The purple storm clouds began to retreat toward the East. Unexpectedly, the wind and rain activity came to a halt. Even so, this thunderstorm left the fussing Mary J muddling through a heart filled with fear.

Chapter

6

MOTHER ADA'S DEATH

For some strange reason the next morning around 4:30 a.m., Ada's eyes were met by darkness. There was no sleep for her, just wide-awake nightmares, along with a monstrous disabling headache, sucking at every morsel of her being. She tried to figure out what was causing her wrenching pain that was invading her temples. As the pain reached the top of her head, Ada felt as if she hadn't slept in days—bursting into tears—feeling death standing in her doorway. Spellbound with fear, Ada reflected upon her Christian faith. She realized that joy should mark her journey from time to eternity. By accepting her destiny, Ada was able to push back a rising tide of anxiety. For some strange reason, her chronic migraine stopped, she quickly drifted back to sleep.

Ada's sleep was suddenly broken a second time from a dream with unique memories. Ada's feelings and thoughts were immediately upon her children. Unconsciously, she discovered memories hiding in her brain. Without realizing it, these emotional memories had been stored deep into her physic. It was like rediscovering streams of living water underneath the sand. She sat up in her bed, gazing at the ceiling with dark, gloomy eyes. She turned and leaned back, with both hands behind her head, her eyes merely questioning. Groping for some positive expression to hang onto, she slid out of bed—scrambled to her feet—washed up and outfitted herself. The house was quiet; all seemed well.

Ada went downstairs to the kitchen and prepared the family breakfast. Afterward, she grabbed her husband's bucket from the pantry to organize his lunch. As Ada looked down the road from her kitchen window, she became somewhat dizzy. She decided to sit in a chair near the stove for a few minutes.

Although under attack by unexplained dizziness, Ada was determined not to build stone walls around her heart. She started persuading her feelings through tears and gestures—a flick of the hand, a turning down of her lips, a half closing of her eyes. Ada began to reflect on her family constitution, one filled with grace, freedom and responsibility. There was no need for any member of her family to be afraid—to feel inadequate, helpless, or alone. She had no problem recognizing that in her family, there were characters with many challenging personalities.

Ada's eyes dropped to her hands, now even more tightly clasped in her lap. She continued thinking about her family; how satisfying life had been with them. She thought about Showalter outstanding musical abilities. Ella's humble spirit. James Westley love for life. Mary J's dream to be a store owner, Lucy's beautiful voice; Alvin desires to travel, Margret Ann quiet spirit, little Willie Welt's mischievous actions and her baby Larraine being only one years old.

Ada's was enthralled by how unalike her children were from each other. She was awe-struck with their uniqueness and different gifts. Ada truly believed that everybody struggles along a rocky road towards their destiny. She kept thinking that her children would sooner or later learn new forms of behavior through their education, successes, and even failures. As this picture lay before her eyes, she experienced a deep thankfulness and joy for her family.

Ada was now struggling with how to provide a future for her children. She began to cry. She sat silently for a while, feeling helpless, she couldn't stop—drawing back into her chair. Her mind went back to Mary J's strong determination to be a store owner. She smiled, knowing in her heart that she would never compromise, even if many failures were lurking directly in her face. Ada reflected on the particular way that Mary J treasured and prized books, although she wasn't adequately prepared to absorb the information. In Ada's current state of mind, she readily agreed with Mary

J's off-the-wall philosophy: May J refused to be someone mere puppet; whose strings could be pulled this or that way. Ada knew that her daughter was right. She believed in the precious gift of life, known as free will.

Ada was growing deeper into her family's reflections as Ella gradually came downstairs; she was moving as slowly as a snail. Finally, Ella was on the last step of the staircase. Ella noticed that there was an unusually cold and icy silence. In the rising light of day, Ella's eyes found her Mother in deep thoughts. "Good morning Mamma, isn't it a wonderful morning?"

Ada spoke with steel in her voice, even though it was soft and slow as ever. "Oh yes, my sweet little girl, let's get your daddy lunch ready.

Ella immediately noticed her Mother's homemade biscuits, country ham, fresh eggs, and hominy grits with lots of butter for breakfast on the kitchen table. Although Ella was having some trouble understanding her words, she knew the routine. She quickly nodded her head in agreement. "All right, Mama, you are right, we just need Daddy's lunchbox."

Ada rose to her feet and stood, staring intensely into open space. She wasn't looking at anything in particular. Her bright thoughts started turning into darkness. As she Clenched her fists, she began experiencing intense and sharp pains. They were jabbing in the back of her head. She felt the worst headache of her life. Ada shook her head, hiding her face in the midst of both hands.

Ada coughed delicately, "Ella, my darling, please get me the Epsom salt box from the top cabinet."

Ella turned hurriedly at the sound of her voice, then speedily took the box out of the cabinet. "Yes, Mamma, I'm here. You're all right! Here's the Epsom salt."

Ada shuffled back over to the kitchen table, forcing herself to sit down. "Yes, yes—well, almost. But, there's something different about this pain in my head. Now Ella, quickly, squeeze out the juice from two lemons in a cup, grate a little lemon crust and add two teaspoons of this Epsom salt. Then, stir it all together into a glass of water for me."

"Yes—oh yes," Ella nervously replied. "Mamma, I will have it ready in five minutes."

Ada pushed herself up from the kitchen table. She was now experiencing stroke-like symptoms: vomiting, dizziness, confusion, and a loss of balance.

Ada fell to the floor—her face became numb—she had trouble talking, along with cloudiness in her eyes. But somehow, as one in a dream, in her heart, she was telling everybody a misty goodbye.

In Ella's mind, things looked very dark. She closed her eyes quickly in prayer. She could think of no medical device in the house to save her. Ella could only think that her Mother's fate must now be in the hand of her God; who had put a sweetness in the sound of her voice, stirring the soul of an entire community.

Ella suddenly became fearful—not understanding, she called out with a loud voice for help. Mag and John Westley came quickly to see what was disturbing her. Seeing Ada lying on the floor, they became afraid and frightened that her injury might be fatal.

John Westley picked up his wife Ada off the floor and placed her on Mag's bed. She struggled for her breath, then threw up her hands. There was a ripple of death that passed over her face. John Westley pressed around her body to only feel a breathless stillness. A bright smile passed over Ada's face as she moved from life to death.

John Westley cried out, "my wife is gone!" He stood there, gazing with his arms painfully folded. "Oh God, this is dreadful." He turned towards his Mother in agony, then wringing her hand. "O' Mother, this is killing me!" He slowly sank to his knees and prayed for mercy on his children, knowing that their Mother was now gone.

Mag, with tears streaming down her cheeks, stood watching her son sobbing on his knees as his wife laid in a frozen state of death. She said to her son, "Ada was a charming and bright woman who had a good life in my opinion: a loving Christian husband, nine healthy children, and an angelic voice for singing. She loved her life and her children. Ada didn't want to die. She didn't want to leave her young children, oh no, not so soon."

Mag wrestled with the bitter thought that Ada was only 38 years old when she died. She had left behind nine children: Lorraine 1, Willie Welt 3, Margret Ann 5, Alvin 7, Lucy Gray 9, Mary J 12, James Westley 15, Ella 17, and Showalter 23. Mag could feel these children agonizing the future without their mother's help. Mag had tears and pity for her little grandchildren, now without a mother.

Mag thought, "little Mary J will be devastated when she finds out about her Mother's death. They were so close. No one could inspire that little girl like her Mother."

Mary J rushed downstairs, hollering for her mother. John Westley picked Mary J up in his arms and gave her a big kiss. Then he said, "Your Mother Ada has now gone into time without end."

Mary J gave-out an intense emotional burst of tears as she squeezed her Daddy's neck. She wept with a steady roar for her Mother; her Daddy could hear and see the internal screams of her agony. Mary J's world appeared to be upside down. Her eyes swelled from crying on her Daddy's shoulder.

Mag reached over and rubbed Mary J's back very gently, as she was crying in her Daddy's arms. "Your mother has completed the first part of her life, and now it's high time for her to move into the second part."

A scream came from Mag's bedroom downstairs, Mother Ada dead! Suddenly everyone in the house was afraid and terrified at these words. Everyone upstairs started running downstairs. Some of the family members cried out, while others fainted from fear. No one knew what might happen next. Some said that she was in a state of collapse. Ada was pronounced clinically dead upon her arrival at the hospital. The confirmation of her death was completed the following day.

James Westley and Showalter's fears crashed on them like a tidal wave when they heard the news. They drew their arms tightly over their chest, while choking back bitter tears. As they shook their heads together, the pain in their eyes was desperate. The sinking paleness of death had fallen upon their jumpy nerves. Showalter went upstairs, sat down at the piano and then began playing one of his mother's favorite hymn. The entire family filled with cries, screams, and assorted tremors.

When Pastor White arrived at the house two days later after Ada's death, he found Mag in the kitchen cooking. Ella was present, so she turned the food over to her. Mag called her son John Westley. They led Pastor White into their living room. Pastor White selected what he called a comfortable overstuffed chair. Mag and John Westley sat on the opposite side of the reading table. As they were sitting down, the usual greetings and pleasantries took place that recognized the death of a person. Mag and John Westley were breathing slowly, trying to forget the pains of their many questions. John Westley, looking like death warmed over, shook his head in a few moments of silence.

The pastor broke the silence of the room. "Since we know the worst of this situation, how are you folks doing?"

"Little bit better today," said Mag, "but we still have to get through the funeral."

"We are working on getting our business affairs straight," said John Westley. "There's going to be a persistent emptiness in our lives with many questions."

"Religion is not science," said Pastor White. "Science describes how the world works, but silent on the question of how the world ought to be. Although scientific knowledge allows us to do and understand many things, it cannot tell us whether or not we should choose to do them. Death is one of those strange occurrences that make no sense to us. Such matters are in the hand of the Almighty God, who oversees the heavens and earth. According to His word, there shall be a resurrection to eternal life. So, therefore, let us be comforted with these words, Ada shall live again."

John Westley's eyebrows rose, and his heart leaped with the idea that God was his only answer. Suddenly bowing, covering his head as though something was hurtling deep down inside of him. Tears streamed down from his eyes. "This is the most difficult period in my life. Death is not natural."

"You're right, my brother John Westley," declared Pastor White. "Death for the Saints of God, only cuts the cord that holds them captive in this present evil world. The sting of death removed through Christ's death on the cross. I believed that the angels will be there to help the Saints on their transferring from time to eternity. Although their journey towards eternal life goes through the valley of death, their pathway will have many signs of victory along the way."

Mag exclaimed, "Praise God! Our failure to comprehend God fully shouldn't strike us as strange. We already accept many mysteries that we can't explain. No one is truly ready to die; who hasn't learned to live for the glory of God."

Pastor White raised his head. "I'm afraid," he said quietly, "afraid that some people these days are making gods out of their imaginations, sets of rules, other humans, and some even seem to be worshipping themselves. As a result, people make a god out of alcohol, sex, fame, success, work, money, or even food. Out of their frustrations, some people will give up on pursuing the living God. They began calling themselves irreligious. I can understand a little. Death is not natural; people were created to live and not die. We are just dealing with the Lord's judgment because of our sin and rebellion."

Mag nodded rapidly, emphasizing the impact of her daughter-in-law's death. She settled back comfortably in her chair. She said simply to the pastor, "thank you for being here at our time of sorrow. Although time may never set things right, this family's broken heart desperately needs the Lord's strong hand to help us. Without a doubt, people need a rock to lean on during difficult periods."

Pastor White's face tightened, and his hand closed softly. "I came here for an exceptional purpose today."

"Yes, I can tell by your manner," replied John Westley.

"Well," said Pastor White. His fingers were rubbing his nose. "I am going to talk with you about death." Now pausing for a few seconds, "Ada is gone from our lives now. She is beyond pain; nothing more can happen to cause her unhappiness or misery. Her life in this flesh has ended for now. She lived a full, happy, and satisfactory life. God knows that woman could sing like an angel from heaven!"

"Oh yes, she could," yelled Mag, "Ada received so much happiness from her children, singing, gardening, and her church."

Pastor White said: "Ada's life here, with her earthy family, has ended in our present world; no one can add nor take away from it. All of our thoughts about Ada must now strengthen us to celebrate a life gone too soon. Our lives, with Ada, were so beautiful. She lived a wonderful life in a short period time."

"Thank you, Pastor White, for your good counsel and your assurance that you will be preaching my wife's funeral this Sunday," said John Westley. "Your word, pastor, has encouraged us with so much delight."

Pastor White recalled his times with Ada during various church services: leading the choir, performing solos, giving her testimony through songs. Abruptly, tears were dancing in his eyes. Then he said: "Ada was the greatest singer I ever worked with during my lifetime. She had lots of fans. Ada loved singing with a sort of uncompromising honesty."

Pastor White's heart filled up with joy at the thought of sharing these reflections. He was not able to finish the sentence. He got up out of his overstuffed chair and proceeded towards the front door. Pastor White went out on the porch, down the steps, then got into his car. He drove away, down the winding road, without any other words left behind, with his eyes full of tears.

Mary J had already came down stairs in the middle of Pastor White's closing details. She leaned upon her Grandma Mag shoulder as he was giving his final comments. After Pastor White left the house, Mary J took a moment to gather up her strength. She was now trembling from head to toe. Mary J made her legs carry her to the staircase; wherein, she began the long climb to her room.

Chapter

7

MOTHER ADA'S FUNERAL

The following Sunday, a funeral service was held at Craven Corner Baptist Church for Ada Bryant Godette. The funeral service was a significant reflection of a diverse community that included both young and old, black and white. The ushers seated the family members in the front centered rows. The wide variety of attendees couldn't take their eyes off Ada's young children—especially her baby—Lorraine. People became extremely sympathetic as the ushers kept telling the children: "Please, don't cry anymore!"

Leaning on her good intentions, Mag spoke words of kindness to her Grandchildren. She knew they were experiencing difficult times. Her words of comfort only caused more tears to flow from their eyes. Mag held baby Lorraine against her breast, using her fingers to tickle her little nose. Mag looked around towards the older children and then said in a soft voice: "It's not your fault; I am so sorry you are going through this hard situation. My children, we will get through this together."

Pastor White delivered the following passionate eulogy for Ada Brant Godette. "Our world is overflowing with massive changes, within a society that's filled with conflicts, tensions, and divisions. Human beings are vulnerable creatures, often experiencing severe emotional pain. Occasionally, their contacts with one another aren't always pleasant. Every so often, those in authority are compelled to use a good deal of force to get others to do disagreeable tasks. Even a careless remark may wound deeply; children sometimes have their whole outlook marred by a single unkind act. Nothing is lost when a person cultivates a kindly attitude towards others.

"The rise of modern science in general, and the evolutionary view of human origins in particular, has posed a significant challenge for our traditional ideas. To suggest that it's time to rethink the Adam ana Eve's Story is terrible enough, but to destroy our Christian moral teachings seem to be immeasurably worse. If this is true, the Hebrew prophets' and Christ's teachings concerning personal sacrifice must be counted as pointless.

"We all know that our Earth is full of living things. We can see with our own eyes many different varieties of animals all around us. We have the fish in the water as well as the bird in the air. The great oak tree is also a living organism wherein its stem and roots grow continually in length and thickness. So is the swaying blade of grass; so are the miniature animals and plants that are too small to be seen by the naked eye. When a person experiences growth, every organ continues its function. The heart as it grows keeps an even rhythm without so much as missing a single beat. Our bones, as they increase in size and strength, continue their functions of support and protection. Try to imagine an automobile or any human-made machine gradually growing in size while continuing in operation.

"Since the dawn of human consciousness, nothing has been more exciting than the chance of living longer, looking younger, and slowing the natural decay of the body. No one knows for sure why our bodies run down and finally stop like a spring wound watch. There is no reason for nature to hard-wire us to croak; it would make more sense for our environment to wire us to live—at least long enough to reproduce and raise our children. There is an agonizing trade-off between life and death for all living creatures.

"Our Christian faith should inspire us to ask questions about life and death. The greatest unknown in life is death and what lies beyond one's earthly journey. When People search for the deepest meaning of their lives, for some reason, they can never quite understand the mystery of death; often portrayed as one of the great enemies of humanity. Long ago, a man named Job asked the unrelenting question of all humankind: 'If a man dies, shall he live again (Job 14:14)?' If so, this would give us hope throughout our years of struggle on this Earth. People throughout human history have continuously sought the answer to this question.

"Usually, when a funeral service is over, people rush back to their familiar world, only to find a weak shelter in the widespread of science. Yet, we cannot avoid a supernatural explanation of an intelligent designer. It is said that King Philip of Macedon, father of Alexander the Great, kept a slave in his palace whose job was to approach the king every morning and cry, 'Philip, remember that you are going to die.' Most of us would consider such a disruption of our morning's work as somewhat low-spirited, there was a courageousness and truthfulness about the order of Philip, which discredits our present-day efforts of avoidance.

"Our contemporary scientists and theologians want nothing to do with mixing science and religion, but rather prefer treating them as separate realms of human thought. Scientists are, in reality, telling us that faith is emotional nonsense, expressing nothing but fear of death. Scientist, through their profound insights, believes in their god- like powers to revolutionize our world, with unexpected marvels and miracles.

"The Christian church regularly appears too busy with this present life, so it can easily escape the troublesome questions of death. The church hardly ever sings the hymns that draw attention to a longing for the other side. Ministers shun speaking on death for fear they will be labeled old fashion since preaching or teaching on eternal life signifies the existence of another order. We have a church that's quickly losing its prophetic voice—their message slowly being replaced by prophets of technology with their predictions for the future. Our sad effort to hide death implies that we don't understand its real nature. The emptiness of our present ways of life is rooted in the unacceptance of Christ's Kingdom. The people in our world want answers to life's greatest mystery; what lies beyond the grave?

"Our dearest beloved Ada took us many times into this unknown zone of death with her songs. I can visualize her singing now, to a pack filled audience, with standing room only. I can see in my mind's eye, some of the attendees almost paralyzed in spiritual thoughts, while others would be rejoicing with tears. Ada could sing in a voice that was so crisp that our spirits and emotions would come alive; especially, when her son Showalter played the backup melody on the piano. Her voice could change from soprano to alto, also blend smoothly within a group. Ada's singing could even inspire people to get happy about the unknown nature of death. Ada dedicated her voice entirely to the Lord. she was ready to sing whenever or wherever the church called for her services.

"We all cherish Ada's wonderful Christian's testimony. As a person, she lived in awareness of her accountability to God. Ada used her God's given talent, voice, and singing to praise the Lord. She was a beautiful person, blessed with an incredible gift; her labor in the Lord was not in vain. We are going to miss her presence.

"Our Christian faith challenges us to give the most surprising answer to this inquiry of death and what lies beyond the grave. I am here to tell you that according to God's word, death is neither the end nor the cancellation of life. Neither is it an ugly heartbreak nor a harsh chance that must be suffered through one's own strength. No, no, no, but rather, death will become the Saint's most significant victory. The sting of death has been removed by the work of Christ on the cross, and His resurrection. Death must be regarded as the gate that leads us to a more abundant life.

"Death has been swallowed up in victory. 'Where, O death, is your victory? Where, O death, is your sting' (1 Cor.15:54-55)? 'For I am convinced that neither death nor life, neither angels nor demons, neither the present nor the future, nor any powers, neither height nor depth, nor anything else in all creation, will be able to separate us from the love of God that is in Jesus our Lord' (Rom.8:38-39).

"As a Christian, death is not the end of existence but rather a doorway to eternity with Christ. Are you ready to face death? You can put your confidence in Jesus because he died for you. Let his angels gather you in their arms."

Pastor White took a seat as the Choir began singing Ada's favorite hymn. He wiped his teary eyes; tears were now flowing from family and friends. Ada's immediate Family's faces were soaked with tears; even her little children were rubbing tears away with the back of their wrists. Almost everybody was wallowing in misery. Mary J began to cry like a baby, thinking that her family had never done anything bad enough to deserve such punishment.

The viewing of the body was brief and immediately after the service. People walked in a single line past Ada's body on their way out of the church. As the family approached the casket for a final viewing, the church was suddenly full of weeping, wailing, and screaming. Ada's children began throwing themselves on the floor in mixed emotional tremors. Ada was finally laid to rest in the old churchyard cemetery.

Chapter 8

AFTER ADA'S FUNERAL

Nearly a year later, after Ada's funeral, John Westley was staring out of his kitchen window. There was an early morning breeze coming through the side door. Tiny hummingbirds were swarming over Ada's garden and flower beds like live coals—vibrant with energy—glowing in the sunlight. The hummingbirds quickly flashed across the flowers with females overshadowed by spectacular males with flaming throats. John Westley watched as the hummingbirds dashed at rivals, competing for Ada's red flowers and favored perches; they had begun chattering, seemingly in constant turmoil.

John Westley commenced thinking about how his life had changed since his wife had passed away. He began gasping for his breath without any tangible reason; little prickles of fear were now starting to travel over his body. Without his wife Ada by his side, John Westley felt afraid, inadequate, helpless, and alone. He strived to make sense of the world around him to determine what was real and what was deceptive. Yet, behind John Westley's fragile barriers, many of his questions couldn't be answered by his physical senses. While he could touch a leaf or smell a flower, he couldn't tell for sure what was fair or unfair for his small children—what was good or bad for his family. To make sense of his world, he found himself depending more and more on his Mother for validation.

Unexpectedly, Mag made her entrance. John Westley being absorbed in his thoughts; he did not hear his mother's footsteps entering the kitchen. John Westley turned towards Mag when something fell out of her hand.

"I'm sorry, son," said Mag. "Did I frighten you?"

John Westley looked down at the old table his wife used to work upon; he noticed that his Mother was leaning upon it. He said slowly, "Mama, what's next? I have been wrestling with this bitter thought of death—while everything around me is dashing with life, even the hummingbirds over Ada's flowers. Oh, how she loved her garden and flower beds! On the other hand, Mama, my wife has passed away and left behind children that certainly need her."

Mag nodded at him as a shadow of amusement came into her face. "My son, after the death of a close family member, we are prone to react emotionally rather than sensibly. Often, this means that we may start attacking ourselves rather than looking for more constructive solutions. You must remember: We have it in our power to begin our world over again. So, you should not let fear continuously overshadow your conscience."

John Westley tried to clear his head and think. "This emptiness that I feel is terrible. I don't drink, and I don't smoke, and I don't go out except for church and work. I don't hang out with ungodly friends except for my own family. I like to be quiet, I'm not troublesome at all, yet I am struggling to keep this family together. It would be impossible without you. Mama, I owe you everything."

John Westley's eyes were filled with tears as they walked into the living room. He quickly noticed a little table that stood in the Corner. He remembered how Ada had worked from that same place. The little table always stood out in front of the fireplace, covered with an ironing cloth or one of his pressed shirts. John Westley's heart became full of tears, because, in some strange way, he could see Ada rubbing away his coarse shirts to make them as smooth as silk. He remembered the many times that his wife would sit down her iron with a weary plunge, just to play with her children or smile at him.

John Westley shivered. "I am so painfully in love with my wife that her death has begun crippling my emotions. It's ruining my judgment and wearying me to the point of self-torture."

Mag spoke to him softly. "My son, your future is just as real as your past, even though you are now living and suffering intensely. It is your business now to repair your family's life, not to do away with it. In the fading light of today, I know that you still miss her. We both do. It will get better; It just takes time. Only gradually, my son, do all these consequences soak in, for this is God's way of easing our pains."

John Westley began weeping, along with short emotional utterance. He fell on his knees, crushed and struggling under the extremity of mental grief: "O Lord Jesus, help us! O' my God, do help us!" All of a sudden, there was quietness, John Westley began to pray more passionately in a loud voice: "Lord help me this day to search for a new beginning without my wife. Thank you for giving me the kind of mother that will stand beside my children and me, especially in our time of need. Help us to raise these children in dignity, respect, and with the fear of pleasing you; O Lord!" He groaned. "Please look down and give us the victory."

Mag knelt near the window, feeling the hard tile of the floor on her knees with satisfaction. She looked up at the heavens. "Lord, my son, will never make it without his wife Ada," she said, "never in this world, unless you help him. My son John Westley has always tried to be a good person. He has been a real community and church leader. He has always been ready to lend a helping hand to the poor and needy. His character constantly shines through his quiet and inoffensive spirit, thank you, Lord, for giving him the victory today!"

Mag tasted salt on her lips and grasped that she was crying, realizing that death left no other path but acceptance. She struggled with the mystery of death in her mind, determined to discover the meaning of life. She shouted out loud to her son: "Only when a person understands death—only then, life becomes a gift day by day—only then do thoughts of death produces love for life. No, no, no, I am not afraid of death; it's just that Ada left behind so many small children that truly need a mother."

A few minutes later, John Westley went up into his room for some private time. Things looked darker to him since his wife's death. It was unbearably painful for him to put on the appearance of cheerfulness, but he had to find a way for his children's sake. He kept thinking to himself.

"Can death be right? That life means nothing—and even if it does, death wipes away its significance."

Being the Sunday School Superintendent, John Westley began meditating upon the Scripture. He belonged to a small church that had a traveling pastor, he found himself during many of his pastor's responsibilities. As he was preparing his weekly Sunday school lesson plan, Mary J burst into his room.

John Westley called out sympathetically to her: "Mary J, listen to me! I'll be expecting you to be ready with good answers for Sunday school this week. We shall leave the house precisely at 9 o'clock this coming Sunday Morning. Your Mother Ada would have expected you to attend all of the church services."

"Yes, Daddy," said Mary J, "do you think that I will still have a store like Aunt Loretta?"

"Yes," replied John Westley, "the Lord will not forget you, even if I pass away. Just remember one thing, my little businesswoman. When the Lord bless you with your store, always try to be compassionate to your family."

"Yes, I will, Daddy," replied Mary J, "but I will not be a fool like Aunt Loretta; who let people steal from her store because she cannot read or write."

"Mary J, I know that you have a little rough streak in you from time to time, but don't forget your family! Your Mother has passed away. Your Grandma Mag will try to do the best she can to help us, but we also need to support each other."

"Yes, Daddy, for example, "when I get my store… Lorraine can come to live with my family and me, how about that Daddy?"

"That the way your Mother and I raised you to think, praise the Lord! Just remember, my little sweetheart, the Lord will make away for you to have your store for his purpose. Now you just run along, so that I can finish my Sunday school lesson."

Mary J's eyes blink slowly the way a frog blinks, then she smiled and nodded politely. "Yes, Daddy,"

Mary J ran out of the room to help her Grandma Mag with her baby sister. Lorraine was a beautiful child with a straight spine, high-held cheeks, and a sweet disposition. Mary J adored her. Distinctively, she respected her. She thought of Lorraine as her little child, mainly because their Mother

Ada had passed away. Mag sure could use the help, especially with her hands full of children. Mag now had to be mother and grandmother.

As soon as Mag began taking Loraine's bath, Mary J started patting the water, examining her little fingers and toes, then cheering Lorraine to laugh at the water splashes. She then started singing to Lorraine, just like her Mother did in the past. Mary J noticed the love and sweetness that her Grandma Mag exemplified in the process of drying Lorraine's limbs, fingers and toes. Afterward, she told Mary J to pick out Lorraine clothes to wear.

"Mary J," said Mag, "after you finish dressing Lorraine, please take her outside to get some fresh air." After noticing Mary J putting on Lorraine's Easter dress, Mag yelled out! "For heaven's sake! Why are you putting on her best clothes to play?"

"Oh, Grandma!" replied Mary J, "she looks so beautiful in this dress. I promise she will not get dirty. Rosie Lee and little Bertha Ray will be outside with me. All of us together will be able to keep this child's clothes clean."

"O' my Lord," said Mag, "children raising children, go ahead, Mary J, but remember, you're responsible for her."

Mary J rushed out of the house to meet Rosie Lee in the backyard. She began to shoo all the children away as if they were yard's chickens.

"Rosie Lee," said Mary J, "come on with Lorraine and me."

Rosie Lee raised surprised eyebrows, her tone deliberately mocking. "Where are you going with Lorraine?"

As Mary J rubbed her chin, she explained slowly, compelled by the demand in her voice: "Let's go over Zack and Ovine's house to get Bertha Ray; then we will have two children to play house with today,"

Rosie Lee smiled. "Come on!" Let's take a short cut across the ditch!"

Rosie Lee grabbed little Lorraine and hastily dashed across the roadside ditch. She wobbles for a second—quickly losing her balance, slipping back into the trench that was filled with wet mud. Lorraine's beautiful white Easter dress was now completely saturated with mud.

Mary J was all-out furious at Rosie lee because she knew that Mag was going to blow her stack. She snapped nervously, "Lorraine! Please stop crying; we will find a way to get you clean. Now, Rosie Lee, you have made a crazy decision—you are going to get me into hot water. I promised Grandma that Lorraine would not mess up her Easter dress. Look at her now; she is covered with mud from head to toe!"

"Oh…oh, my goodness," said Rosie Lee. "You think I'm crazy! What about Grandma Mag! How could she let you talk her into putting on Lorraine's Easter dress to go out and play? Why does she listen to your crazy ideas? By the way, your daddy is going to be mad; he will be home shortly from work."

Mary J lapsed into a silence of resentful acceptance. For a surprisingly short time, there was a calmness instead of turmoil. Mary J tried to work out a plan of action. "Here what we will do, one of us must sneak back into the house and get another dress. Then, we can clean her up at Ovine and Zack's house."

While Mag was in the Kitchen, Mary J sneaked into the house and ran upstairs. She took one of Larraine dresses out from the closet then rushed downstairs. As she returned back to Rosie Lee and Lorraine, their Aunt Salland was walking along the road to her house. She began hollering out, "you children wait right there for me."

Rosie lee shouts out to Mary J, "We have a gift from God…there is Aunt Salland."

"What are you girls doing to baby Lorraine?" Salland asked dryly.

Mary J closed her eyes and raised her face. Thank you, God, she said conversationally to herself. Next, she remarked directly to Salland. "We are in trouble because Grandma Mag told us not to get Lorraine's Easter dress dirty. My crazy cousin Rosie Lee jumped the ditch on our way to your daughter's house. Lorraine fell into the mud. Grandma Mag is going to be very mad at us, but she should only be mad at Rosie Lee."

Rosie Lee's anger swelled. "This was not my idea to dress Lorraine in her best clothes, and then go to Ovine and Zack's house."

Salland set her little hard chin towards them: "Mary J! Please don't blame your cousin Rosie Lee—because you are both at fault. You must learn to judge fairly the conduct of others and give another person a chance. Now, Rosie Lee, you need to remember this: When life isn't fair, don't dwell on it. Move on. Ask yourself: Will this matter tomorrow? Or in a month? Is it big enough to warrant a major upset with your best friend? Come on home with me, girls, while I help you all get out of this mess."

Silence now overshadowed Mary J and Rosie Lee as they made their way to her house. Salland thoroughly washes Lorraine: put fresh clothes on her, then placed her dirty clothes on the clothesline to dry. Afterward, Salland sighed. "You girls just go to my daughter Ovine's house and pick up my granddaughter Bertha Ray; then go out into your backyard and playhouse. Later, I will go and talk to your Grandma Mag, and hopefully get you girls off the hook!"

"Yes, Ma'am," said Mary J and Rosie Lee, then they went skipping down the road to Zack and Ovine's house to pick up little Bertha Ray. Mary J made sure that they didn't try to re-cross the ditch, but rather, they walked back along a little path near the roadside.

At the end of the roadside path, they met Mary J's uncle Charlie, which was Rosie Lee's daddy. He had a few drinks as usual on a Friday afternoon. Charlie never drank at home because his wife Annie Cleo wouldn't allow the consumption of liquor there. Annie Cleo learned a long time ago that the devil rode on a popping whiskey cork. Charlie wouldn't have done it any other way. He believed that a man didn't drink in front of his wife and daughters, but rather, in the woods, along the side of the road or at the whiskey house.

Charlie was not a church-going man like his brother John Westley. Although he was surrounded by people that dedicated themselves to God, it wasn't religion that forced him to hide his drinking. Men like Charlie allowed themselves to become squeezed between their affection for families and their love for the taste of liquor. He came home only when the whiskey was finish. This may seem unusual to have a man drink himself half-blind and then stagger back to his family. Especially, when everyone knows all the bad things it brings into a family environment. Nevertheless, this was one of the reasons why Mary J loved her uncle Charlie. His sweet nature was not turned ugly by drinking whiskey. Charlie drank while he laughed, sang, told stories, and usually went to bed, smiling. Charlie liked living, so he didn't drink to hide something, but rather, for its taste and good feeling.

"Hey, my Uncle Charlie," said Mary J, "It's Friday! Where is the candy?"

"I have two pieces for you and Rosie Lee," replied Charlie. They both ran to him at the same time to take the candy out of his hand. They grabbed his hand and took the candy out of it. Charlie was feeling so good that he also asked them to reach in his coat pocket and get some more.

"Rosie Lee," said Charlie, "go and see if your Mother has our dinner ready."

"Yes, Daddy," said Rosie Lee.

As Rosie Lee approached the house, Annie Cleo came out onto the porch. At that moment, she hollered out to Charlie: "Dinner will be ready in thirty minutes. She also added, "Honey, I sure hope you are not drinking today—times have been hard enough—you better leave Tom Bell along tonight! People are still talking about how the law kicked down his back door looking for illegal moonshine. Everybody knows that he doesn't have the brains God gave a water bug. How can whiskey run like water during these hard times?"

Annie Cleo was a little tired from working in George Ball's fields, digging potatoes, and chopping her vegetable garden. But as a faithful wife, she always had the family dinner ready. On her stove, she had a pot of pintos simmering with ham hocks and fatback. There were also golden cakes of cornbread in an iron skillet with an irresistible smell. The smeared bacon grease around the skillet, and the smell of hot bread could draw people into her front yard.

Mary J decided that she and Lorraine would eat dinner at her Uncle Charlie's house today. Charlie's face was full of laughter, as he walked into his house to prepare for dinner. He just let his wife fussing roll down his back about his Friday night drinking. For now, it was dinner time!

After dinner, Charlie was now ready for Tom Bell's place to further his drinking activity. Whiskey ran through that place like a river. Charlie worked hard during the week, but he was a weekend whiskey man. He was not averse to stopping off at somebody's house that had a large jug on their table. Charlie was wearing his ragged work overalls that had faded to gray. It had red spots all over the bottom of his pant legs. Right after dinner, Charlie was dressed in his Sunday-go-meeting' clothes, not his overalls. His face was staring out from under his favorite hat. As Charlie prepared to leave, he began singing senseless rhymes.

> "I am not going to town
> I am not going to the city
> I am going on down
> To Tom Bell Place
> Just to Rock and Roll until the place shakes"

When Charlie arrived at Tom Bell's place, the doors were left wide open so people could hear old Tom Bell play his guitar. Some of the other folks inside were singing with his music. As a drinking man will do, Charlie commenced dancing. There were no shags, no reels; just people buck dancing. Charlie knew the steps, but he couldn't have told you where they came from at the time. One of Tom Bell's children jumped on the piano, and everybody went wild.

Charlie was undoubtedly the oddball of his family, but even so, he didn't want his Mother Mag to know of his behavior. The men and women at Tom Bell's place acted like wild turkeys. Their language alone could knock a regular God-fearing person flat on his or her back. It wasn't that they didn't believe in the Bible. It was that they believed in other things as well. Unfortunately, they all had one thing in common, poverty! They lived in houses that were not much better than shacks.

Annie Cleo began dressing several of her small children for the revival meeting to be held at the church. In a special way, Mary J felt Annie Cleo's pain because of her husband's drinking habits. She said sadly to Annie Cleo, "Why don't you make Uncle Charlie go to the mourner's bench again? So. he can be a good husband and daddy—just like his brother."

"Well, said Annie Cleo, "your daddy is the kind of man that's made in heaven. They are few and far between. But don't worry about me, because I have faith in God." Then she started to sing her favorite song:

> "He'll be your friend when you are friendless,
> He's a mother for the motherless, a father for the fatherless;
> He's your joy when you're in sorrow,
> He's your hope for tomorrow;
> When you come down to the Jordan
> He'll be there to bear your burdens,
> He's going to step in just before you,
> At the judgment He's gonna know you."

Annie Cleo would end up singing her chorus lines several times. Mary J and Rosie Lee played the role of backup singers by blending in with vocal harmony during her melody lines. They would respond each time: "surely God is able!"

After listening to Annie Cleo's song, Mary J said, "how about me, my brothers and sisters? We have no earthly mother to love us."

"Oh, Mary J," said Annie Cleo, "your Mother was a great singer for the Lord and a dedicated servant. God will take care of everybody in your family. The store that you have been dreaming about will come true for you; now, just obey your Grandma and your Daddy. Just be a good girl! When the Lord bless you with your store, at that time, you can also help your family through their struggles."

Mary J's face was a picture of embarrassed discomfort. She said to Annie Cleo, "your words sound perfect, except my mother can't come back from the grave to help us." Mary J now had tears rising in her honest eyes, holding Lorraine by the hand. She continued: "We miss our mother every night."

Annie Cleo hugged and kissed Mary J and Larraine, then sent both of them home. She stood there by her door, staring at them. Annie Cleo couldn't take her eyes off those two little girls with no mother. In her thoughts, she could visualize their invisible guardian angels traveling along beside them, especially as they were walking between the two clumps of trees. Annie Cleo now shaking with anxiety-tears, flowing down her cheeks. She asked God to be merciful to them. Being mindful, their Mother Ada's voice was no longer there to guide them; she felt their emotional pain. In Annie Cleo's mind, as Ada's children travel through the rocky and thorny roads of childhood; They need both of their parents.

DEATH OF DAD AND ELDEST BROTHER

Showalter felt overwhelming joy when he saw his newborn baby boy being born. But within hours, he was living a horrible nightmare. His wife had died of a pulmonary embolism that instantly stopped her heartbeat. Within seconds—she was gone; there were no previous warning signs as she vanished from the family that loved and needed her. Showalter and his wife had four young children: an infant, a toddler, a four-year-old daughter, and a six year-old-son.

Just like his Dad, Showalter missed his mother and now his wife so much. He rocked back and forth with the sway of the wind: Shivering throughout the night while trying to sleep. There was a continuous nervous feeling dwelling within the pit of his stomach. He was trying to drain all the bitterness out of his heart—weeping with saddened eyes—wondering how he lost his way. Thinking as he looked out of dirty windows with tattered draperies, *What a shame—tragedy has struck our family again— with the death of another mother—leaving behind young children, why God! My poor Grandma Mag, in her old age, must now be simultaneously a mother, grandmother, and great grandmother...all rolled into one. My Dad and I have no one else to help us.*

After his wife's death, Showalter occasionally spent long hours at night before bed, gazing into the night sky. He would be wondering if his wife and mother were somewhere out there. Using his divided heart, dragging emotions, and painful experiences, Showalter would become passionately charged up by a sudden release of energy to write a new song, tunes about loneliness and feelings of isolation. The melodies most often came first, then the lyrics as he sat down at the piano—fiddling with the keys. Singing and playing his songs mostly during family gatherings, dedicated to his wife and mother.

It was early Friday morning, long before the sunlight began dancing in the sky through a rainy mist. Showalter, still in bed, had just dreamt that his wife was calling his name from somewhere far away. Unconsciously, he pressed his hand against his face and then along his tightened throat. His heart was racing, along with dropping eyes. He stopped, gasping, struggling to clear his mind. He quickly sat up in bed and let out a silent yell. It was hard for him to ignore the dream—slowly breathing—trying to forget the pain of loneliness. His eyes were red and swollen from weeping. He forced himself to smile. Yet, he had no desire to frighten his children.

Later in the day, as the sunlight began filtering down through the rain, Showalter decided to drive his children over to spend the weekend with his Grandma Mag. They traveled mostly on dirt roads; his children loved the bumpy ride as they twisted and dipped in low spots washed out by the rain. Manipulating the gears and speed from the pedal in the floorboard, Showalter kept looking over at his children with smiles and encouraging words. They were mostly giggling and laughing at each other.

As Showalter approached Mag's house, his nerves were very much on edge. Thinking, where is God when things keep getting worse? But somehow, the sound of his voice comforted him as he entered through the side door with his children. The atmosphere was surprising to him. There was none of the previous coldness of death like moods that had usually encircled the family's environment. The living room floor covered with a fresh area rug, along with new matching rose colors draperies on the main windows. Candlelight poured brightly over polished silver trays, distinctly located on two small tables.

Showalter turned his head; he heard sounds of laughter that were overshadowed by singing from upstairs. Over and over again, there were constant sounds of laughter, followed by singing. The music from the piano was like a bridge over trouble water for him. He smiled, thinking, *this is the way*. It was as if the family was having some weird kind of shift. He felt a sense of fatherhood again, supported by a trust from divine protection.

Showalter occasionally worked at the local sawmill, but mostly he toiled with his Dad: building houses, barns, pounding shingles, and farming. He thought this would be an excellent time to plan a trip to town. He sat down next to his Dad on the couch. "Let's go shopping in Beaufort tomorrow morning. We will be able to get Grandma's supplies and make a down payment on our construction and building materials."

After a long silence, John Westley only shook his head. He hardly noticed Showalter's solicitous and troubled eyes that were weak from sleeplessness. He knew that his wife's death had caused him to experience excruciating emotional pain. It was hard for him to watch hope die right before his eyes. John Westley looked startled, then please—he took a deep breath of delight. "I would love to, my son, as long as you stay overnight with us."

As Showalter looked up, his heart quickened to the magical rejuvenation of life. "Why not," he said out loud with wondering certain: "I'm not going to die because of losing my wife. After all, it's Friday night, that's not a problem. This way, I can spend some time with my brother and sisters. Also, I would like to see Uncle Charlie and his family."

James Westley came into the house from the side door to check on his Grandma. He found Mag sitting down in her room. Next, he stuck his head in the Livingroom after hearing his brother and dad discussing their shopping plans. "Brother Showalter, I would like to go."

"Oh certainly, my brother!" said Showalter, "Dad and I will be leaving around eight o'clock, so be ready."

After hearing the voice of Showalter, Mary J ran joyfully downstairs, shouting out: "Oh my goodness! My brother Showalter! What are you doing here?"

Showalter, with his gorgeous voice, called Mary J's name over and over again. He pinched her cheeks softly with his fingers. "Well, I am here to see you, my little sister! Don't you worry, I am going to help your daddy to build your store when you become of age."

Mary J drank in his words that somehow got mingled with her fading thoughts. "Mama, before she died, was going to help me. So now, I'm going to be counting on you and my daddy to assist me." Mary J paused for a moment. She became terrified, tears running down her cheeks, thinking that something might happen to them. "Oh, my Lord! I sure hope nothing else goes wrong."

"Oh my little sister," said Showalter, "I will be right there by your side. Maybe you can give me a little place in the corner of your store to play my guitar."

Mary J's fears crashed on her like a tidal wave. "Brother, you got it, but I am starting to feel some anxiety inside of me. I know this may sound strange, but inside—well, I'm feeling worried and uneasy as if something going to happen—whenever I pick up my mother's shoes, I shudder just a little thinking how short life can be—what am I going to do with my life? Mary J let her head droop towards the floor, then looked up again. "Now Daddy, when I get grown, you are going to build my store, right Dad?"

John Westley had a big grin on his face as he winked his left eye several times at Showalter: "Mary J, you can count on it; if the good Lord keep breath in my body—six- year from now, when you become twenty-one years old, we will start building your store."

Unexpectedly, the rumble of a crowd came from outside of the side door entrance. Charlie commenced banging on the door as if the world was coming to an end. Expeditiously, he just opened the door and made a grand entrance. Some of his children were standing behind him, just playing around and having fun. Charlie threw back his head and roared with laughter so loud that it became contagious throughout the house. Everybody began talking excitedly to each other—laughter filled the air.

Because of the whiskey scent on Charlie's breath, Mag came out of her room, steering down at her nose. She said with a firm voice: "My Lord, Charlie," pushing her way to a corner table, sitting drown in her favorite chair—crossing her legs at the ankles, placing a Bible on her lap. She immediately resumed her cross-stitching and needlework selections.

Mag frowned over her glasses at Mary J, then cleared her throat with several intense emotions, as if to remove away a lump. "Mary J, bedtime is a rule we must follow."

Shortly after eight o'clock, Mary J went upstairs. Her eyes were still shining as she undressed for bed. She folded her clothes neatly, said a little prayer, blew out the light from the kerosene lamp, and then leaped into bed. She lay sleepless for several minutes, thinking about how Showalter and her Daddy would someday build her dream store. She felt like jumping to her feet and shouting out with jubilation. She thought with a sense of relief. *Although I have lost my mother, yet my dream lives on.* She got up one more time and opened her room door so she could hear the chatter and laughter of her family downstairs. She then returned to bed and quickly fell asleep.

John Westley began yawning, "it is ten o'clock! I am going to bed. Showalter, you and James Westley need to go to bed soon so we can get an early start tomorrow morning."

Charlie cleared his throat, and then he said, "Good night, my brother! We are going home."

All of Charlie's children said, "Good night Uncle John Westley!"

John Westley grinned as he stood up from his seat very quickly. He slipped his arm around his brother, "now Charlie, are you sure that we can't give you a ride to town in the morning? I know this is short notice, but maybe you could reduce your drinking schedule tonight."

Charlie's face brightened, then darkened with what was almost his last breath, "oh yes, another day perhaps." Charlie's voice went stubborn, quickly lashing out: "Now my brother, let's talk about something else."

Showalter looked at Charlie's fat face and slack mouth. He reached out towards him with a long and gentle hand. "Come on now, Uncle Charlie, Dad, has a great idea! We will pick you up early tomorrow morning. We won't stay in town for too long."

Charlie said with a haughty laugh: "I wouldn't count on that because the night is still young for me. I tell you what; my Son Clyde Edmond can go in my place."

"Ok," said, Showalter, "You tell him to be over here at eight o'clock in the morning. Better yet, Uncle Charlie, my brother James Westley and I will walk home with you and deliver the message directly to him."

"Well," said Charlie, "Let's go."

Showalter, James Westley, Charlie, and his children all left together. They walked out of the side door near the kitchen. Charlie's children went on ahead, while Charlie, Showalter, and James Westley stayed behind in a lively conversation.

Charlie swiveled around in a happy mood. "Well, now, it's time for my medicine," he announced. "I have a little jar of white lightning in the weeds alongside the road. We can get us a little taste before we turn in tonight."

"I am not sure about that, Uncle Charlie," said Showalter. "Our Dad would be mad at us, especially if he ever found out about us drinking whiskey."

Charlie said, after noticing that everybody was in high spirits: "Well, my nephews, I wouldn't worry too much about that being a problem. Boys, it's Friday! We'll just have one little drink, at least I'm going to have a little taste."

They walked out of the yard and made a left turn and then walked approximately 100 feet down a dirt road. Across the ditch, behind a tree surrounded by weeds, there was Charlie's jar of whiskey. Charlie picked up the container and screwed off the lid and took a long sip. He then turned his eyes towards the boys and said, "Come on, boys, you want a taste!" He looked directly at Showalter.

"Ok," said Showalter. He then took a short sip. After that, he felt somewhat unhappy. His Dad had always encouraged him to set a good example for others, especially before his younger brothers.

James Westley stared at his brother Showalter, and then quickly took a big swallow. It robbed his breath away, eyes bugged out and faced turned red—in his mind, lightning started flashing and thunder crashing, "shhhoooh," said James Westley, "my God, this whiskey is too strong!" He asked Showalter to take a look at his throat to make sure everything was still there. He thought it had burned out his tonsils.

"Look at me, little James Westley!" Grumbled Charlie. "The best thing you can do right now is to take another big swallow. Then, you will be just like your Uncle Charlie."

Poor James Westley immediately took a second swallow. He began to tremble. Sharp pains were running through his throat; he became dizzy; he was now gasping for his breath.

Charlie shook his head. "Glory to God, what is wrong with you tonight?" He then noticed tears in his puffed-out eyes. "You mustn't upset yourself," repeated Charlie several times.

Showalter's heart gave him a sickening wobble. "You shouldn't be drinking James Westley, give it to me! I am going to take me another one." He became half-drunk from the second drink; nevertheless, he maintained a serene calmness. In an ordinary course of events, Showalter would never have taken a sip of whiskey, but somehow this night felt strange and different to him. He just wanted to enjoy his family.

Charlie glanced around at them, as his eyes flicked over the lines of his whiskey bottle. "It's Friday night, and the feeling is right—you boys need to keep up with your uncle."

Showalter was silent for a long moment. Then he said, casually, "Uncle Charlie, we have to take Daddy to town in the morning, so tell Clyde Edmond to be ready by eight o'clock. Let's go, my brother; Daddy will notice if we don't get in bed by midnight."

Drinking liquor always bother Showalter's conscience. He had grown up with the idea that drinking was immoral, sinful, and that drunks went to hell. Showalter began to think about his Dad's position as a deacon and superintendent of Sunday school. His Mother, Ada, although dead, was a gospel singer as well as the mother of the church. He was now the head church musician and directed the adult choir. Showalter didn't want his younger brother James Westley to start sneaking around drinking with Uncle Charlie. He knew this would break his Daddy's heart.

Showalter was now coming to the point of realizing how drinking whiskey affected people's interactions with others. In his opinion, it always created an atmosphere of fakeness that produced phony conversations and deceitful relationships. He started to think about how his daddy and grandma Mag had shaped a Christian culture in their home; their values didn't even approve of drinking on special occasions. A tear came to his eyes as he reflected on his brother, James Westley, taking his first drink of whiskey in the shadow of his presence.

With these thoughts in mind, Showalter wanted to send a message to his brother. "Come on; Daddy doesn't approve of drinking. We will get into a lot of trouble with him. Let's go home and prepare to take him to town early in the morning."

Charlie started to have a change in his temperament. His typical personality traits began to disappear; they were now being replaced with egotistical behaviors. Charlie started speaking loudly and then laughing for no apparent reason.

Out of nowhere, Charlie said, "I am going to have another little sip; come on James Westley, this stuff is good for you." Afterward, he stumbled, Showalter grabbed his arm. He regained his balance and then started towards Tom bell's speakeasy, known as the blind pig. Showalter and James Westley went home to bed.

Grandma Mag rose early the next morning to make breakfast before they left for town. She made some biscuit, fried up a batch of smoked ham, eggs, and potatoes. She also made a variety of natural fruit spreads. Mag stares at John Westley, Showalter, James Westley, and Clyde Edmond while eating, as if this was their final meal.

After breakfast, they were ready to go to town. John Westley had a righteous glow spreading all over his face as he walked out of the side door. He looked back at Mag. "Mother, anything else you need this morning from town?"

Mag spoke quietly from the porch between the Kitchen and the living room. She began to cough, then tried to clear her throat. "Please don't forget the coffee."

"Beg your pardon Grandma," said Showalter with his head lifted, and eyes widened. "Now, you know we wouldn't forget your coffee. We all love our lives too much."

Mary J finally awoke and heard the laughter downstairs. She ran to the window to see the chirping birds. Through the window, she saw her brother Showalter going toward his car. Mary J dressed quickly and ran downstairs to catch up with him. "Oh, Brother Showalter, I am glad to see you this beautiful morning!" She then flung her arms around Showalter Neck. Showalter begins to pull Mary J closer for a broader embrace. Mary

J also hugged her daddy, James Westley, and her favorite cousin Clyde Edmond.

"I love you all," said Mary J. "When daddy and Showalter build my store, you may all come and stay at my house. You may eat all you want free!"

Grandma Mag stood there on the porch gazing at them; she began frowning at Mary J for not washing up before putting on her clothes. "Mary J," she said sternly, "please go wash up and then come to breakfast. You need to leave them alone, so they can get to town and come back. You act like they're never coming back."

"Yes, Ma'am," Mary J replied as she ran on the porch and then proceeded towards her breakfast food on the table. She hollered, "someone gets the fly squatter and kill that fly on the table near my plate! I will be right back in a few minutes. She went to wash her hands.

Ella stopped washing dishes. She picked up the fly squatter and killed it with the first stroke. "I hate flies," said Ella. "Like Mama used to say, 'flies are not only dirty with a lot of germs but also dangerous to our health.' They can also cause illnesses."

Everybody went on the side porch to wave goodbye to the men going to town. Mag worst fear was losing her son John Westley and grandson Showalter. She knew that their children needed them, even more so now, since their wives' death. For some reason, Mag seeing her son and three grandsons ride away felt strange. She felt like some kind of curse must be on her family. She just couldn't accept another shocking tragedy.

It was now raining, as they drove off for the town of Beaufort. Everyone watched as they drove out of the driveway and made a right turn onto the dirt road. They could see the car making a signal to turn left at the end of the road. Their car soon faded out of sight, as Showalter drove toward town.

"Showalter, it's raining, so slow down, "said John Westley. "We have James Westley and Clyde Edmond in here with us, you know!"

"Yes, Daddy," said Showalter. "This rain is so bad; I can hardly see the road. Hold on! I am going to make a left turn onto 101 towards Beaufort."

After driving for several miles on highway 101, Showalter noticed that his windshield wiper on the driver's side was not working properly. He was within a mile of the dangerous Core Creek Bridge, which was structurally deficient and in poor condition. Showalter was concern that his defected windshield wiper could cause an accident.

As Showalter began to approach the bridge, James Westley and Clyde Edmond both yelled-out with frightened voices, "lookout for that car coming off the bridge!"

James Westley said, his voice now shaking, "Oh my God Showalter, just pull over for God's sake! Brother, your windshield wiper isn't working correctly; oh man, you can't see the road!"

John Westley managed to get his mouth working, but it was hard. "Showalter, you need to do as they say and stop this car now."

Suddenly the situation became a matter of the utmost urgency as Showalter's driving frightened James Westley and Clyde Edmond. Usually, John Westley was warm, gentle, and easygoing, but now there were traces of anxiety and downright gloominess.

Showalter said quietly, "All right, Daddy, but let's first get over the Bridge to the other side."

Showalter then pressed the gas pedal down slightly until the engine speeded up just a little. At the same time, a car was coming off the bridge from the other side. Simultaneously, there was a torrential downpour of rain, Showalter's defective windshield wiper was now squeaking louder and not able to clear the moisture. Now he was approaching the bridge entrance; another car was coming off the bridge traveling head-on towards them. Showalter slammed on his brakes and started jerking his wheel back and forth. His car nudged into a spin after skidding across the wet road then collided headfirst into the bridge. Showalter was thrown from the car when it hit the guard rail of the bridge. The vehicle was flattened from the impact on the front end. The car wheels were up in the air lying on the riverbank, just narrowly missing a plunge into the Intracoastal Waterway. Showalter was killed immediately on impact.

The driver of the westbound vehicle was uninjured. After seeing the damaged car, he ran over to help. He saw John Westley legs sticking out of a partially opened window, which he then broke to gain access. It was too late. John Westley died shortly at the scene of the crash. The other driver was able to help James Westley and Clyde Edmond to get out of the Vehicle. It was amazing that they were able to crawl out from the wreckage.

James Westley had a front tooth knocked out, and Clyde Edmond severely hurt his back. Both of them screamed with bitter tears for Showalter and John Westley, but now, it was too late.

When Mag heard about the accident, she tried to hold back an outburst of bitter tears for another death tragedy within her family. Mag was still dealing with the death of her husband John Kit, daughter-in-law Ada, and grandson Showalter's wife. The question in Mag's mind, who will take on the responsibility of raising John Westley and Showalter's young children? Were these Children now without a mother or Daddy? Mag finally burst into tears, questioning God in her heart. She was in a daze, fumbling for wisdom to deal with a feeling of helplessness and her grandchildren's bereavement.

Mary J came downstairs and sat next to her Grandma. She gently closed her eyes, leaning her head alongside Mag's right shoulder. She had tears flowing from both eyes. Mag comforted Mary J by moving her fingertips into her hand. Then she began cupping her head, rubbing in a slow and sensory manner. Mag thinking that her house was so full of delights just the night before, has now become a gloomy place, filled with strange darkness.

Mary J said in a pitiful voice, "Grandpa John Kit gone! Mama Ada is gone! Daddy John Westley is gone! Showalter is gone! Grandma, how are we going to survive? What will happen now with little Lorraine, Willie welt, Margret Ann, Lucy Gray, and Alvin? How about Showalter's Infant Arthur, his toddler boy, and his little girl Ethel Jane. They are like us with no daddy or mother. I truly thank God that at least James Westley and Clyde Edmond are still alive! When I get my store Grandma, then I can help you with these children. But now, my momma and daddy are dead; they promised to help me. I am certain now that only the good Lord knows who will help me with my store."

Mag took out her handkerchief, wiped her eyes, and then said, "Sometimes I feel like a broken branch hanging by a splinter. I know that isn't true because I am a branch rooted in the true Vine. Years without my husband John kit, now my son John Westley, and grandson Showalter, a part of that branch, has died. I find myself like a broken branch today in need of healing from a damaged spirit."

Nevertheless, my children," with her arms around Mary J and Lorraine in her lap, "this is the time we need to give thanks for what we have, not for what we want. We know God is sovereign and has never failed us. He won't fail us now. We are a fruitful branch, drawing from the living Vine. The Bible says, my children, at Matthew 28:20, 'Lo, I am with you always.' God is here. We are not alone." Mag wiped her tears away, but Mary J could still see a light of faith shining through her eyes.

All of a sudden, Mag only surviving son Charlie walked into the house through the side door, along with his wife Annie Cleo and their children. All of their eyes were full of bitter tears for John Westley and his son Showalter. Although Clyde Edmond would always have internal injuries, yet they were glad their son had survived the accident. Charlie lapsed into silence for a few minutes as he drifted toward the living room windows. He began thinking and staring at the old oak tree in the front yard. From his point of view, that old oak tree symbolized so much of his family's past activities. He could remember how he had played with John Westley under that tree, heard Ada sang like a mockingbird, and Showalter playing the piano, guitar, and harmonica like a master.

Abruptly, Charlie turned around and faced his family. He asks everybody in the room if he could have their attention for a few short minutes. "I like to honor the fallen soldiers of our family today. I mean right this very moment. I need to get this out of my heart and mind. They were just as brave as military people on the battlefield. Although I am not a churchman, yet I feel compelled to say a few words about my brother John Westley and his Son Showalter. I still can't believe that they are gone from us."

"This is the right thing for me to do today. My brother John Westley and I lived next door to each other. We have been together all of our lives. Our babies were handed from lap to lap. Our families ate at each other kitchen tables, and our children grew up together. Our houses shook with laughter and dripped with tears. Our children were very close companions and friends. We told our family stories over and over again to each other.

"One could only ask the question, who in this family could ever forget the tremendous musical talent of Showalter? Somehow, he had the mysterious ability to establish lasting rapport with onlookers. He played mostly at churches, community homes, and many times on our front porches. Many other times, in front of the local barbershops, during lunchtime for farmworkers, in the backwoods and on corners of dirt roads. He would occasionally play some secular songs in juke joints for Saturday night dances; only if his Daddy John Westley was not around to hear about it. He was a singer, songwriter, and musician who used the piano, guitar, and harmonica just like vocals instruments. The man had a bulletproof smile and a pocket full of dreams, but now he is dead.

"The quiet and gentle spirit of my brother John Westley will always be cherished by his family and friends who knew him. He alway had on a carpenter's apron. He built my family a beautiful little house; so that we could live in a fine-looking home, not a shack. My wife, Annie Cleo, and I couldn't thank him enough for standing with us through the thick and thin valleys of our lives together..

"My brother, John Westley, completely remodeled and transformed our Mother's house into one of the biggest and most beautiful homes in our community. He took an old run-down house and made it beautiful again. He kept up the repairs on our Aunt Salland's house. She has a daughter name Ovine that married a man called Zack; again, John Westley built their house. Whenever his family needed help, he made himself available for them; his kind-heartedness became one with his character."

Standing there, Charlie could look back and see his whole life. Unexpectedly, he sounded old, wise, and calm. An awful sense of loneliness had fastened down on him; tears poured from his eyes. Yet, he could somehow still feel their presence, deep within his heart and spirit.

Charlie's family brought with them the best of Annie Cleo's cooking: a pot of Pinto Beans simmered with ham hocks and fatback, several cakes of cornbread, pork crackling, mixed into a meal, lard, and buttermilk; along with, fried okra, squash, onions, tomatoes, and chicken.

Charlie said with tears in his eyes, "I want to say to you children, we are all one family. You can always count on us to stand by you and your Grandma Mag. My house is your house."

Mag's only daughter, Annie Miller, walked in through the side door with her three children: James Miller, Annie May, and Clarence. Annie loved her brother John Westley and his Son, Showalter. As heartbroken

71

as she was over them, she couldn't help feeling sorry for the children left behind without a daddy or mother. In her mind, this was a shocking tragedy that was a curse within itself.

With tears in her eyes, Annie said to her nephew and brother's children, "Look-up my children, so that we can remember the precious love ones that are no longer here with us. Each one of these short lives will always be a heartbreak. We must uphold the words of Job that say: 'The Lord giveth, and the Lord taketh away.' I have always loved my brother John Westley and his Son, Showalter. They will alway hold a special memory within my heart.

"I can still hear and see Showalter playing his musical instruments right now. He was such a talented musician in both words and music. He could reach out and snatch a melody from the sky to produce beautiful sounds on his musical instruments. His voice was that of an inspired singer with a natural passion. He could draw out of his throat the very soul of his music.

"Likewise, I can see John Westley speaking to his church congregation, teaching a Sunday school class, or using his Sunday afternoons to pray in the home of the sick and shut-in. I have shared both of your parents' tears and dreams for their children. John Westley was determined to build Mary J a store, just like her Aunt Loretta's store. But you children, don't ever give up because those opportunities will be realized, according to God's plan and purpose."

Despite Annie's tears and words of encouragement, one could easily witness those previous little happy faces fading into shocked and painful expressions. The younger children were bouncing around because they couldn't make sense of the situation.

Mary J had always prayed for her Daddy's safety since her mother's death, nearly three years ago. She began to think within herself: Why didn't it work this time? She had prayed continuously, but her prayers hadn't been answered, according to her expectation. She looked up in bitter tears and said to herself, "Was it time for my mother Ada to die three years ago, or my daddy John Westley and brother Showalter to be killed in a car accident this very week? Look at all these small children around us? I am only fifteen myself!"

72

Mag looked at Mary J with a startled expression, then nodded her head and said to her: "My child! I know how you feel. I have lost a wonderful son and grandson. Just like my daughter Annie, I can still hear your brother Showalter's wonderful music as your mother sang her favorite Hymns. I can hear your daddy's gentle and kind voice. They had planned to build you a little store someday, so please don't feel discouraged because of their deaths. God works in mysterious ways. Maybe, someday, the Lord will send you a good husband so that all of you can build a store together. All things are possible with God! You have had so many heartbreaks from the deaths of your loved ones." Mag 's face was now lit up with a big grin again. "I don't possess the talents of wearing a carpenter's apron like your Dad, but I will help you anyway possible. I believe that you will be a good store owner, just like your Aunt Loretta."

James middle, who was around Showalter age, said, "You just listen to our Grandma, Mary J, that's the main thing! The Good Book warns us not to dwell on the past. Instead, it urges us to keep looking forward."

Mary J, with tears in her eyes, began to remember not only what could have been, but also the present reality of what was, she wondered, "if the years to come, would be better than the past." The dream of her store ownership seemed now to be fading away; with the passing of her Mother, Dad and Brother.

"Hey James Miller," said Mary J, "I don't think my mother, daddy, or brother missed out on anything in death, because they truly loved God, music, and singing."

During the following week, John Westley's and Showalter's bodies were brought into Mag's house for two days of viewing, in the family's living room. Several times during day, viewers would assemble around the open caskets while meditating in prayer or reading a Bible verse. Although this was a community tradition, it felt strange to Mary J that her dead relatives were in the same house with her. She would cry along with her siblings and grandma, especially as various stories were being told about their lives; this was hard, especially now, since their mother Ada had preceded them in death. The family sat in silence, remembering John Westley and Showalter's lives, before their deaths, around an open casket.

73

James Westley and Clyde Edmond were in the car with John Westley and Showalter when they met their unexpected deaths. At the viewing of their bodies, James Westley was visibly upset. He kept thinking out loud: "this must be a mistake; just maybe, this is someone else, how can they be gone? We are still alive; why did God help us and not them?"

It was tough for James Westley to believe that his father and brother were not in their midst, telling everybody jokes, making them laugh, and giving a few winks. Everything was a blur for James Westley because he was in a state of shock and denial. James Westley mourned their deaths and couldn't understand how they were able to escape death and not them. He thought of Mary J's dream to own a store and talked to himself out loud: "Poor little Mary J, she will never get her store now; mother Ada, daddy John Westley, and brother Showalter—all had planned to help her. Mama was going to work in the store with her; Daddy was going to build the store; Showalter was planning to provide the music and songs, but now, it is a hopeless situation."

These double funerals were held at Craven Corner Baptist Church. The church grounds were crowded with hundreds of people, during the funeral service. Reverence White, the minister of the Craven Corner Baptist Church, was also the family's pastor. A great number of people, living outside this community, were still buried and married by Reverend White.

As Mary J sat listening to the Reverend White big booming voice, eulogizing her dad and brother funeral, she could recall them standing in the doorways of their home with delightful smiles all over their faces. Great wreaths of flowers surrounded their caskets with colors and fragrances. Grandma Mag wore a long black Sunday dress: a large wide-brimmed black hat with a veil, along with a black coat. Mag smiled and greeted everyone as Mary J and her siblings walked with her to the three front rows near the caskets. Reverend White waited until all the mourners assembled in the church. He smiled at Mag and the children, then opened his Bible, and began to read from the book of John.

Reverend White began his comments after the reading, "this was the story of Jesus' special friend Lazarus of Bethany, whom Jesus loved. Apparently, Lazarus had grown ill and died before his sisters, Mary and

Martha, could get word to him. The Apostle John, an eyewitness at the scene, remembers how Jesus wept when He was led to His dear friend's tomb.

The people watched in disbelief and joy as Jesus said, 'Lazarus, come forth! I am the resurrection and the life.' Jesus said to them that day. 'He that believeth in me, though he was dead, yet shall he live.' Both John Westley and Showalter were believers. They chose to believe in the promises of God through his Son, Jesus Christ. The good news is that Jesus is the resurrection and the life, anyone who believes in him will live again, although death has taken them."

The overcrowded funeral procession stretched around the church, more than a quarter-mile long. John Westley and Showalter were buried in the family section of the Church cemetery, on a hilltop next to their wives. Mary J and her family were able to look back down the hillside at the steady stream of people. They had gathered to pay tribute to their Daddy and Brother. The grass had been trimmed and smelled garden-fresh. The trees were changing from green to bright orange. The countryside itself appeared decked out for this celebration. There were lots of flowers adjoining the caskets; nearly all the mourners dressed in black.

Mary J was indifferent towards the preacher comments. She was more interested in the crowd of people stretching out from all directions to recognize her Daddy and Brother. They had come to honor them: Showalter—who brought beautiful music to their ears; John Westley— who watched over most of the church and its community activities.

Reverend White finished his address with a stirring reminder that "God's is a forgiving, loving and kind Father through His Son Jesus Christ." He then took out his handkerchief and said in conclusion, "Now we must commit this family; especially, these little children," he hesitated for a second, then said, 'into the hands of the Almighty." Again, he paused for a second, then said: "I know that He will sustain these children through this difficult period."

Days after the funeral, Mag would often retreat from the world and reflect on Reverend White's final words of encouragement. She would sit on the edge of her bed; sometimes, she would be singing one of her daughters-in-law Ada's favorite funeral songs from earlier years. At other times, she would sit in the shade, Lorraine in her lap, the other children clustered around, and singing in a sad, pure tone:

> *In the sweet by and by*
> *We shall meet on that beautiful shore*
> *In the sweet by and by*
> *We shall meet on that beautiful shore*

Mag truly missed Ada, John Westley, and Showalter terribly; so much so, that in her mind, she still spoke with them, from time to time. The little children, including Mary J, would start to cry. Sometimes, little Lorraine's lips would begin to tremble for a mother and father that she would never know. The boys would shake their heads in sorrow. Sometimes, the younger children would fall on the ground, grieving the death of their parents. They would have a sudden outburst of tears triggered by their memories. During these times, their Uncle Charlie, with tears in his eyes, would try to comfort them.

In time, most people will forget dead people as if they had never been at all. But when people talked about John Westley, Ada, or Showalter, they always raise their hands, and a smile would creep across their faces. They would say, "Hey, remember the musical talent of Showalter's playing his guitar, piano, or harmonica. How about Ada's powerful singing voice? Better yet, what about the amazing Spirit of God upon John Westley as he taught our Sunday school lessons and led the congregation in worship and prayer." A great legacy for loved ones to be given in their death, by a family that refused to forget them.

Now, the human eyes of this community fell upon Mag, she was the only cradle for raising these young children that were left behind. Many times, she would appear to be in some type of mysterious thoughts. Nevertheless, without even being said, everyone knew that all Mag's grandchildren had down-to-earth love for her. Let's just put this on the record: a lot of people say, 'They have given their complete lives to their families.' But with Mag, she had the proof to back up every line. Her fingers were hurting from sewing clothes, brown spots upon her face, and hands from the hot fields. The continuous hard work of raising a garden and maintaining fruit trees to provide food.

Mag's hairs of gray were already beginning to emerge, along with little white scars received from wading through the brier's patches of the fields. The country was at the height of the Great Depression throughout the 1930s; times were still hard for everybody, even more so for an aging widowed grandmother with no husband. Mag had given birth to three children. Now in one day, she had lost her son John Westley, who left behind six small children to raise without a mama. The same day, in the same car, she also lost her grandson Showalter, who left behind three young children in her care without a mother.

During the bleak years towards the end of the Great depression, Mag was now focusing on raising her parentless grandchildren. She understood these times would be long and severe; since her grandchildren's support now rested primarily upon her shoulders. As Mag's worries started to pile up, she was determined to keep her grandchildren together under one roof. Mag constantly created a way out of no way, by pushing through the dark curtains surrounding her family. She was always shining out a beautiful smile to her community. Mag's dominant attitude became like flipping a light on—in a fully stock pantry, even when it was empty.

Chapter

10

MARY J TAKES A HUSBAND

T he years surrounding World War One and the Great Depression called traditional religious beliefs into question. Some cast off the tie-ups of creeds and biblical thoroughness; others came to regard science, especially Darwinism, as a threat, rather than an ally. The destruction of World War One, along with the massive economic devastation of the Great Depression, had shattered a simple belief in the goodness of human nature. Life during the Depression had been brutish and cruel; delivering to many firsthand, the gnawing pains of hunger.

Mary J was born shortly after the end of the First World War; she grew from childhood to adulthood during the Great Depression years. The Depression ended with the coming of World War Two, Mary J's life had changed radically over the years. She was now twenty years old—her life had evolved during some of the most challenging times in America's history. Dark shadows had fallen all around Mary J's life, especially after the death of her parents and eldest brother. Nevertheless, somehow by the grace of God, she was determined to live fully in the present—free from inflexible inner values surrounded by walls—free from an excessive need to conform to the social prescriptions of her time.

Mary J held onto her dream of owning a store throughout the Great Depression years. Even though her pathway towards achievement was not quite visible, she kept on pursuing this long-range goal. Although, Mary J had won no significant battles towards the realization of her predetermined goal; she just kept thinking, *my parents and older brother are dead—my old widowed Grandma cannot do everything—who will the Lord send to help us?*

As fate would have it, on the other side of the Creek, her Cosmetic pendant of Prayer for an entrepreneur partner was in the process of development. Pap, a local man from the Harlowe community, was willing to work tirelessly in the trenches, helping to lay a foundation for business growth in the Harlowe's community. Even though, he never accepted his Mother's strict religiosity; Pap was considered by his community to be a diligent, honest, and upright man—who was a good citizen, as well as a kind and helpful neighbor. A man of his time that was sensitive about his community economic challenges, and willingly accepted high risk opportunities to meet them.

Although Pap wasn't bothered by long work days or an unpredictable environment, he took what fate brought him with a steady eye. Pap and his business associates recognized that at the heart of securing social and economic advantages was the need for people to work honestly together. They felt that people could change the social forces underlying their troubles. Pap and his business associates didn't care how society perpetuated social inequalities. Instead, they focused on building and bringing together a network of social relationships, which were tied together for a common good.

Pap made his living as a full-time farmer and part-time moonshiner. He had a direct advantage as a moonshiner because he lived on his Grandparent's 120 acres of waterfront property. This is where he established his bootlegging operation. Pap knew every square inch of their property, from the marshlands to its voracious predators. He understood how the tides moved forward and back across the intersecting rivers and creeks, stranding the blue crab and fish inhabitants. He noticed that various animals could find food in plenty, but only at the risk of providing meals for creatures better armed than themselves. For Pap, this was his battleground for conquering the pearls of life. Right here, where Clubfoot Creek flowed into the Neuse River at the mouth of Mitchell Creek. The place where his bootlegging operation was nearly unchallenged by local law Authorities.

Pap's Grandfather, Solomon, created a farming area on this land when it was saturated with beautiful long-leaf pine trees. Solomon soon learned that the sap from those trees could be used to make tar, pitch, rosin, and turpentine. He sold those products, called naval stores, to wooden boat-builders and other businesses. After a while, these woodland's jobs gradually came to a standstill, especially once wooden ships and boats were replaced with mostly metal structures.

Now when Pap came along, the woodland's jobs were nearly gone. There were only a few ways left for a man to earn a living for his family. As a small farmer, he had to become a jack-of-all-trades. Normally, small farmers grew just enough to stay alive and ate what they raised; this allowed them to live from hand to mouth. There was very little time for books or book learning—people's primary education was mostly shaped by meeting others or winning over difficulties from their daily work.

During Pap's times, moonshine flowed up and down the East Coast. Around the waterfront, moonshiners would haul out their finished product in rows of containers tied onto trotlines, then towed behind boats. The crew would cut the lines, causing the kegs to sank, then retrieved the finished product later. Federal Revenuers used late night's raids that shutdown many stills. Nevertheless, production in most areas continued for years; the moonshiners often outsmarted the law; sometimes, they were in cahoots with each other and drinking buddies.

Moonshiners hired runners to carry their whiskey in cars. The runners would transport the liquor after midnight when the roads were clear. They had the fastest cars on the roadway that could out-run the Revenuers. Moonshining was so profitable that moonshiners could lose every third car with a full shipment and still made a profit. Moonshiners organized pre-order delivery routes with their clients to guarantee immediate deliveries upon release—just like the milkmen, going from one place to another.

Being a way out of poverty, many white and black men became bootleggers. A local brand of corn liquor, known as Craven County Corn, had strong recognition throughout the Northeast. The reason these men peddled moonshine whiskey was to keep their family alive, to hold onto a rooftop over their heads, and keep clothes on their backs. Most of these moonshiners were hard-working, prayerful, churchgoing, and honest people. They sweated hard to make some money, simply to survive from day today.

Prohibition created a vast market for the production and sale of alcohol. The cancellation of prohibition in 1933 only slightly reduced the request for moonshine. Craven County Corn whiskey continued to be profitable and in high demand for many years, even throughout the 1940s and 50s. The know-how of moonshine distillation and distribution swept through many rural communities. Most families living in these communities had operated a still. At the least, they would have known someone that was running the mash or resetting the barrels for the next run. Moonshine had been a part of North Carolina culture and tradition for many years. Moonshine was sold throughout its eastern swamps to the mountains.

During these hard times, many of the beautiful homes in rural North Carolina Counties came directly or indirectly from the sale of intoxicating liquors. Moonshine production and distribution became a valuable business. Many mom-and-pop operations sold whiskey right out of their homes. Moonshining became the next engine to drive economic growth. Men like Pap began to say to themselves: "Wait a minute! I got an idea; anyone likes to purchase a jar of moonshine?"

On New Year's Day 1940, Pap stopped at the Beer Garden in his community to conduct business with Luke, the owner. James Westley, Mary J's brother, was there in need of a ride home. After doing business with Pap, Luke walked over to James Westley with a cigar in his mouth. He placed his left hand on his shoulder as he took a puff from his cigar.

Luke blew the smoke right into James Westley's face without a second thought. "Pap meet one of my good customers: James Westley."

Pap responded with an enormous smile, "glad to meet you, James Westley."

"Glad to meet you also," said James Westley in a high pitch voice, simultaneously coughing from Luke's cigar smoke. After regaining his voice, "Pap, I have heard nothing but good things about you."

"Well, thank-you, but aren't you kin to James Miller?" Pap said with a sparkle of sarcasm, with some humor beneath his words.

"Oh yes, that my first cousin! To tell you the truth," said James Westley, now in a lower pitch voice. "I was waiting for James Miller to pick me up, so I can go home. But now, I am not sure he is coming to get me."

James Westley was looking-for a ride back home to Craven Corner, which was a section of Harlowe named after its local church. This section of Harlowe was separated from North Harlowe by Clubfoot and Mitchell Creek.

"No problem," said Pap, "you just live on the other side of the Creek; if you want, I will give you a ride home in just a few minutes."

Pap swayed around, then he yawned, and stretched. He rubbed his hand over his chin. James Westley could almost hear the rasp of his unshaven whiskers. He had shadows under his eyes from working all day on his Mother's farm and late into the night at his moonshining operation. His black hair was messy, standing upon his head, along with an untidy appearance.

"Ok, that wonderful!" said James Westley, grinning from ear to ear. "Pap, I am ready when you can take me."

"Well now, James Westley, here is the proposition," said Pap, "I heard you got some beautiful sisters, and I would love to meet them."

"Well then, let's go, Pap! I would be glad for you to meet my family."

James Westley was a handsome and dashing young man—very well-dressed—a man that loved women and a good time. He was a confirmed bachelor that had considerable trouble handling his whiskey and money on weekends. Pap usually wouldn't associate too closely with a man that couldn't control his alcoholic beverages.

Pap always kept changing clothes in his car. Luke allowed him to use his private facilities to freshen up. Afterward, he and James Westley walked towards the front door to exit the building. Pap had several people that wanted to talk to him on his way out. He excused himself with the following comment: "I will stop back boys after taking James Westley home."

Pap and James Westley walked out of Luke's Beer Garden conversationally, then got into Pap's car and drove away. James Westley couldn't stop talking about his beautiful sisters and loving Grandmother. He told pap the sad story of how both their parents had died when his sisters were youngsters.

James Westley cleared his throat as he persistently kept telling his family's story. "My Mother, Ada, died shortly after giving birth to my baby sister, Larraine, leaving behind nine head of children, most of them were stair-steps, not even teenagers." James Westley had a tearful look in his eyes as he continued: "My daddy and oldest brother were killed instantly in a car accident less than three years later. My cousin Clyde Edmond and I were in the back seat of the car; we just narrowly escaped death ourselves. If it wasn't for our Grandma Mag, only God knows what would have happened to my family, and my brother Showalter's little children. Grandma always made sure that my sisters walked the straight and narrow paths of life. I couldn't be prouder of them. They are the essence of what women should be, thanks to Grandma." His voice now stuck in emotional quicksand. "You know, Pap; I will do anything to help my family, include giving them my right hand, if necessary."

"Alright," said Pap with a warm understanding smile, "let's go check out the merchandise!" Pap was teasing, knowing that James Westley had a couple of drinks; nevertheless, James Westley was very much in control of himself. By this time, Pap was making a right turn down a dirt road towards his house.

James Westley said, "That's my house on the Left, with all the people on the porch." Pap slowly turned into his driveway.

"James Westley! Who are all those good-looking girls on your front porch?" Pap said in a humorous but an appealing manner; then, he began to laugh again.

James Westley was surprised by his penetrating voice. "They're my sisters and cousins—would you like to meet them?"

Pap glanced at him, amazed. "Yes, especially the little short one over there. I have always liked a short woman."

James Westley's eyebrows rose, and his heart leaped. "Oh, my goodness! She's a very high-spirited young lady that's full of energy, but has quite a good business mind. Come with me on the porch; I will introduce you as my good friend."

Pap got out of his car dressed for the occasion. He was wearing his favorite black pants, a white shirt, along with his hair all slicked back. This was far different from his usual farm outfit that consisted of work pants, no shirt, and barefoot with a brown paper bag on his head.

Pap and James Westley went on the front Porch. James Westley introduced Pap to everyone, including his Grandma Mag sitting on the swing with Mary J. "I like for everyone to meet my good friend Pap, who lives in North Harlowe."

James Westley went into the house towards his bedroom. People came pouring through the open door, talking, laughing, and pausing on the porch, reluctant to see the end of a joyous evening. Suddenly, there was a laughing avalanche of young people running across the front yard.

Mag offered Pap a seat to sit down; he accepted the invitation with a warm smile, and then extended the conversation by saying, "I see that James Westley has a very nice family; it is my pleasure to meet all of you."

Pap began laughing along with the crowd; his laughter was extremely friendly, even admiring. He acted as if they had always been his good friends.

Mag smile, then glanced at James Westley, "Thanks for bringing him home in good condition." She then threw up her hands while groping towards a better understanding of Pap: "Now tell me, who is your family?"

Pap said gracefully, knowing his Grandparents' good character. "You may know my Grandparents: Solomon and Susan Lennie Fisher!"

"Yes, I do," said Mag, "your Grandmother was a midwife who delivers babies in Harlowe, especially in her younger days."

"Yes, ma'am," said Pap—sharing her perceptions and feelings. "My Grandma, Susan Lennie, believed in delivering babies as a call from God. She did not say no to anyone, whether the person had money or no money!"

"You are sure, right, Pap!" Mag exclaimed. "she didn't care whether the person was black, white, rich, or poor. The weather didn't hinder her either, it could be raining or the sun shining, Susan Lennie would be there."

Pap said. "Yes ma'am, she loved her work and could even make medicine for minor ailments like the flu, fevers, and chills."

Mag quite unconsciously, interacting with Pap in her subtle ways. "I also knew your Grandfather Solomon, who sold wood by the cord or by the pen. My husband, John Kit, brought home some turpentine, pitch for his boat, and several chair seats made out of ropes from corn husks. He also got a rocking chair from him a few years ago. By the way, making seats out of corn husks is an ancient craft. Well, Pap, you certainly came from a good family. I mean a hard-working family."

"Thank you," said Pap, as his head went up and down. He was continually giving Mag lots of positive validations. He could tell that James Westley's family liked him right away from their self-disclosure statements. He also began disclosing himself as much as possible.

James Westley walked out of the front door that led back onto the front porch. He asked Pap if he would stop him off at another resident. One could quickly tell, from Mary J's smile, that she was impressed with her Grandma's comments about Pap's family. Everybody said "goodbye to Pap" as he began to walk out with James Westley.

Pap responded likewise by saying, "good-by to everyone on the porch," with a unique smile towards Mary J.

Pap and James Westley got back into the car and started down the road. James Westley looked at Pap, then said, "I could tell from you all conversation that my Grandma likes and respects your family."

Then Pap said to James Westley: "whenever you need a ride home again, please let me know; I would love to see a little more of Mary J if that's all right with everybody."

"Well, you know," said James Westley, "Grandma Mag is stringent on my sisters, but I will let Mary J know that you would like to see her again."

"All right," said Pap, "maybe you will need a ride somewhere this Saturday if so, I can pick you up." He was looking directly into James Westley's eyes, feeling his response. Instantly, James Westley accepted the ride for Saturday; it fitted his plans perfectly. After Pap dropped-off James Westley, he went to work for the rest of the day.

James Westley returned home later that night. He said to Mary J, "My friend Pap will be picking me up this Saturday evening. He hopes to see you again."

Mary J responded by saying, "I'll see how it goes! I may not even be here. Why does he want to see me anyway?"

"How do I know!" said James Westley with a frown on his face, as if he was disappointed with her attitude of self-importance. "Pap must be impressed with you as a person for some reason. You know, I can see a little flame in his eyes when your name came up. But now, listen to me, Mary J, Pap is a smart man, single, from a good family, and that's all I know about the situation. What a shame that you're always such a fussy young woman!" James Westley shouted, lifting his hands, turning his back to the door, then began speaking in an unnatural tone, "maybe that's all you need to know!"

"Brother James Westley," said Mary J, "have you been drinking? If so, your word is not worth anything in my book. If Grandma Mag ever found out that you came into this house drinking! You will get a piece of her mind. Let me think about this; I might even tell her."

"That's my business," said James Westley. "This is your oldest living brother talking to you now, Showalter is dead." James Westley's temper flared up. He angrily walked out, then proceeded upstairs to his room.

When Saturday rolled around, Mary J felt the need to dress up just a little and did a beauty fix on her hair. She had no idea what James Westley was trying to do by boosting this relationship. Mary J didn't trust James Westley's nonverbal signals that were aimed at influencing her actions. His prompt communication indicated his desire for her to feel what he felt, and to agreed what he had decided. She didn't like the messages that he was conveying to her.

Pap came to pick-up James Westley exactly at 4:00 p.m., just as they had set-up earlier. As he drove up, Mary J was walking out on the front porch. When Pap got out of his car, a watchful rooster appeared out of nowhere, acting very aggressive.

Mary J walked out towards Pap. "I know you not afraid of this old rooster. He is too ancient to attack anyone. This old rooster is just like a lot of people, all show and no action."

"Now! I am not like that old rooster," said Pap, "because I am a little slow but full of action, that why I am glad you came out to help me."

Mary J interrupted, "Why is that so important?"

"Well," said Pap, in a playful mood. "I am hoping to get to know you. Your brother James Westley was telling me how smart you are and the good common business sense you possess. He also said that you wanted to own a grocery store someday. So, you are like me, full of action."

"Oh, Pap! That's so true. My Aunt Loretta had a little General store. I always loved working in her store since I was eleven years old. My mother and Dad used to take me there when they were alive. My Daddy was a top-notch carpenter, and he had promised to build me a store someday; my mother also had promised to help me by working part-time. But that plan will not happen now; God has taken both of them away from me."

"I am so sorry to hear that Mary J, but I am confident that you will find away. Especially if you believe in God's purpose for your life, He will open a door for you."

"Well, thank you Pap, it's good to meet a man that believes in dreams. What would you like to become?"

"Well, for now, I have a little side business and runs my daddy's farm since he died three years ago. Also, I look after my Mother, Rachel, and teenage sister Alma Tucker. My Brother Fred also still lives with us; he is currently working at Blades Sawmill."

"Pap, that is so responsible of you to fill in the gaps after your father's death," said Mary J. "You must be a nice person, like my brother James Westley told me. You can't always believe him, because he loves to joke, way too much. He is known to drink too much whiskey, date a lot of girls and never make a commitment to any of them. You aren't like him, are you?"

"Oh, no, Mary J," said Pap, "I can see that you are someone exceptional. I know that anyone blessed enough to have somebody like you, would want to do the right thing. I always wanted to meet someone—just like you—a woman with a good moral compass. A woman who knows exactly the direction she should go; especially, when force to make decisions involving right and wrong. I would love to see you regularly; so that, we may enjoy the benefits of each other company."

"Well Pap, if you want to come see me, my Grandma will have something to say about that!" Responded Mary J, laughing and giggling at Pap's statement.

"That sounds good!" Then Pap looked around and said, "Here comes your brother. I will be back with him in a couple of hours." As Pap left with James Westley, he tossed his shoulders back with a big grin that was bubbling with joy.

"Come on, Pap, let's go!" said James Westley.

After several more visits to see Mary J, Pap made the acquaintance of Zack Hodge. Zack played a crucial role in helping Pap to establish his relationship with her. He was a first cousin to Mary J's Mother. His wife, Ovine, on the other hand, was the daughter of Salland, who was Mag's sister. This made Mary J kin to them on both sides.

Zack and Ovine were neighbors of Mag and lived just across the road. They were in many ways just like second parents to Mary J, since her parents' death. For Pap to gain their endorsement, was indeed a big deal. They helped pave the way for Mary J and Pap to pursuit their dreams. Mary J had a lot of confidence in Zack and Ovine. Likewise, they loved her.

Mary J, along with her brothers and sisters, lived with their Grandma Mag, under her supervision. Mag didn't approve of Pap because of his age, which made him nearly ten years older than her. For Grandma Mag, this was a significant concern. Mary J didn't want to upset her Grandma Mag with any kind of issues. She typically sought-out Mag's consent on all her actions; so that, she didn't have to hear her fussing day and night. Mag would even go and get the preacher after Sunday services to help resolve issues when necessary. This was the last thing Mary J wanted to happen.

As a compromise, the home of Zack and Ovine became a perfect meeting place for Pap and Mary J at the beginning of their courtship. This way, Grandma Mag wouldn't have to approve of their relationship right away. Zack and Ovine had a small two- bedroom home with a two-seated swing on their front porch. Now, when Pap came to pick-up James Westley, he could meet him at Zack and Ovine's house. James Westley would let Mary J know the night before, so she could meet Pap over to Zack and Ovine while he waited for him. Pap had also won over another member of Mary J's family, her first cousin James Miller. He became quite warmhearted towards Pap and supported their relationship.

Mary J believed that in time her Grandma Mag would come around. Pap and Mary J were quickly going through their preliminary steps toward marriage. For this couple, marriage was becoming a realistic possibility extremely fast. Due to the death of Mary J's parents, Zack, and Ovine became Godly mentors and counselors for them. Mary J was not the kind that would allow Pap to be kissing, necking, and cuddling around with her in dark rooms or squirming in parked cars. She maintained safeguards that ensured a real noble courtship. Her Christian standards, certainly was a tribute to her deceased parents, Grandmother Mag, Zack and Ovine.

Pap and Mary J shared a storybook relationship that went on for several months; then, it became clear to both of them that they were in love. The two of them were inseparable in spirit. Mary J was now twenty years old and would be twenty-one on December 16, 1940. They eloped and was married by a country preacher in Beaufort, North Carolina, on December 21, 1940. Mary J's loyal friend and confidant, Ovine, was the only one by her side when she and Pap were pronounced husband and wife. Somehow Zack must have known because he waved his hands as they went by in Pap's car.

Now, on the way back, the plan was for Mary J to go home to her Grandma Mag. Pap was to come by later. He dropped-off Mary J's to Ovine's house. Mary J walked home from there to see Grandma Mag. Afterward, she planned to figure out how to tell her. She had no idea that little Bertha Ray, Zack and Ovine's daughter, had already told the secret marriage plot.

The very second that Mary J came into the house, Mag gave her this challenging question, "Mary J, I certainly hope you didn't marry that old man, did you?" Mag sat down and pulled out her knitting-work. She had an unfriendly look upon her face. Nevertheless, Mag continued knitting her fabric until Mary J finally responded to her question.

"Yes, I did, Grandma," said Mary J, with a trembling voice. She thought that her decision might be saddened her Grandma Mag. Mary J always wanted Mag to think highly of her.

"Well, you shouldn't have because of your age differences," said Mag. "But I forgive you now, sweetheart, because Zack, Ovine, James Westley, and James Miller thinks so highly of your new husband. So maybe you made the right choice, I could be wrong. Pap comes from a good family. From all I have heard of him, he is a very responsible person. By the way, I am making you a new dress as a wedding gift."

Mary J knew that her Grandma Mag was an outstanding dressmaker. She had a way of combining various styles of sewing and knitting. Her creations could be trimmed down to fit several designs and then streamlined to add a lot of lace, ribbon, and trim. For the youth, she would create a youthful style dress that embraced bright colors with floral patterns. Mag had built a thriving little business making customized clothes for children and adults. Additionally, she made garments for the poor and was admired for her charitable works.

Mary J, with tears in her eyes, tightly embraced her Grandma with a hug, then said, "I love you, Grandma!"

Suddenly, there was a knock upon the front door. Zack and Ovine burst through and announced their support for Mary J's marriage. Ovine gave a longwinded version of the marriage ceremony, while Zack added the particulars; he had received some of the details from his wife Ovine on their walk over to see Mag. Mary J's parents were dead; nevertheless, she found a beautiful friendship in her relationship with Zack and Ovine. They were first cousin to Mary J on both sides of her parents. Most of all, she found peace with her beloved Grandma Mag. This paved a positive transition to her new family, with a new last name. Now, she is Mrs. Pap Fisher.

Chapter
11

MARY J MOVES TO FISHER-TOWN

Mary J got up early the next morning to complete her packing; she was contemplating the wider issues of joining a new household. She walked quickly to her dressing table; she touched her shoulders and throat with perfume. She felt like a fascinating blend of silk and steel, a conflicting mixture of modest sensuality and vigorous independence. Although she had few personal possessions and looked like a poor little lamb; yet, Mary J felt too noble to care much about what she took or what she left behind. For most of her life, the house she grew up in had never given her much thoughtful pleasure, especially after her parents and brother's death.

Pap came mid-morning to take Mary J away from the only family she had ever intimately known. She hunkered down in deep thought as she waited for her husband to finish putting her things in the back of his pickup truck. Mary J couldn't help thinking about her new life ahead. She had already experienced both sides of family life that included love and conflicts. She had immediately accepted the idea that no family would be exactly alike; certainly, her new family would be drawing from different cultural experiences. Even so, Mary J was determined to build new sets of experiences that would enhance her childhood's dream of owning a store.

Mary J shook off the uncertainty of joining a new household, along with the reality of the Great Depression years that had chilled her youth. Lost in her daydreams, Mary J began to focus on the idea of marriage and family. For the first time, she now had figured it all out with these words: "no sense being apprehensive when you have a sure thing." A sudden gleam came into Mary J's eyes; she had now fulfilled a personal aspiration of having an entrepreneurial husband by her side. In her mind, Pap was that slight edge—heavens had given her one of its stars. She could believe again; store ownership was once again within the realms of possibility.

Mary J unhurriedly walked downstairs and sat down in front of a small table. She then crossed her legs upon it in a restful manner. Quickly, she got up out of her chair after realizing it was time to depart with her husband. She went into the kitchen and living room to share words of good-byes in the uproar of her joyous reassurance. Before leaving, she turned and gave all the children at tap on their shoulder—plowed into her pockets and produced a handful of pennies. "Go to my Aunt Loretta's store and buy yourself some bubble gum and candy. I'll be back to see you all soon!" Mary J then hugged and kissed everyone. She was laughing with tears as she walked out of the front door.

Mary J and Pap got into the truck and drove along the dirt road. They could see the sun shining outside the window, turning the brown grass to gold. Together, watching people—older people, young people and children, they all seemed to have somewhere to go. So did Mary J, she was going to join her new family. Most of all, she and Pap were enjoying themselves with laughter, gossip, confidences, and harmless intricate conspiracies. They were all extremely wrapped up in themselves, along with their love, hopes, dreams and fantasies.

"Look here Pap," said Mary J, "Tell me a little more about your family before we get there, especially the background of your grandparents and parents."

Pap chuckled as he put his arms around her, then said: "Solomon and Susan Lennie, my grandparents, originally had 120 acres of prime waterfront property. This waterfront landscape intersected both the Neuse River and Clubfoot Creek at the mouth of Mitchell Creek. Together, they produced a continuous flow into the Neuse River. Grandpa and Grandma had five children: George, John Allen, Martha, Eliza, and Genettia. Grandpa gave my Daddy thirty acres of prime waterfront property for his wedding gift.

"Grandpa was a woodcutter who sold wood by the cord. He mostly used axes and crosscut saws to bring-down a tree, and then dragged it from the woods with a mule. He used to make tar, pitch and turpentine from North Carolina Longleaf pine trees. He was also well-known for his chair bottom's seats made from corn shucks.

"Susan Lennie, my grandmother, was a midwife who delivered most of the babies in our community. When a woman was ready to give birth, she would be right there to help the family. She mostly took care of women who couldn't afford doctors. Grandma was neither in a position of power nor made a great deal of money. She was neither an organized business person nor did she see herself as a professional. Yet, she was a passionate midwife that made her community a safe and nurturing place to birth children. She also made medicine for colds, fevers and the flu. She was just a plain person that had an extremely peaceful spirit, along with a big heart.

"See Mary J, that why I love you, because you remind me so much of her. She had her own little business, just like you want your own little store. My Grandpa always supported her because she had to go here and there, sometimes several days. Now, I will do the same for you. When I am not on the farm or working at my side business, I will come help you in your store. Now you should have a similar attitude about my work. I expect you to do the same for me."

Mary J was so happy to hear the word store. No sweeter word was ever spoken. For her, money wasn't what store ownership was all about. It was about freedom. Freedom to care for the poor, widows, orphans and those down and out in her community. Freedom to get her head above the crowd. Freedom to be her own person. Freedom to have an idea, and to turn that idea into a business, and that business into something special for her family and community. And, if it all works, freedom to fuss everybody out—freedom to tell all her oppressors the devil with them.

Quickly, Mary J rubbed the back of Pap's hand across her lips. Now with a face full of smiles, she said, "Tell me about your parents."

"My parents, John Allen and Rachel, built a beautiful two-story house on their thirty acres of waterfront property. Our home consisted of two hall ways and five bedrooms. As you will see, there is a porch upstairs with an outside door leading to the master bedroom—porches downstairs with three outside doors, along with a winding staircase inside leading back upstairs. The house is without a fireplace, but we have several wood stoves throughout our home. Instead of regular paint upon the house exterior structure, it is whitewashed with lime and water. The house stands at the end of Fisher-town road with an amazing waterfront view. It shares the backdrop of Clubfoot and Mitchell Creek as it blends into the Neuse River.

"After my daddy died, I took over his role as head of the household and now runs the family farm. We will live with my teenage sister Alma Tucker, Brother Fred and Mother Rachel. The rest of my siblings have already left home. I will be giving a considerable amount of my time to farming, raising hogs and being engaged in a little side venture as a moonshiner. You can help my Mother and Alma Tucker take care of the garden and chickens. Also, you can enjoy everything from a quiet afternoon sitting by the Creek or the thrill of catching fish. Just make sure, the fish you catch is not bigger than Mama." Pap raised his hand and shook his head teasing her.

Mary J kissed Pap on his right cheek. "You were molded and shaped from your hard-working family. They taught you the value of hard work, of persistence, and of improvisation. You have become a racehorse that can make things happen. You have inherited the ability to make the seemly ordinary into the extraordinary. One who doesn't know what it means to say something can't be done. But above all, you aren't the kind of person that values security over the thrill of the chase."

"Lesson number one," said Pap, "running a business is a matter of pressing on, in spite of an unending series of bewildering difficulties and failures. My Grandpa said, 'people need a mental compass to guide their minds and hearts.' We can't be the kind of people who like to follow everybody else procedures. Labor achieves very little unless we dream up ways to organize it."

Mary J took a deep breath. "Well, now, what's your Mother Rachel's story?"

Pap hunched his shoulders to lift his collar higher on his neck then nodded vigorously. "My Mother, was born on December 28, 1881 to

Gilbert and Cassie Jane Falls. Her Mother Cassie Jane was a Carter before marrying Gilbert Falls from Maryland. Mama always worked as a housewife and gardener. She loves fishing on Clubfoot Creek in front of our home or on the point of Mitchell Creek behind my Grandparent's house. There are many reasons she loves to fish. It's relaxing for Mama and a good way to sooth her distressed nerves."

Mary J watched him with a look of amused indulgence, then turned her head slowly from side to side. "What if... I can't fish."

"Don't worry, said Pap, "fish is one of our most important sources of meat for our family. Mama will gladly teach you the tricks of the trade. Also, Mama knows how to preserve jams, jellies, fruits and all kinds of vegetables from our garden. She makes clothes on her old fashion sewing machine; she washes our clothes each week in an iron pot using a washboard. Of course, Mama is the religious type who loves to sing hymns like: *Must Jesus Bears the Cross -Along*."

Mary J patted Pap's hand again, as though he had been a loving friend. She whispered several pleasant things in his ear. She then said, "Oh! Pap, your Mother and I can learn to sing together. I can see us now singing and fishing together on the banks of the Creek." They both burst into laughter. Then Mary J said in a high pitch tone, "Now, tell me about your Dad."

"Now my Daddy, John Allen, he was born March 5, 1878 and died May 8, 1937 at the age of 59. My parents were married for 37 years, since July 11, 1900. They had eight children: Lester Alward, Fred Allen, Bertha Jane, Warner Haney, Hugh Marshall, Ina Chester, and Alma Tucker— then of course me: Beleather—better known as Pap. Dad main farm crops were cotton, tobacco, white potatoes, sweet potatoes, peas and corn. He also planted each year a family vegetable garden. Of course, there were chickens, turkeys, ducks, geese, hogs, and a cow for milk. Dad would walk nearly five miles every Sunday to attend Piney Grove Church, where he served as chairman of the trustee board. He loved to play jokes, fish in the Creeks, used tobacco and occasionally swigged a little whiskey."

Pap gently turned into his driveway—he slowed down as his family came out to greet his new bride. Pap said to his new wife: "Come on sweetheart, we are home!" He parked under the pecan tree, while his mother Rachel stood in the doorway to welcome her new daughter-in-law.

Chapter 12

MARY J'S NEW FAMILY

The home of Pap's parents was highly unusual, the front of the house faced Clubfoot Creek instead of the road. However, the house was perfect for the family's lifestyle. The background scenery was beautiful, with a wraparound porch from the kitchen to the front door entranceway. There was a second-floor porch also facing the waterfront. When someone walked outside in the front yard, he or she would immediately be viewing a stunning waterfront. There would be a water pump on the left side, chicken coop on the right side, and a vegetable garden towards the road behind the coop. There was a pecan tree in front of the porch with nearby fruit trees and berry vines. If a family member were out fishing in a boat or standing on the edge of the shore, they would be visible from the house.

The house design captured the more refreshing Creek breeze throughout the hot, humid days of the long Southern summer. The early morning breeze off the Creek usually stirred outside over the porch in front of the kitchen. The coldest time of the year had just passed through the community. This will be Mary J's first spring, summer and autumn with her husband's family; approaching the time of year when Rachel starts canning her summertime goodness to enjoy during the winter months.

Rachel's primary canning season started around harvesting time for her garden, usually early to late summer and early fall. From Rachel's point of view, food must be treated as a precious gift from God, never taken for granted; Rachel loved a pantry bulging with food. Seasonal fruit and vegetables were picked from her garden—washed and prepared for canning. Rachel had strict standards for the blanching of her vegetables as well as sterilizing the jars.

Early before the good morning-dawn, Rachel called for assistance from her daughter, Alma Tucker, to help with the 'putting up' process. As soon as Rachel began strolling downstairs, Alma Tucker could hear her Mama demanding voice once again. "Alma Tucker," said Rachel, "come out here and remove the ends of these string beans and cut them into the proper lengths. The cucumbers need their blossoms and stems remove, and then cut them into small circles. A little later, you can peel some tomatoes for sauce and juice to be canned. We also have some early corn to be shuck and corn kernels to be cut off the cob. There is a sharp knife on the kitchen table."

Alma Tucker hastily jumped out of bed—made herself ready to join her mother downstairs. She was easily over 6 feet 4 inches tall in her heels. She believed that every woman was a queen, so she attended to matters of posture and grooming before rushing downstairs.

"Good morning Mama," said Alma Tucker as she paced down the stairs. Slowly, methodically, rigidly, unemotional, "All right, tell me about these apples on the stair steps."

"Oh yes," said Rachel, "we are going to make applesauce; it will be so good with our breakfast during the winter months."

Alma Tucker, chuckling and walking, "How about those ball glass jars already filled on the table? You have arranged and packaged them into a portrait worthy of Vincent van Gogh's signature."

"Now Alma Tucker, you know those glass jars need to be placed within our canning racks. Glory be to God!" Rachel looked around until she located her. "What's wrong with you this morning? Come along, child; we have a lot of work on our list today."

Alma Tucker stretched and yawned as gracefully and unselfconsciously as a cat upon entering the kitchen. She paused in a passing moment of awkwardness on seeing all the work to be done. Alma Tucker stood smiling as she took in the situation at a glance. Then she said with a smile in her voice, wringing the last bit of fun out of it. "Oh Mama, can I go and get, Mary J to help us?"

In the kitchen, Rachel grinned uncertainly at Alma Tucker from her habitual corner behind the stove. She noticed her standing in the doorway. "Don't worry; Mary J will be down soon. What you need to do is get started with your work, maybe she and Pap have other plans for today."

Alma Tucker stood still for a moment; her face was quiet. "Pap left for the farm at least one hour ago." Suddenly looking down, shaking her head from left to right; "Oh no, I forgot that Mary J washes on Mondays."

With a special kind of quietness in her aging face, Rachel shuffled across the floor. "Mary J is going to need those two tubs outside filled with hot water, please heat some water on the woodstove. She will need one tub for washing her clothes and the other tub for rinsing them. Also, give Mary J our hand roller, so she can roll her clothes into the rinsing tub and then the clothes basket. If it starts raining or drizzling outside, let Mary J know that she can use the clothesline on the upstairs porch."

As Mary J came downstairs towards the kitchen, she had no need to charm or conquer anyone, because she was completely accepted by her new family. Mary J could now turn down the spotlight, so someone else could be the center of attention. There had been very little fun in Mary J's life, except for the dream of store ownership, and her childhood family's vigor for music.

The Fishers had a charming effect upon Mary J, primarily because of their affection and helpfulness toward one another. She had never known anyone just like them. In some surprising ways, they put forth the energy to maintain an ideal home that wasn't easily pulled asunder by outside interest. She had been noticing that within the Fisher's family, they shared love and happiness as naturally and unconsciously as they shared the air that they breathed.

Mary J realized that she was gaining something that she had lost too long ago to remember. She was now becoming more like them, genuine, off-the-cuff, and open to happy-go-lucky joy. She could now shed some of the deceptions and scheming that she had learned to use during her battles for conquest and dominance, especially growing up without her natural parents.

Mary J no longer had to fight for attention. Yet, she was sad and heartsick. She felt a degree of pain in her heart, sometimes a hundred times a day, particularly when she thought about her baby sister's lack of adequate care. With an ominous quietness in her smooth and attractive face, she kept thinking that her Grandma Mag was just too old to handle all those children. The death of Mary J's parents created many unresolved emotional issues, with feelings of hurt and betrayal, acted out in her childhood's family daily experiences.

Mary J was determined to find a way to support her sister emotionally. She wanted Lorraine to share the joy of her newfound happiness. Nothing in Mary J's past troubled life had ever hurt as much as those reflections. Suddenly, she calmed herself again, shrugged, and then began looking around the house. She was breathless as soon as she stepped on the last step. She immediately hollered out in a cheerful voice. "Well, bless my soul! Where is everybody?"

From inside the kitchen, Alma Tucker stuck her head out around the door. She called out urgently but caringly, "Mary J! Mary J! We are in the kitchen. Come on in here with us, my sister-in-law! I am just getting ready to heat your hot water for washing today. You know, today is Monday!" Alma Tucker quickly observed that Mary J was trudging slowly along with an unusual sympathetic expression upon her face. She continued, "What's on your mind, my sister-in-law, so early this morning?"

"Well," said Mary J, "Pap and I have been talking about my little sister Lorraine. She is only nine years old, with no mama or daddy to look after her. Grandma Mag is doing all she can, but there is also little Willie Welt, Margret Ann, Alvin, Lucy Gray, and Showalter's children that also need her assistance. Of course, Ella and James Westley can help, but my heart goes out for little Lorraine. Pap and I have decided that we need to raise her. So, Mother Rachel, would it be all right if she comes to live with us?"

Alma Tucker's earthy goal was to be a preacher's wife so that she could plant inspirational seeds in other people's minds. She was someone who compassionately cared for other people. In her mind, good citizenship meant working with others to build beautiful communities. She thought of people like a library with untapped potential—crying out to the world: *We have all kinds of interesting and helpful information, so please make somebody happy, just come and use one of us.*

Alma Tucker thought that people weren't limited to only one chance, because every day there were new beginnings. She wanted people to believe in the infinite abundance within themselves. Alma Tucker would tell others: *Don't worry, there are new opportunities all over the place, just look within your mind.* Then she would say: *You don't have to carry all the problems of life on your back at one time, just take your breath one mouthful at a time.*

It was a very emotional moment. Alma Tucker faced twitched and was wet. All of a sudden, she laughed. "Mama! I got an idea. Just think about it, she could sleep in my room with me."

Rachel's face lit up with her trademark gaze, suddenly she smiled reassuringly: "Ok, Mary J, that sounds good; you and Pap can bring her anytime. Furthermore, this is now yours and my son Pap's home as well. You are my daughter now; your family is the same as mines. Larraine is just a little girl; she needs your help. If God has put this in your heart, you need to please him!"

The very next day, Mary J and Pap went to pick her up. When they arrived at Mag's house, Lorraine was sitting on the porch. Mag looked-up and saw them turning into the yard, she hollered out, "Hey, you all, Mary J and Pap are here to pick up Lorraine."

All of Mary J's brothers and sisters rushed out of the front door with great joy. They began hugging and embracing Mary J with smiles and caring words. Unexpectedly, people were coming from everywhere to see the Newlyweds. Uncle Charlie's children came from their home next door. Zack and Ovine, along with their daughter, Bertha Ray, came from their house across the dirt road. There was laughter, jokes, and congratulations with an atmosphere of celebration. Their daily lives had not been the same since Mary J's departure. Annie Cleo came wearing her new white Apron, holding onto her husband's hand.

"Mary J," said her uncle Charlie, "what is this I heard about you living in a big house on the waterfront. You better not forget about your old Uncle Charlie." He began laughing out loud while offering his hand.

Mary J straightened her shoulders and lifted her chin. "Now Uncle Charlie, who could forget you with your crazy self!"

"Hey Pap," said Charlie, "if you come over here, I got a little something for you in my back pocket. You know, I have always been weak in philosophy. I flunked religion 101 because I refuse to spell 'he' with a capital. To tell you the truth, I'm a little scared of it." Suddenly, he laid back his head, sipped a swallow from his bottle, and then roared with laughter.

"Uncle Charlie," said Mary J in a firm but a happy spirit, "you just leave my husband along; he is not drinking with you today. This is our wedding celebration! Also, we are going to take Lorraine to live with us,"

Charlie smiled at her. "Mary J, I love you because of your great big heart. So many people think only of themselves, but not you. No, no, no! You treat everybody with equal kindness from the ditch digger to the undertaker. You are a soft, feminine woman on the outside with an interior that is as formidable as a coal miner. May the Lord bless you and Pap in every possible way."

Mary J then hugged her uncle Charlie with a big smile. "Oh thank-you Uncle Charlie, I am also going to pray for you to stop drinking and spend more time with your family. God surely wants us to be happy, healthy, and good, so don't let the devil spoil it all!"

Annie Cleo hugged Mary J and said, "Let me run back to the house and get some pies and cakes to share with everybody."

"Pap," said Mary J, "let's get our food out of the car."

Pap and Mary J brought with them all sorts of fish, vegetables, and fruit. Additionally, Pap's Mother, Rachel, and his Sister, Alma Tucker, sent several combinations of freshly baked blackberry and blueberry pies. It was now suppertime, so the timing was perfect. Pap and Mary J had both hands full of food as they stepped back upon the porch.

"Come on in the house," said Mag, "we are going to cook these fish right now."

Mary J had a pleasant glow spreading all over her. Of course, she had to talk big about her grandma's cooking. She said to Pap, "My grandma Mag is a self-taught cook. All of my family knows that she is the best fish cooker on this side of the Creek. 'Fresh fish is wonderful,' she always told us. She won't even touch frozen fish. She loves to cook fish on the bone and lift off the fillets after cooking it. She frowns on overcooking any fish; she always insists on using her private recipe. This includes dusting her fish into cornmeal with a little salt and black pepper. Grandma then fries them perfectly, so that the outside is crisp. This always leaves the inside moist and flaky, with a delicious, muddy taste."

"Hmmm, not bad, not bad at all," Pap said slowly while merrymaking with her. He clapped Mary J's hands with delight as they smiled companionably at one another.

Mary J's eyes were overflowing with emotions as she continued: "My Grandma Mag always fries potatoes along with her fish. She uses an Irish potato recipe that was passed down from her grandmother Eliza. Oh, for goodness sake Pap, don't mention her cornbread made from a meal that is mixed in milk. She also adds some diced onions and a little cubed-up sharp cheese. Now, rather than deep-frying her cornbread mix in little round balls, she spoons the mix out into hot grease, within an iron skillet."

The porch was more crowded than ever now since the word got out that Mag was cooking fish. Mag was just about ready to serve everyone. Mary J yelled out to all the folks to find a place to sit down, so they could eat together. All the people began to gather around wherever they could on the porch, kitchen, or yard; they started eating, siting, and talking until it was too dark to see. This was a spectacular family-friendly event that demonstrated the beauty of a loving family.

After several hours of socializing, the family all joined in together and brought Lorraine clothes to the car so that she could move to her new home. Everyone gave Lorraine hugs, kisses, and a lot of gifts. Lorraine got into the car with Mary J and Pap; then, they slowly drove away.

Chapter

13

BLENDING FAMILIES

The next morning, Alma Tucker scrambled out of bed after smelling the aroma of breakfast that had floated up from downstairs. "Good Morning, little girl," Alma Tucker said emotionally to Lorraine, then grabbed her by the hand. "It's morning! Let's get up and explore our new day. Don't you smell the scent of ham coming out of our kitchen? Your clothes are on hooks behind the door; your shoes are all jumbled together on the closet floor. We can fix that later, perhaps after breakfast."

Lorraine looked up at her with carefully concealed curiosity and a racing heartbeat. She moved soundlessly from the bed, then forced herself to smile as they began making up the bed together. Lorraine said softly, "it's nice that you're planning to take me fishing, school, and some of your community events."

Alma Tucker grabbed Lorraine by the wrist as she looked down at the worried expression upon her face. She leaned over and kissed her on the top of the head. "You going to be just fine here, so don't worry."

Lorraine breathing slowly, trying to forget the pain and distractions of leaving the only home she ever known. "I thought so, but what if the other children at school don't like me, you see, I'm a stranger here."

"Just remember one thing when you deal with others. The biggest key to a woman's success in life is her beauty. You are a queen; it's that simple! Charm is the art of making others feel good about you. Good heavens! You are a pretty little girl, just develop a sense of humor by putting a shield of impenetrable protection around your little soft heart. A woman must balance her sensitivity with defensive detachments. This way, you may enjoy the sweet times in life without continually complaining about hardships.

Lorraine was now smiling again as her fear broke apart like splintered glass. She began to turn around faster and faster—spinning and whirling—freely around the room. Afterward, she stretched to put on her new dress with a roar, "Good, good! Grandma Mag raised us by drilling certain ideas into our heads: you should never drink; always say thank you ma'am; be on time, go to church; clean up your room."

Alma Tucker grinned cheerfully at her. "You have a sweet and wise grandma. Nothing is more important in people's lives than their ability to get along with others. So be a strong and secure woman that compliments others in their faces and behind their backs."

As they smiled companionably at one another, Lorraine's heart leaped, thinking about her Grandma. "My Grandma feels that a woman should create warmth wherever she goes. She told me before I came here that I should be warm and inviting to everybody in this home. Grandma always told me: 'More flies are caught with honey than with vinegar.'"

Alma Tucker laughed. "Young lady! I like that—that's good. What your grandma means is for us to be gracious, thoughtful, and always considerate of others and their feelings."

"Well now, don't tell Mary J," said Lorraine as she leaned back and ran her hands through her hair. "Sometimes, I feel that I am missing something. My emotion occasionally causes me to experience feelings of unhappiness, separation, and even loneliness—just like your brother Fred. But now, believe me, I would never drink whiskey like him to solve my problems."

Alma Tucker's eyes scrutinized Lorraine again. She grinned abruptly with smiling eyes. Her lips spread into a beam of heartbreaking tenderness. "My little sweetheart, conflicts will arise no matter how much people care about each other. However, many times, struggles will deepen rather than weaken people's relationships. Learning to mix with others is a lifelong process. We learn from our surroundings how to develop a sense of self. My daddy always told his children: 'There are no big 'I's and little 'You's.' We're all the same in God's eyes. God has placed miraculous possibilities in your mind. They are just waiting for you to stimulate them."

Lorraine's eyes became slightly tearful as she thought about the children that were living across the road. "What happened to your cousins' next door? They are like my family with no daddy."

That' right," Alma Tucker said. "That's precisely right. My brother Lester died in 1938 at the age of 35. Lester's wife Eva continued to live right across the road on our homestead. They had eight children together: Clifton Louis, Cherry Haney, Della Jane, Samuel, Henderson, Ella Mae, Phillip Roy, and Garson Lee. So, you see, you have lots of friends to play with after school and weekends."

For a moment, it seemed that Lorraine might not answer. She looked away over her shoulder; all of a sudden, her eyes met Alma Tucker again. She said in a whisper, "Oh yes, I believe that everything will be alright. My sister Mary J will get her store someday. Since our Mama and Daddy are dead, they can't help her. So, I guess, I will be her helper."

"My dear child," Alma Tucker said. "Mary J is a good woman, but sometimes I feel sorry for her leap of imagination, especially to build a store with no resources. This idea of building a new store is like a star in her mind. She is too eager to hear the rings of hammers on fresh wood—expecting the earth to open for her new store's foundation. But somehow, nature and fate are working against her. The curse of death upon you all parents have given Mary J blind panic and unreasonable confidence in this illusion. I believe that fate is trying to defeat her dreams. Death took, you all, mother away much too soon. Death also took away, you all daddy and eldest brother, who were carpenters; they had promised to build Mary J's a store when she became a young woman. But for some reasons, their deaths happened during her childhood. And you, my little darling, don't even remember your parents. It almost seems like fate has been working against your whole family—children can't control their destiny."

Lorraine's ears perked up, and her heart jumped. "Well," she said, "Grandma said that Mary J has that certain something that up-and-coming people possess. She calls it personal motivation. Of course, Mary J is fussy and hard-headed at times, but she must find a way to fight back against fate. Grandma is praying that your brother Pap is the answer."

Alma Tucker frowned and then smiled: "But, it just seems, I don't know, maybe a little overoptimistic. I sure hope you're right about Pap with our small, petty farm."

"Of course, I know it," Lorraine said, almost hissing in an effort to keep her voice low. She then looked at her thoughtfully. "But my grandma said, the whole world stands aside for the people who knows where they are going."

Alma Tucker struggled with that for a moment and then said in a calm voice: "Well, there never lived a more ambitious woman than your sister Mary J, nor one more self-confident. During hard times, she never loses heart; in good times, she shows her charm and thoughtful consideration. Her energetic personality is the reason why her internal stars shine under challenging times.

Lorraine's mind now flooded with memories. Mary J truly knows how to greet life's potholes of disasters and mishaps with determination. She recognizes a critical thing for sure. Personal motivated people prosper in life while bitter people don't—she uses her power of choice to choose her destiny.

Alma Tucker smiled, and then put her hands on her hips. "Oh, my God! Enough of this kind of talk, come on, little girl, let's get ready to go downstairs."

Lester's children were waiting for Lorraine downstairs. They showed up for breakfast to welcome her to Fisher-town. Samuel introduced everybody to Lorraine as Rachel's grandchildren and her future playmates. Della Jane began to discuss with her the way to have fun living in Fisher-town. Phillip and Henderson smiled at each other and were silent most of the time. After everybody finish breakfast, they said goodbye, promising to return later in the evening after their farm duties.

Lorraine quickly went to the window as the door slab behind them. She was watching Lester's children walk back to their house. Suddenly,

Larraine noticed the boys were jumping over a drainage ditch between two stunted trees about four feet high. Lorraine started to think about her other brothers and sisters that she had left behind, prior moving to Fisher-town. Under the hurt, she felt an unusual rage that she hadn't even known was possible. The world had given her something, and then quickly snatched it away. *Hopefully*, she thought, *Mary J won't let this happen twice to me.*

The following Saturday morning, Zack came to Fisher-town around 10 a.m. He brought with him a carload full of family members. Zack drove extremely fast into the front yard, almost killing several chickens. He immediately got out of the car to check on the chickens.

When Lorraine saw a car turning into the driveway, she ran excitedly out to the car, greeting everyone. So delighted that her eyes were filled with laughter, joyfully thinking, it's going to be a beautiful day.

Mary J came to the front door behind Lorraine to find out why there was so much commotion. She stood looking at a distance with absorbed eyes. Suddenly, after seeing her family, she immediately went outside to greet them.

When Zack's eyes caught Mary J, he shook his head, giggling. "Where is my buddy, Pap?"

Mary J said enthusiastically. "He's out working in the field."

"Ok, the gang is in the car," said Zack, "I am heading in the direction of the field to see Pap."

Everybody began hugging each other, laughing, and making small talk to one another. Subsequently, separate groups started dispersing in different directions, some wandering around the side of the house while others went across the yard towards the waterfront.

Mary J joined the older folks gathering around the pecan tree; where they could enjoy the breeze coming off the waterfront. Rachel and Alma Tucker went out of the house together, also joining those under the pecan tree. Everybody was engaged in making small talk, creating several small groups.

"Lorraine," said Rachel thinking nothing of it. "Please bring all your family inside; so, we can have some pie and cake."

Lorraine took her Grandma Mag, Lucy Gray, and Ella inside the living room. Others began poring through the open doors, talking, laughing, and pausing on the porch. Reluctant to see the end of the evening, Mary J and Alma Tucker went inside the kitchen to bring out more fresh pies.

"Mary J," said Alma Tucker with a big chuckle, "we always have the best fun when your family comes over on Saturdays. My goodness! Girl, your grandma looks good to be nearly 90 years old. Now, sister-in-law, if you take care of yourself, maybe you will reach that nearly one hundred mark as well."

Alma Tucker and Mary J were an unusual looking team. Mary J was only 5 feet 2 inches, while Alma Tucker was towering over 6-foot-2 inches. When they walked out with the pies, Fred was sitting on the porch.

Fred said with a teasing attitude. "Hey, my sister in law! I think you should give me the first slice of that pie!"

Mary J said: "My goodness, well, if it isn't my brother-in-law. You don't need any pie! I don't know why, but your Mother, Rachel, left you a whole pie on the kitchen shelf. You know the place, just above the stove. By the way, Alma Tucker and I have a wonderful deal for you; we would be glad to trade you a slice of pie for your whole one."

Fred responded half tipsy from whiskey. "You know Sis, I may be a little slow, but I wasn't born yesterday. But just to show you my heart, give my whole pie to your family."

"Well, Fred," said Mary J, "you'll be alright when I get my store business. Someday, you can come and spend the whole day eating cakes and drinking soda pops—but now, no whiskey! My community store will help expand your social world. You will have available to you a whole new network of friendships. You may even find yourself a girlfriend."

Fred stared at Mary J long and thoughtfully; suddenly, there was a dancing light of amusement in his eyes. He laughed silently, thinking about how he lived intensely and suffered deeply because of his social isolation. An appalling sense of loneliness fastened down upon him. He felt that Mary J had given him an honest analysis of his life. It was like putting together the pieces of a jigsaw puzzle, finding the answer to a riddle, or solving a mystery. Yet, his bleeding vanity yearned for one word of comfort to heal his wounded heart.

Fred looked at his dusty fingers and shook his head. "All right, Sis," he said, "Now I have already flunked religion and is preordained to be a bachelor. My fate doomed from the day I was born." He reached for his whiskey bottle in his back pocket, sipped a small taste. "You see, the Lord doesn't make any mistakes."

Mary J smiled sickly. "People like you, who depend on whiskey; they are unable to establish suitable relationships. You must be very unhappy with a lot of worries and frustrations. Look at me, all the people that promised to help me get a store have died. This includes my daddy, mama, and brother; nevertheless, fate will not overrule me. You have allowed fate to dominate your emotion. Now, just get off your knees, my brother-in-law, don't let the world know that you are defeated—find the stars that God has for you in the night sky. Whiskey is going to bring you down, so low that no woman is going to want you."

Fred kept on eating his biscuit and smoking his cigarette. He just let Mary J's fussing roll down his back. The harshness of Mary J's words took his breath away; yet, he knew in the innermost center of his soul, the place where there should be no lies, she was trying to help him. All the same, he realized that his hurt feelings wouldn't change the truth; Fred felt like he was somewhat of a longer by temperament; his genes were doing what God had designed them to do. On the other hand, he had a reputation at the Sawmill of being able to handle the entire lumber yard with very little assistance. But for some reason, he still desperately needed his whiskey on the weekends to soak up his loneliness.

The extravagant mockery of it all seemed to shine like a ball of fire to Alma Tucker. She appealed to her brother Fred. "So, quit worrying and drinking so much. You must have ice on your brain! You have to get through this life just like everybody else. Now, why don't you go out and give Pap a break on the farm, then he can talk to Zack?"

"Zack here! Well," said Fred, "thank-you Sis, I am going out to the field with them."

As Zack approached the field that Pap was working in, he began to walk briskly. He went past several trees with branches alive with birds; a banded woodpecker kept rapping hard on a standing dead tree near the edge of the field. Next, he noticed that a red-bellied woodpecker had just alighted on the side of a pecan tree. Its stiff tail feathers braced against the trunk. Its strong yoked toes, two in front and two behind on each foot—firmly grasped the bark. Swiftly anchored vertically, the woodpecker reared its head and delivered a series of trip-hammer strokes, with its chisel-like beak. All of a sudden, the birds quickly flew away, leaving bright darts waving through the leaves.

Finally, Zack got to Pap's location. He hollered out, "Hey, Pap! Hey Pap!" there was a shortness of breath in his voice as he kept moving towards him.

Pap waved his hands towards Zack—commanding him to come on over. Pap had a pleasing disposition that people respected because of his business type personality. Amazingly, he could say the most exaggerated things in very crafty ways. People would never get mad at him; they just laughed as if it was a joke. For this reason, Mary J and Pap were the perfect twosome, she could make people mad through fussing; he could defuse it through his serious humor.

Zack finally got there. "Hey, my friend Pap, how's the farming business?"

"Well, Zack, here is the proposition," said Pap, "farming is a sun-up to a sun-down job. Attempts to make farming easy have not met with success. The profit is thin because of the crows eating the seeds. Many times, low rainfall will cause poor growth and low production. The best part of farming is getting down and dirty with a hoe, would you like to try it!"

'Pap," said Zack, "I will take your word for it." He just smiled and laughed at Pap's way of using his word choice.

Pap continued lacing his conversation about farming. "It got so bad last year Zack that corn dropped to five cents a bushel. The plain truth is that coal cost more during the winter. Frank Carter tells of doing repair work on farmer Martin's house; afterward, they paid him with 250 pounds of potatoes. There is almost no cash available in the farm business. I guess as long as the farmer can raise his vegetables, fruit, and grind corn for cornmeal, we will be as happy as anyone else. We also need to have hogs and chickens for meat and eggs. We have to find a way to shift from survival farming to profitable farming."

As Pap turned to his right side, he saw Fred coming toward them. He refused to accept Fred's craving for whiskey, as just a weekend outlet. Pap would occasionally have a drink of whiskey with a person, but if they became highly intoxicated, he usually wouldn't drink with them again. Pap had little respect for people that couldn't handle their whiskey.

"Oh, my goodness here comes Fred," said Pap. "We are going into the weekend; Fred is most likely looking for whiskey. You talk to Fred, so I can finish plowing this small section." Pap went back to work just as Fred came near Zack's location.

Fred shouted out, "Hey Zack, how are you doing, Buddy?"

"As wonderful as a duck in water," replied Zack

"Come on, let's get Pap to take us to his still for a little drink."

"Sounds good to me, Fred, but don't you take too many."

"Now Zack, I work at the Sawmill every day, Weekends are my time," said Fred with a wink and a roar in his voice. He was dressed in denim overalls and wearing old shoes that were too big.

Pap came down the field to the end where Zack and Fred were talking together. Pap had a paper bag on his head, no shirt, work pants, and barefooted.

"Fred," said Pap, "take this mule and finish plowing these two or three rows for me."

"Ok, Pap," said Fred, "I am here at your service."

Fred took hold of the mule and started to plow, but the mule hated Fred for some strange reason. The mule didn't want to pull the plow for him. He began to holler at the mule, "get on up, you crazy mule!" Nevertheless, the mule refused to go in a straight line for him.

Pap said to Zack with a straight face, "if this mule could talk, he would have more sense than Fred! Let me finish these rows before the mule drag the plow all over my field. Fred's intelligence is almost as complicated as the federal tax code."

Zack started to laugh and laugh at Pap's comments. Pap never cracked a smile; he just simply threw up his hands and gave up. Zack said, "Please send Fred over here to me Pap, so I can explain to him how to treat a mule."

Pap relieved Fred immediately of the mule and plow. Fred went over to be with Zack; they broke into laughter as their eyes made contact.

"Zack," said Fred, "here are two foot-tubs, you can sit on this one, and I will take the other. Pap will be finish in less than an hour. His still is only about ten minutes away from here. He knows how to make some good whiskey."

"Fred," said Zack, "the way you handled that mule, I am not sure that Pap wants to give you a drink of whiskey."

"Zack! What are you talking about, man? My brother Pap is as good as gold. His wife also, that's your people, right?"

"That's right, Fred," said Zack, "I love Mary J just like my own child."

"Let me tell you," said Fred, "Mary J is better than gold to me. But now, it's just one little problem. You know, Mary J wants her grocery store."

"So, what wrong with that Fred," said Zack? "I believe that if you don't want anything, you will never have anything. Pap and Mary J are both hard workers; together, they will make a great business team."

"Well," said Fred, "I tell you one thing; the money is not going to come from this small farm, that's the problem!"

"Fred," said Zack, "you are making a good point. I certainly agree with you. This country is just coming out of its pains from the Great Depression years; nobody has any real money. Moonshining, especially for a poor man, is the only door open to get hold of a few dollars. I don't consider moonshining immoral for an honest man like your brother Pap."

Fred shouted, "Now you got it! Pap better get his butt in the woods and make some whiskey so that Mary J can get her store. The sooner, the better, because you and I need a drink right now." Fred began laughing with Zack. "Furthermore," said Fred, "who taught Mary J to think so high and mighty, like money grows on trees. I got to give my brother credit; he is working day and night like an ox."

'Well," said Zack, "the idea came from her Aunt Loretta; when Mary J was a child, she grew up around her store. Now Fred let me say this about Mary J; she just wants to be her own boss, that's all. Mary J doesn't like taking orders from anyone; she rather give them. When people have that kind of personality, they have to go into business for themselves. I believe that she is doing the right thing. Mary J senses that somehow, as a business owner, she can find a way to provide for her family and help others through the grace of God. She is willing to work hard and isn't afraid of failure. There is no greater blessing to a man than a devoted and dedicated wife by his side. For a man's best development, a womanly influence is necessary."

Fred had to laugh: "I hear you, Zack. I believe that my brother Pap is just too good; he needs to send his wife's butt out into these fields to work or get a house-cleaning job. I tell you one thing; she is a bossy little thing. You know, she tried to tell me what to do, but I told her that I have the weekends off. If I want to drink on the weekends, that's my business. On the other hand, my Sister, Alma Tucker and Mother, Rachel, just loves the ground she walks on. Now forget Pap, he treats her like she is the Queen of England."

"Alright now, Fred, just leave my people along," said Zack! I notice you don't have a woman!"

"You got that right, said Fred! I rather drink on my weekends off. You see Zack, these few women around Harlowe are just a real headache. I wouldn't have one of them, even if their rumps were made of pure gold. By the way, I have a half-pint in my back pocket."

Fred took the bottle out and shook it to show Zack the fine beads. Zack knew it was respectable stuff because good whiskey always had tiny bubbles along its surface, especially shaking it. Fred put the pint bottle of whiskey to his mouth, then he closed his eyes and raised his face to the trees, and quietly announced: "My friend, Zack, this is real whiskey!"

"Come on, Fred,' said Zack, "you know that stuff isn't as good as your brother Pap's whiskey."

"Well," said Fred while rolling in laughter, "it will do till Pap and that mule finish those rows. Come on Zack, you can drink this little bit left."

"I think it will be better for me to wait on Pap," said Zack with his hand on Fred's shoulder. "He makes the best moonshine whiskey in the state of North Carolina."

Pap finished up his plowing and then joined Fred and Zack. He said, "All-right fellows, come on; let's check on several cases of whiskey that I need to deliver after sun-down tonight."

Pap never went the same way more than once or twice. He would always circle his still area at least once as a precaution. An old man had told him, 'A dog does this so that he wouldn't lay down on a snake.' Pap relied on the same approach when sleeping at night in the woods near his still. His instincts more or less shielded him, just like the wild animals making use of the natural law. He learned this attitude by observing the ways animals used their instincts to protect themselves. He noticed that animals refused to rebel against nature. Pap also noticed that a fox sleeping on top of the ground would cover its face with its bushy tail; a hen slept at night with its beak tucked within its feathers. A mule stood with its back to the wind. Pap realized that nature already had a well-worked-out plan. By observing how animals followed nature's law, Pap was able to survive at night, making moonshine.

They went deep into the woods behind his farm towards the waterfront. The still was a mile away. Pap had found the perfect place. He had discovered a deep sinkhole, more profound than a man is tall, and had carefully scooped out a cave on the inside to place his whiskey. Then, he would cover his products with vines and honeysuckle. Pap had cleverly not worn out a walking path to his still. He would ease through the weeds on a slightly different route during each of his visitations.

Zack walked slowly behind Pap, noticing how Pap observed the flight of birds, the crawling of earthworms into their burrows; the movement of the leaves on a plant. Zack looked at him from time to time with admiration in his eyes, smiled, and shook his head. "Oh, my goodness," said Zack, "unless a person can fly, there is no evidence of a path anywhere."

As they approached this quiet location, Pap picked up a jar of whiskey from under some tree branches. "Hey Zack, here is something you and Fred may sample."

Zack took a big swallow—then held his breath and drew up his nose and said, "Now Fred, this is what I am talking about, 'the real thing,' not that soda pop you have been drinking!"

Zack put his hands-on Pap's shoulders. "How many cases are you moving tonight?"

Pap leaned over towards him. "We have an order for ten cases to be deliver after dark."

"Well Pap," said Zack, "just let Fred and I head back to the house. I know you got to take care of your business. You got customers, and I know Mary J will be waiting on the money." They had several laughs, knowing Mary J's ambition to be a store owner.

"Here the proposition folks," said Pap, "I was born at night, but not last night. Life isn't a spectator sport. The only way people can derive any satisfaction from life is to get their feet wet. This way, we will be able to experience the satisfaction of producing as well as performing. Here boys, take one more sip for the road!" After the drinks, Zack and Fred returned to the house.

Pap remained in the woods to prepare for his deliveries. He generally went to his still during the black of night, when the deep woods could keep a secret. From there, he watched the seasons come and go with their beautiful contrast of trees and flowers. He also was filled with curiosity about the ways of the animals and birds, even about the sun, the moon, and stars.

Pap would sometimes be in the woods all night long. Supported by his trust in divine protection, he lived through many hazardous situations, hastening through the nights towards his destiny. During those innocent times of shadows and darkness surrounding him, he would speak to his Creator, out of the depths of his heart. Godly thoughts would start to bear down hard upon his heart, the idea that without the sure hand of guidance from God, he would be only a straw in the wind. These thoughts and meditations provided a wide shade net for his conscience.

After Zack arrived back to the house, He told those that came with him to get ready for departure. Everybody walked slowly towards Zack's car to see them off. There were many hugs and kisses between them before getting into the car. Eventually, Zack back out of the yard and went down the dirt road with a cloud of dust swirling behind his vehicle. The car's red tail-lights grew smaller as its sound diminished to a low roar. The car quickly disappeared as it went around the deep curve.

Zack always drove his car with caution while drinking; he was good at everything except right turns. Zack always thought he had a little more room than he did, so from time to time, Zack would hit a few mailboxes. But with Grandma Mag in the car, he was hoping that today, everything would work correctly for him.

As Mary J witnessed their departure, she couldn't help reflecting on her dream store. At last, she had found people who didn't think that talking about money was taboo. Her new in-laws were like her, willing to work hard, and determined to make money from it. Although there were many trade-offs, Mary J wanted to be a winner and not a loser. Nevertheless, she was mystified at the inexplicable delays that constantly plagued her efforts. She only hoped that Pap hadn't forgotten her dream to be a store owner. She realized that they would never save enough money from running Pap's daddy's farm. Nevertheless, It did put food on the table.

Oh, my Lord, Mary J thought, *what options do we have available?"* These were painful thoughts, knowing that she could never compromise her dreams.

Chapter 14

THUNDERSTORM

Mary J has now been married for three years. Lorraine unofficially adopted as a permanent part of her family. With two little girls of her own, Mary J's family had become an important source of companionship and intimacy. Although in a heartless world, she fully accepted them as a wonderful treasure. She now felt unrestricted to disclose herself more completely, share her hopes, rear her children, and grow old. She regularly reflected on her small children's state of being. She kept thinking; they must learn how to act, how to love, how to touch and be touch, even how to fit into their culture.

Many times, Mary J's thoughts returned to her childhood's dream of someday owning a community store. She felt that the years were slipping away. In most people's estimation, her childhood dream appeared to be somewhat logically impossible. Yet, Mary J refused to make a single compromise. She would say to herself over and over again: *when the Lord closes a door, he will always leave a window open.*

One early morning between sleeping and waking, Mary J's restlessness interfered with her sleep. She began tossing and turning in bed with jumpy nerves. During dead silence, Mary J was willing to be a little girl again, imagining her mother tending to her emotional needs. She kept thinking that growing up without parents was a mistake. She couldn't recall why it hurt so much: her heart was tired from a wounded inner spirit. Growing up, without a mother or father, produced a hurt that pressed and pressed and pressed throughout her worldly life.

Now reflecting on various seasons of life, Mary J's heart sank even lower. She could neither see a pathway nor a doorway, not even an open window to start her progressing towards store ownership. Mary J began shaking just as if she was going to fall apart—trying to cry—gasping and making strange little noises as though she couldn't get her breath. She was forced to go down stairs to get something to drink before the shaking could stop completely. Yet, she maintained her stubbornness, refusing to give up. Thinking as she walked downstairs towards the kitchen, she spoke softly to herself. *The world can't always be so bleak—things aren't always what they seem to be; humans aren't necessarily trapped in their present situation.*

Unexpectedly, baby Dora Lee woke up. Mary J could hear the faint stirring noises she made, so she waited, knowing almost to the second when she would start to cry. As Dora lee whimpered once, then howled, Mary J quickly rushed back upstairs. She picked her up, balancing Dora Lee neatly in the crook of her left arm. Mary J made several small clucking sounds as she walked her around the room. Dora Lee's eyes crossed blissfully; she then went back to sleep.

Things became quiet within the house again, except for the sound of Lester's children's dog that had begun howling, barking, and whining outside of the kitchen door. Mary J thought the dog had genuine separation anxiety from being left alone. She said to herself. *That dog is having an unusually painful experience.* When she looked out of the window, one of Lester's children came and took the dog back to its pen.

Mary J went back downstairs to help Alma Tucker clean up the kitchen. Without warning, there was a noise of thunder. The thunder rolled again, then came flashes of lightning, with ringing thunder even louder. Lightning flashed through the trees; the thunder sounded like drums playing real music. The leaves on the pecan tree danced on its edges from the wind coming off the waterfront.

Mary J heard drops of rain hitting the roof—smattering like a handful of shotgun pellets on a tin plate. She ran to sit down on the living room sofa; Mary J began hugging her knees. Her heart was pounding so loud that she could hear it. The rain came down hard. Mary J kept sitting there; she was waiting for the roar of the thunder, along with quick flashes of lightning. It began to rain harder, and the earth seemed to celebrate along with it. The clouds were moving into a steady black mass. The thunder cracked closer, and the rain began to roll into small beads from the edge of the roof.

The house was quiet as Rachel came down the stairs. Like always during a thunderstorm, Rachel sat in her favorite rocking chair. She stared out of the window towards Clubfoot Creek. The rain came down and down, swept through the field, and fell along the edges of the yard. There were small pools of water gathering in the roadway. By now, this was a ferocious thunderstorm; lightning was flashing every few seconds—thunder made the house shake. Rachel knew that there was no way that Mary J was going in her bedroom to sat through the storm. She had noticed that during the black of night with the sounds of thunder, lightning flashing, and Pap out working, Mary J would go into Alma Tucker's room until the storm was over.

Mary J was terrified as usual for what seemed like hours, just knowing she would die. Although Rachel believed it was an irrational fear, Mary J was surprised, not saying a word. Swiftly, there was a crack of lightning and an immediate boom of thunder very close. You would have thought that Mary J was going to have a fit, especially by the way she embraced herself. She sat there for one hour, waiting for the storm to pass over. Mary J was prone to voice her opinion more than most women of her time, but not during a thunderstorm. She soon realized that living on a Creek, during a thunder and lightning storm, was not a pleasant experience.

Mary J began to worry about her husband out working in the woods and farming near the Creek. She said to Rachel, "I surely hope Pap is not working near the creek; if he is on that little rowboat, he needs to return back to land."

Rachel calmly put things in proper perspective. "Pap knows these woods and waterways around here; there is no need to worry about him."

Alma Tucker looked out of the living room window, then gave her weather report after going on the porch. "Mary J, it's no need to fear! This storm is passing over."

Mary J gave a great sigh of relief after realizing that the thunderstorm was close to ending. Now suddenly, the last sounds of thunder caused her babies to wake-up. Alma Tucker told Mary J, "You just sat right there with your scare self! I will take care of our babies."

Alma Tucker, along with Rachel, started to laugh, knowing how frighten Mary J was during a thunderstorm. "Alma Tucker," said Rachel, "bring Elise May and Dora Lee down here, so I can take care of my grandchildren. Mary J is right, this is the Lord's work, and we need to be respectful of Him."

Alma Tucker dashed upstairs to Mary J and Pap's bedroom. She came back downstairs with Dora Lee and the nearly two-year-old Elsie May. Holding Dora Lee in her arms and little Elsie May by her hand, she gave baby Dora Lee to Rachel and the little toddler Elsie May to her Mama.

"Mary J," said Rachel, "little Dora Lee is hungry. You can just go in that side room to breastfeed her, just let Elsie May sit and play on the rug. We will look after her." As soon as Mary J placed Elise May on the rug, she became dramatically upset over a toy that fell out of her hand. It had rolled under the couch.

"No, Mama," said Alma Tucker, "I will keep little Elsie May with me."

Alma Tucker began to play with Elsie May as she walked her outside on the front porch. They heard the cat make a soft mewing sound. It was Alma Tucker's warning that the cat was getting hungry. Being excited by the external world of nature penetrating her brain, Elsie May fingers gently touch and then pulled the cat soft wisp-covered head. The cat jumped off the porch and began to hide his face in the ground with meticulous care, to cover his track.

Out of the blue, Lester's children's dog was in the yard again. He started running and trying to play with the chickens. When the dog saw the cat, he began to behave in a hostile way. He started to chase after the cat instead of the chicken. Elsie May, seeking a more in-depth understanding, enjoyed all the commotion going on.

Being highly emotional, Alma Tucker took Elsie May back into the house. "Mama, please hold Elise May while I get those chickens back into the coop. Lester's children dog is out in the yard; he may injury one of them."

"Now," said Rachel, "be careful how you roundup those chickens, don't injury them! You might as well clean the coop before putting them back, please also bring in our eggs. If you see Samuel, Henderson, Philip, or Della Jean outside, tell them, I said come get their dog before I tie him up. I don't know why they can't keep that dog in their yard."

"You're right, Mama," said Alma Tucker! "He is a no-good egg-sucking dog. After the hens lay their eggs, he goes to the nesting boxes and gets the eggs. We must keep him out of the chicken coop. You know Mama, we never had any trouble with that dog eating-eggs before last month. I would highly recommend not letting that dog hang around our chickens."

"You are right, Alma Tucker," said Rachel. "That dirty old egg-sucking dog needs to stay out of our yard."

"Alma Tucker immediately went outside towards the chicken coop, then said, "you, dirty old egg-sucking dog, if you don't stay out of our hen house, I'm gonna stomp your head into the ground." At that very moment, she saw a pail of water on the front porch; she was so mad that she threw the entire pale of water onto the dog. The dog quickly took a flight back to his house.

When Mary J returned to the living room, Rachel said to her. "Why don't you come and go fishing with me? Alma Tucker and Lorraine can take care of the children."

"Ok," said Mary J, "just give me a few minutes to get ready."

"Good," said Rachel, "I will start getting our fishing equipment and lure organizer together."

Rachel loved going fishing as much as possible, especially after a big rain downpour that usually cooled down the temperature. After the cloud droplets went away, she knew the intensity of the bite often increases a lovely seafood dinner for her family. Sometimes, the cat even got a good meal. Rachel only had to decide whether to use her little rowboat or just sit and fish from the banks.

Alma Tucker returned from rounding up the chickens and agreed to help Lorraine take care of the children. Mary J and Rachel took off for the morning fishing routine. Rachel loved taking someone with her; sometimes, she would take one of Lester's children if no one else in her household would join her.

Rachel and Mary J rowed the small boat a little way into the Creek; they began casting their lines. This was a good day for fishing after a brief rain. They were certainly going to have fish for dinner. As they were sitting in the boat, this gave Mary J and Rachel a little time to small talk.

"Mary J," said Rachel, "I am glad that you and Pap are living here with us. You know, since my husband passed away, Pap has been an anchor for the family. I know you want to get your place. Also, there has been some talk about you wanting to own a store."

"You are right, Mother Rachel, I have had this dream since I was eleven years old; I want to own a store just like my Aunt Loretta."

"Just remember Mary J, we are coming out of what they called the Great Depression years. The 1930s have produced some of the toughest years in our country's history. So, it may take some time. You and Pap both are hard workers and full of determination. Yet, otherwise, I know the Lord can make a way out of no way, especially if you trust him."

"Well, Mother Rachel, I surely trust him. I believe that your cousin Luke has some ideas that he wants to discuss with Pap and me. I know that money has been scarce during the Great Depression years. Nonetheless, Luke believes that World War two will drive out the Depression and boost our economy to new heights of prosperity. There is a military base now being built in our area. We will have thousands of new people relocating here; this means many new customers and opportunities."

"Oh, is that right, Mary J," said Rachel graciously, "well now, but you will still need money to build a store. You know Pap is always welcome to run my little farm here, but that's no jackpot full of money."

"Yes, Mother Rachel, Luke is in the process of building a little house out there on the Corner. Pap has worked out some type of deal with him, just maybe we can start a little business right there. Luke already has a store in the same area, maybe something good will happen for us. The Corner is an intersection where three roads meet—full of little businesses. The location would be perfect for a little house business."

"Well, you all be careful! There are two little children to think about, including your little sister Lorraine."

"We will be careful, Mother Rachel," said Mary J, "but we have to try. As you said, we must trust the Lord. From my early childhood, my parents taught me that the only true foundation for faith is in God's Word. Pap is not perfect, but he does have strong faith in the Lord. He prays every night very beautifully. I would love to see him go to church more regularly with us, but Pap said that he must work hard to get my store. As you said, the effects of the Great Depression still linger with us, so we must do everything possible to make each penny count."

Rachel looked at the water, then up at Mary J again. "I admire your willpower and determination. I have heard Pap grandfather Solomon say that willpower and commitment is more important than ability or even education. This world is full of people too scared to try anything, especially our women. To be a good business owner means putting others needs ahead of your own. Now, if you do it well, like old man Solomon said, you will receive rewards for your hard work."

"You know, Mother Rachel, I believe that a person's work is part of a calling; no matter what our family background, we are equal in our ability to glorify God."

Rachel said thoughtfully, "You are right, Mary J, our work must have value to other human beings. There is no time to think through every idea when you are trying to build a business. They must be woven into the very fabric of one's soul."

Mary J nodded, then she explained slowly, compelled by the demand in Rachel's tone. "Of course, Pap and I don't have a lot of time to think; however, we can thank the Lord for godly parents that sent us to church and Sunday school."

Rachel struggled for the right words. "I still say, money is the biggest problem you and Pap must overcome—so... just pray on it."

Mary J eyed her hand, then swallowed hard. "Yes, oh how true, by the way, you are right. Nevertheless, but somehow, we must trust the Lord in our weaknesses—who is laying the foundations of our lives."

This statement hit close to Rachel's heart because times had been hard for her, especially since her husband passed away. She had given birth to eight children, buried one and a husband as well. She needed Pap to stick with the farm and help provide for her household. Mother Rachel lifted her eyebrows, stared deliberately at Mary J, and said, "It seems to me that without any money, you and Pap are headed for trouble. Nobody around these parts has that kind of money except bootleggers or moonshiners. My son Pap better not be messing around with that business!"

Mary J didn't want to add any more wearisome situations to her mother-in-law's life. She knew that occasionally Rachel would worry over her son Lester's young death that left behind a wife with eight stair-step children. Like others of her times, Rachel's attitude of life had been greatly affected by the great depression years that left behind many dark shadows. Mary J admired her for being able to push through those dark curtains. In Mary J's mind, it was like suddenly flipping the light switch on in a flower shop at midnight.

Mary J and Rachel rowed the boat back to the shore with beautiful smiles on their faces. Rachel was always happy when she caught a lot of fish, even if there was no fancy ice chest to preserve them. She would just carry several old buckets for her catch. As Mary J and Rachel got close to the shoreline, Samuel and Philip, two of Lester's children were standing on the banks.

Samuel yelled out, "Grandma! We will clean the fish and put away your boat."

"All-right, boys," said Rachel, "we are going on to the house."

Philip screamed out with a high voice, "Look at this big fish here! Don't you worry Grandma, we know exactly the best way to clean them."

Mary J cleared her throat, "Phillip, there is a smaller tub over towards the end of the boat for you and Samuel to take home."

"Yes! Of course," Samuel said with a smile. "Thank you; Mama said she would sure like to have a fresh fish for her supper."

Mary J turned her head to look directly at him. "Well, you tell your mother Eva, we caught those fish, especially for her."

Mary J and Rachel walked back toward the house from the glittering Creek to a dim and cool front yard. They stood a few minutes under the pecan tree to enjoy the fresh breeze blowing suddenly through its branches. Mary J decided to sit on the porch while Rachel went into the house to fix supper. Her eyes brimmed with emotion as she began to ponder over Rachel's statement about faith in God. Mary J couldn't believe what she had heard from Pap's mother about his bootlegging activities. Pap was moonshining right under her nose, yet she acted as though there was no awareness on her part.

Mary J had never forgotten how hard it was growing up during the Great Depression years as a child, without parents, and along with eight other siblings. Now she knew for sure, after talking to Rachel, that her family must leave the Fishers' homestead to intensify their efforts toward new paths of opportunities. Regardless of whether or not dark times were ahead, Mary J felt that she and her husband must choose what was right for their family instead of what was stress-free. She was determined not to allow the lack of money to halt her dreams. In short, Mary J kept asking herself: *Are there any interpretations that will show my goals and dreams to be incorrect or in any way to prove them wrong? If so, what is my life all about?*

All of a sudden, Mary J looked up towards heaven, praying with expectation. Then and there, she promised the Lord that if she succeeds in establishing her store, she will dedicate her business to assisting others. She would give back to her community by helping local churches and ordinary people—especially those who were permanently scarred by poverty from the Great Depression years.

Chapter

15

BUSINESS CHALLENGES

After breakfast the next morning, Mary J went back upstairs to get a quick nap before her girls woke up. The lack of sleep was beginning to show on her face. It was still motionless dark outside; Pap was at work from the previous day. She knew that bootleggers worked long hours, sometimes all night. Mary J lay down on her bed but couldn't sleep. She began thinking about her husband's work activities. Now she could see so clearly in her mind; Pap was one of those salt-of-the-earth type people that worked hard. He was known as a man you could trust. When he gave you his word, it was as good as gold.

Mary J started scrutinizing Pap's bootlegging set-ups with Levy and several other partners. *Why not? There is no other way for us to make money. But* she thought—*if only Pap could keep people from stealing his whiskey. He certainly needs to stop people like his brother Fred and Levy's brother Eli from drinking-up so much of the profit. I need every extra penny for my new store. Now wait a minute—in all fairness, Pap does take on most of the responsibilities for us: two little girls, my little sister Lorraine; his mother Rachel as well as his sister Alma Tucker, who is two years younger than me. The farm is hardly making any money; this means that he must team up with several partners to make some money as a bootlegger. We just need to get some real money*. After tossing and turning for a little while longer, Mary J finally went to sleep.

Pap and his business partner Levy were busy working at the still engaging in a process they called Sweetening-up. The smell of the mash was strong even from a distance. Pap walked towards some of their mash barrels. He pulled the covers off several of them to get a closer look at the mash. He told Eli, his partner Levy's brother and a crew member, to fill the boiler as he removed the cooker cap with a wrench.

Eli spent several minutes trying to figuring out how to unstick several stuck buckets. Pap walked over to Eli, turned the buckets upside down so that their open ends faced the ground. Next, he put his foot through the handle closest to the ground. The stuck buckets quickly came apart. Eli smiled nervously; then, he made his usual trips to the water pump with two 5-gallon buckets. He promptly returned with more water for the boiler, only to drop both buckets after he notices a small flock of birds scrabbling for bits of his biscuits.

"Now listen," Pap said, placing both hands on Eli's shoulders: "No sense thinking about that now, just get two more buckets of water. It requires only common sense, not native ability." The rest of the crew, including Eli, just laugh as usual, like a big family.

The smell of alcohol was intense; the odor steamed up into Eli's face each time he scooped up a bucket of the mash. The more he scooped, the more he had to lean into the barrel to reach the mash. Toward the bottom of the barrel, the cornmeal began to swirl as he tried to scoop the last of the mash out. One barrel of mash filled the little cooker perfectly as if it had been made just for this purpose. The mash was about eight inches from the top of the cooker neck.

As Pap inspected Eli's work, he simultaneously began to put the top back onto the cooker, tightening each bolt snugly. The steel pipe extending from the cooker top coordinated perfectly with the doubling keg inlet pipeline; Pap only had to connect the two pipes together with a wrench.

"Eli," said Pap, "make sure that the valve is open so it won't blow up."

Eli replied, "I am inspecting the lever valve between the cooker and the doubling keg right now. It's open right now; thank God! We just avoided an explosion."

"Now Eli," said Pap, "This burner will make steam from that boiler; it runs right down into this pipe. Just look at the bottom of the cooker, you can see steam traveling from the mash to the boiler—pushing out the whiskey. The alcohol comes from the cooker and then flows directly into the doubling keg—utilizing the purifier and the worm. The whiskey will come out here. You got to be sure that you keep water in this worm barrel cold, so that the whiskey won't steam out.

Suddenly, the wind freshened the treetops; it swept a few leaves in the air that landed on the cooker. Eli began quickly dusting the leaves off the cooker. "My goodness Pap! This is top of the line, just look at how this stuff is dripping slowly from those clean copper tubes. I tell you, my friend, no one will ever find a dead possum floating in our mash or catch us using a rusty radiator. Would you like a little taste?"

Pap knew that he had to learn how to communicate more effectively with his crew. He was now facing the problem of altering his crew's habits and attitudes. A skill that he recognized as coming mostly from observation, experience, and studying each situation. His training process was very focused on teaching a simple sequence of planned behaviors. Pap was not the kind of man that flaunted his authority rudely and disrespectful. He needed only to figure out, when and where to use his power without damaging his workers' morale.

Pap observed Eli for several moments with concealed curiosity, trembling with rage. "Eli, just keep on sweetening it. We can taste a little bit later on. You should have enough cornmeal and sugar to set up four or five more barrels. That ought to give us another six cases with this operation. I am going over here and wake up your brother Levy, so that we can get more wood."

Pap and Levy returned with more wood three hours later. As they entered the still area, they found Eli somewhat tipsy—resting on a crate. As they approached the crew working area, Eli jumped to his feet—gave a little wink with a slight head nod—made a small hand motion with his right hand.

Eli pursed his lips. "Follow me. This stuff is just as clean, pure, and safe as Kool-Aid. I tell you one other thing; there is no trace of lead salt either. Man, this stuff is good!"

128

Eli was now feeling good. He became tipsy from tasting the whiskey at the still so often that his co-workers gave him a nickname: Mr. Feeling Good. The crew would often say to him: *Hey there! If it ain't Mr. Feeling Good—What's going on brother?"* Eli was proud of his nick-name, which always lit up a big smile on his face with the following remarks: *Shoot, what are you talking about, man! Brother, I am hanging in there*! The crew would always burst into boisterous laughter.

Levy leaned over one of the barrels and smelled a strong present of whiskey on Eli's breath. He also saw a whiskey bottle under his arm and a bag of biscuits in his hand. Levy gasped like a land fish—vibrating with anger. "This can't be true! Oh my God, Pap! Why did we leave my brother, Mr. Feeling Good, at this still without anybody watching him? Maybe next time, we will invite your brother Fred to stay with Eli in our absence; this way, we will have two people half-drunk destroying our operation."

Remembering that Eli's had been warned many times about his drinking on the job, Pap walked away with a compassionate heart. He looked away from Eli towards the other crew members: "Well now, my fellow Americans, rarely do I recommend therapy for a crew member, but now, one of our most dedicated workers, Mr. Eli—in my opinion, the man must be a scientist testing his proposition through experimentation with our whiskey. Gentlemen, I sure hope his conclusion is in the form of payment."

The crew was on their tiptoe with excitement as they tried to resist the urge to roar with laughter. They huddled close together to hear more of the conversation. It was as if they were sipping champagne at a comedy show. The ethical questions for the crew were highly inconsequential because it was a typical occurrence at the still.

Elli cheerfully shouted; I hope you all brought oak wood because those other types produce too much smoke." Then he added, "By the way, Dallas and his brother Hap picked up several cases of whiskey... just about a couple of hours ago. They left here driving a huge truck."

Levy hit the fan when he found out that Dallas and his brother were delivering their whiskey. "Oh my God, my brother, Mr. Feeling-Good, don't you have a bit of sense?"

Pap looked at Levy and his crew thoughtfully, never cracking a smile. "Eli doesn't have the sense of a coon. I think a coon might be even cleverer."

Because Eli was the acting boss when Pap and Levy were away, the crew had been whispering behind their hands for several hours, watching Eli sneaking drinks of whiskey. Now that Eli had got caught drinking on the job, the whole crew was roaring with laughter. They started cheering for Mr. Feeling Good, screaming their battle cries in support of him. The crew members were plotting something; there were side bets placed on whether or not he would get caught. The entire crew knew that Eli would never get fired by his brother and friend.

Levy rolled his eyes at Eli. "My brother, how many cases did you give them?"

Mr. Feeling Good said, half-staggering: "I'm not sure; I just told them to go back there and take it all with them. So, they put everything in their truck and drove away."

Pap maintained, as usual, a thoughtful facial expression—muttering under his breath with his hands in the air, "I am through with it."

Levy now has a tear in his right eye: "Oh, my Lord, our investment has been stolen! We might as well have left a jackass here."

Pap throws his hands up in the air again without cracking a smile. "Now! If you put Eli's brains in a bird, the poor creature would fly backward."

The crew members, along with Eli, just roar with laughter at Pap's comments. Pap had a way of correcting a tense situation, with a no-nonsense persona, using firm but laughable statements.

Pap felt rightly upset with Eli; nevertheless, he held the rest of his views back for now. He had developed the philosophy: Never trust a man with a drinking problem. Pap and Levy would take a drink, but just one, and then continued with their work. Their brothers, Eli and Fred, were excellent workers but couldn't be trusted with decision-making authority; especially, if they had a shot of whiskey running through their veins.

Pap looked at Mr. Feeling Good, then said with a firm look while shaking his head: "Never trust a hungry dog to guard your chicken coop or smokehouse."

Levy's jaw snapped shut, and his teeth clicked. "Dogs, smoked meats, and chickens don't naturally mix, nor do thieves and bootleggers."

After these comments concerning Dallas and Hap, Pap walked away with a slight smile, then slapped Mr. Feeling Good on his left shoulder. Pap was that kind of a guy, who could tell you straight up his opinion; but somehow, he would leave your dignity intact rather than allowing you to feel less than a real person. But then again, there was one kind of person Pap hated immensely: a thief.

Levi hollered out to Pap, "My brother Mr. Feeling Good doesn't have a bit of sense, especially when whiskey takes over his brain. Eli is not just cable of giving the dog our chicken coop, but also the smokehouse. I can tell you right now, Dallas and his boys are worse than dogs. They will even steal from their friends and neighbors. Now get ready for this, Dallas may call the law for meanness to report our still. I truly believe the dog is better!"

The next day Levy and Pap followed up with Dallas and his crew, only to find out that none of the whiskey picked up from Eli was delivered to customers. Dallas shared a story of mechanical problems with his vehicle—claiming that his crew had to leave his truck to get tools for repair. Dallas told them that after leaving the truck alongside the road for a couple hours, somebody stole the whiskey. Pap and Levy—in their hearts, knew that Dallas and his crew were the real organizers behind this fraudulent scheme.

Because Levy and Pap hooked themselves onto a shoestring budget, Levy now felt like their situation was hopeless. Levy felt himself gagging; he put down his head—thinking, *it couldn't be; no one would do such a horrible thing. It had to be an accident.* Because of his broken spirit, Levy's heart was in his imagination. His pride and joy had now left him. Levy just couldn't take anymore.

Levy looked back up at Pap: "Dallas and his boys have stolen our whiskey—right from under Mr. Feeling Good's nose. We are now financially broke. We need money to provide for our families."

At this point, Levy's eyes now clouded over with tears. He had mentally thought it all out. Levy had considered not only the dollars spent but also the real personal cost. He began with all the significant trade-offs: Sacrificing one thing to obtain another—away from family frequently, long hours in the woods with dangerous animals, sometimes all night. As part of Levy's thinking, there were also legal implications with laws in a constant state of change.

Pap looked down at his hands and then raised his eyes towards his partner. Without any signs of resentment: "We will make it through this some kind of way; even if, we have to eat a lot of string beans from our gardens. Thank goodness that my mother knows how to catch fish! But now Mary J, she will be very unhappy with me for losing so much money. You don't need to worry, Levy; I am confident that we will make it on the next run."

Levy had already borrowed money from everyone he could, including his mother and brothers. He had hock everything he had just to get into business with his partners. The Great Depression years had hit his family hard, just like all the others around him. A succession of business failures would be financially devastating for him. He had only one consuming obsession: Growing his business and make money. His voice was now croaky and hoarse from dealing with all of his firm convictions. He broke down and wept bitterly. The impact of this nose-dive operation on his life was immeasurable.

Levy raised his thick black eyebrows, then took out a white handkerchief to wipe his eyes. "I sure hope so, because all the money that I have to my name is in our next patch of Whiskey. But one thing for sure, my friend, if I ever get my hands on a sizable amount of money, you can count on my help, for any amount necessary, even to help Mary J get her store."

Pap's heart was in his throat. He lifted his chin higher. "We don't need shoes in bed or under a bush. Let's think about our opportunities. The purchase of more farmland and a new store is mutually beneficial with our moonshining operation. We could grow our corn on the land to make a low-cost mash; a store would certainly enhance our bootlegging operations. This way, we can filter our money through Mary J's store. But anyway, thanks for your kind thoughts of generosity towards helping my family."

Levy looked at him with old, old eyes. "What isn't earned by a person's own hands is a charity, but to me, we are family. I would also like to thank you for being my business partner. You are one of the most honest people that I have ever known. Today, I am as broke as Mark Washington. The story goes that all of Mark Washington's worldly possessions could be kept within a tiny hobo bundle, dangling over his shoulder. He could squeeze into any vacant corner of a room to sleep. If he walked into three rooms with several corners to choose from, he wouldn't be able to decide which corner to sleep in for the night. You know Pap, they tell me that he survived in the past by hopping on one train after another in New York City. He doesn't even have a spare shirt or any extra pants. On the other hand, when I last saw him, he had on fake military clothes. So, if he can make it, we can as well."

Levy then reached into his pocket and took out two hand-rolled cigarettes and gave Pap one. Pap reached into his pocket and pulled out a box of matches and lit their cigarettes.

"Thanks," said Pap, "there is no value in looking for an opportunity in hindsight."

As they stared at each other for a long silence, two birds squawked at each other in a nearby tree. Well now, Levy said. "Here are some tiny cloth pouches used to hold cigarettes. Mary J can use these to put on sticks and make dolls for your little girls."

Pap just put the cloth pouches in his back pocket without cracking a smile. He then looked up and saw birds in the tree. Pap grinned. "For some birds, there are no nuts too hard for them to crack."

As Pap was about to walk away, Levy shouted out: "Here is a little bit of advice, never get married to a young woman that you can't afford to make her dreams come true."

Pap and Levy began laughing together; their spirits were so much higher than a few minutes earlier. They were now ready to depart, knowing that one more mistake would be disastrous to them financially. At that precise moment, Eli showed up out of nowhere. He came over to apologize for his stupidity in trusting Dallas and his brother Hap with their whiskey.

Eli's misery was like a sickness that had crept over him and paralyzed his faculties. The very air had a restless smear for him; a sense of an inescapable destiny of betrayal was convicting him. With a despairing cry, he called out to them—turning saddened eyes toward the clouds—staring as if wondering: "How did I lose my way on the road to righteousness."

Eli shook his head and bowed it low before them. His body being helpless and grim, he stumbled down on his knees—clenching himself in his misery. With a catch in his throat, "I should have known better; I am very sorry. Now it's clear to me, I have caused a great deal of emotional distress and pain to you and your families. An angel of death is hanging over my head; may Heaven forgive me!"

All of a sudden, Levy made an impatient gesture, then slowly forced himself to calm down. For a few seconds, the silence was so great that one could have heard a bird stir in its nest. Eli's humility was most impressive because of the visible signs of his overwhelming grief. His pain and sorrow were hastily turning into tears of sadness, raising a broken voice of constant sadness.

"Well, Eli," said Pap, "as long as you have learned something… we can move on."

As the bitterness slowly began draining out of their hearts, Levy and Pap speechlessly gazed with uncertain eyes into each other faces. They were restored with a mixture of practicality and forgiveness. Now with an extremely inadequate budget, they were experiencing entrepreneurial fright, which was their ultimate fear of an adventurous life. They knew from previous experiences that when entrepreneurial fright entered the activities of the mind—it always left one's conscience filled with little monsters, which included subjective thoughts that prevented sleep by causing wide-awake nightmares.

Pap and Levy now left with a paradox instead of a compromise. This hindered them from grappling with significant issues and tough questions. They yearned for a general reconciliation that would unify their crew. Nevertheless—in a spirit of harmony, they departed peacefully in different directions.

Pap went home and told his wife the bad news. "We were hoodwinked by real live vultures. Dallas and his brother Hap pulled the wool over Eli's eyes while he was feeling too good from our whiskey."

Mary J never understood how Pap and Levy could have knowingly risked their business with so many incompetent crew members. Mary J's head sunk between her hunched shoulders—her thoughts possessed by confusion and panic. There was no doubt that turbulent times were now in their future. Shame mingled in her heart with a timid and dark hope—questions rushed through her mind like an unseen strong wind.

For a moment, Mary J was terrified; a feeling of unbearable loss squeezed her heart: "Oh, what buzzards they are! Eli should have known better than to trust Dallas and his brother. My goodness—when Eli is drinking whiskey, I have more faith in Mark Washington."

Unconsciously, Mary J pressed her hand against her face and along her tightened throat. She began staring outside her window into the darkness; the news of their loss became more than a shock to her. Mary J didn't want to believe the true depths of their situation, so she went on and on with her fussing and grumbling.

Pap felt sad that he had to be the bearer of bad news to his wife, which meant lost opportunities for his family. Pap's feelings were deeply wounded, so he just went to bed. While lying down, Pap's imagination began drifting—moving between the past and present. He swallowed his pride and took a deep breath. He began thinking within his inner self: *We are just a poor, struggling family with dreams. My family isn't trying to be the wealthiest folks in town; we only wish to have a beautiful place to live and a legal community business. It's about being able to feed ourselves, then having something left over to share with others. The only way that I can get a community store, for my wife, is by seizing every business opportunity on the right and left.*

After acknowledging that Mary J's childhood mission had not changed, Pap turned quickly and restlessly on his pillow as he glanced out of the window. He realized that life was much more than sleeping and eating. There was no doubt in his mind that fate had unquestionably been a significant obstacle against his wife reaching her personal goals. He saw his wife as a mystique bird sitting on a tree that never troubles itself about the branch breaking, because the bird's faith was in its wings, not the branch.

Pap continued thinking about his family agonizing times ahead, due exclusively to loss financial opportunities. Suddenly, he began considering the big picture. *We have these problems in the wrong order of importance. We are personally responsible for our torment. These things happen to all entrepreneurs at one time or another. The important thing is to get through our encounters without complete failure. What I fear, I suspect, is that we might just become another member of the herd that has passed into obscurity.*

Pap's mind briefly shifts to his Dad, John Allen, who was born and raised upon this very homestead. He was poor money-wise—just like everybody else during the Great Depression years. Pap could remember as a child the time he saved up enough money so his Dad could buy him a pair of shoes; only to find out after trying them on, they were large enough for his brother's feet as well. He accepted that his Dad did what was best for his family during those hardscrabble times. Pap could still see in his mind's eye—a shovel in his Dad's hand. He could never forget how his dad did miracles when times were hard, especially with the little money he received from his crops. Sometimes life would kick him down to the ground—he would each time get up again. Although his Dad had fallen down many times during his life, yet he continuously got back up again. Pap felt that his Dad was always ready for the next round of life's experiences.

Three years before Pap's marriage to Mary J, his Dad called him to his death bed while still in his fifties. Pap could even visualize this experience as if it was right before his eyes. He could again see his Daddy putting his hands on his right shoulder with tears in his eyes. 'Pap, I am depending upon you son to pull the family through, it is all left up to you.' One week later, his Dad passed away. Pap could still hear his dad's voice: 'I am depending upon you, my son, to see the family through.' From that day forward, Pap took over the family farm and began taking care of his mother and her household.

Now, Pap had his own family; they were all living together in his mother's house. He was farming her land. He knew that his wife was craving for her own land, home, and store. She had been pushing him to make a move. Pap began thinking: *What shall I do?* He felted Mary J had understood that he had promised his dad, on his dying bed, to see the family through the hard times ahead. Pap always carried this snapshot in his mind. Nevertheless, he was determined to find a way to make his wife's dreams come true. Lying down silently near his wife, he became lost in his thought over ideas that were somewhat difficult to grasp. Within a few minutes, Pap fell asleep with a troubled mind—that had divorced itself between his reason and emotion.

Mary J shook her head as hideous memories and dreams had broken her sleep. She could no longer bear to think of the future. Entangled with terror, her smile and pride evaporated into darkness. Mary J tried to believe, but found that she was too disturbed.

All of a sudden—her mind started dancing, like a veil falling; it changed. She unexpectedly regained her childhood's survival instincts. *Strange day...* she thought as she felt the thrill of her convictions. The fog over her mind began to evaporate—she could think again: *I believe in the sacredness of my husband's word; God will make way for us. We must do something to breathe life and excitement into an otherwise dull and mundane world. I will never allow anyone or anything to let my God-given dreams become air castles.*

Chapter

16

COUSIN LUKE

L uke was continuously looking for an excellent business opportunity. He believed the secret of success could be found in people that made demands of themselves. In Luke's opinion, they would always be purpose seekers by nature, with an entrepreneurial spirit. At the same time, armed with worthwhile and predetermined goals—unafraid to deal with gut-wrenching pains, especially as they try to free themselves from a private world filled with monsters, sucking at every morsel of their being.

Luke would always tell his associates: *Budding entrepreneurs must be decision-makers—forming their own opinions, without depending on other people. When they do the unthinkable, ask for advice—they will surely be called nuts to start a new business. Why? I will tell you why—most people are reluctant to make choices—any choice that may be independent of the advice of others. Their fear of failure is too high—their self-confidence is too weak.* Most *people would rather have the punishments of someone else's choice.* Luke would then rest his case, concluding with strong feelings: *You know why? I will tell you why—because they want to have their cakes and eat it too.*

Luke had known plenty, potentially successful men like his cousin Pap, who married women without much thought of the future. They found themselves burdened with wives who couldn't keep up as they rose in the world. Their wives' constant fear of failure had unconsciously sabotaged their chances of success. In so doing, these women attract even more omissions and mistakes, mostly from their imaginary minds. Their personal feelings had affected their perception of factual realities that could have produced golden opportunities. But for some reason, they couldn't see beyond what met their eyes.

Just like her Aunt Loretta and Uncle Sweet, Mary J knew that she wanted to be a store owner. She had made this decision on her 11th birthday. Mary J was determined to make it through the pearly gates of opportunity. She had created a mental track to run on, a course to travel—a goal to achieve. Her strategy wasn't to eliminate risk but to increase the odds of success. Therefore, she placed her bets on making hard choices. Now with Pap by her side, she had the stubbornness and stamina to start a new business from zero. She felt like a woman full of confidence, with the vigor of a young warrior.

Pap's cousin Luke was the perfect person to be informed of this information. He and his wife Eunice owned land, a night club, and a small general store. After moving to Fisher-town with her husband, Mary J began going out some evenings to sit with Luke's wife Eunice at their general store. This first-hand look, at her store operation, was an easy way for Mary J to get knowledge of the retail business.

On Monday afternoon, Pap dropped Mary J off at Luke's general store to spend the evening with his wife. After Mary J got out of the vehicle, Pap slowly drove away to take care of a few business deals. When Mary J walked inside the store, Eunice was handling a long line of customers. Mary J took a seat near the sales counter. The store featured an ongoing circus act of characters from the comical to the political—from the law-abiding to criminals. For Mary J, this was a dancing light of amusement.

Because more and more customers came into the store, There was no chance for Eunice to say a word. She would look at Mary J from time to time with an apology in her eyes. Mary J would just smile and shake her head. There was no need to apologize because Mary J was more than pleased just to be there. At last, there was a brief moment; all the customers had departed. Eunice mumbled something under her breath as she walked from behind the sales counter.

Eunice had an extremely cheerful smile upon her face as she approached Mary J: "I am so happy that you are out here with me today. Your companionship and friendship have been a great benefit to me. My husband, Luke, has been gone since yesterday." She looked down and began running several fingers through her hair. She continued: "Have you ever experienced a complete change in your feelings? For example, you go to bed one night, and everything's fine. You wake up the next morning, and nothing's fine. Nothing you can think of accounts for it. Yesterday you were happy. You were looking forward to a great day. But something happens, and your responses are different. Your feelings, actions, and interpretations of the very same thing that took place yesterday are very different today. I know that we are not alone in this world—God is here—sometimes, I feel that Satan is even closer. At times in the morning, I feel that demons are sitting right on the side of my bed, looking for an opportunity to destroy my marriage."

Mary J thought it all out for a few seconds. "Well, now, you are consumed by your marriage. Luke is emotionally draining you so much that it is affecting you both mentally and now physically. Do you know how the devil wins? He tries to get you fouled out of the game of life. He sends an evil spirit that wants to turn your natural mood of depression into spiritual defeat, doubt, and unhappiness. You can count on one thing; Luke is extremely knowledgeable in making and keeping his money. Just remember one thing, those women will never get Luke's money. Just look around your environment; you are personally running a store that's making a profit. Luke has several other businesses, including an active farm. You are not like those helpless women out there, running around with an alcoholic husband that has poor money-making skills. I don't see you cleaning anybody's house or being a field hand. Plus, think about this, when Luke is dead and gone, these things will become your belongings, girl you just hang on in there!"

Eunice couldn't help it; she was like a soft, timid, brown field mouse. After tapping her hand kindly, Mary J kept talking, laughing, and teasing her about being too uptight over patty matters.

Eunice paused indecisively, while hobbling across the room towards the sales counter. She was now talking to herself again, although promising not to punish herself with negative issues. Eunice's mind started assessing and analyzing the facts of her marriage. She began thinking: *conflicts are inevitable, even among the best of friends. Like Mary J' just said, 'conflicts should deepen rather than weaken my marriage.'*

Eunice dropped her eyes as if she was embarrassed by her situation. She strolled aimlessly back towards Mary J, looking somewhat confused but determined. "You are right, but don't forget one other thing; Luke has the susceptibility of being a womanizer."

The harshness of her words took Mary J's breath away. Mary J shook her head and then spoke with loving patience. "My poor darling: Guess what? So are most of the other men in our community. We all suffer because of the evil in this world. We aren't living in some dreamland or perfect world. Let's face reality, you and I need to be strong women—we're going to do business in a man's world. Being businesswomen will make it easier for us to create the lives we want for ourselves. My husband, just like yours, is either on the farm or taking care of business deals, God only knows what they are doing."

Looking surprised, Eunice drew a deep breath of delight. "Thanks, Mary J, for that advice, you certainly know how to turn something bitter into an extraordinarily sweet spirit. Whenever there is bad news, there is always a lot of good as well. Unless we learn to deal honestly with bitterness, we will be living in a glass house."

Mary J said with a soft smile, "Now remember Eunice; you may have Luke all wrong."

Eunice replied in a sad tone. "I won't let it upset me; I won't. I can't let anything bother me now, not when I need to be at my best with customers. You know, Luke has a son by Clarence Fenner's wife."

Mary J almost fell out of her chair in shock. "You mean to tell me that Walter Dennis is Ada's child."

Eunice gazed at Mary J with misted eyes. "Oh, yes! I tell you something else. Her husband, Clarence, will not stop at our store because of that mess. When Clarence's drive passes this store, he will not even wave his hand.

A mix of fear and anger dimmed the happy excitement that Mary J was feeling earlier. After thinking it all out, she said: "Now I have heard from my cousin Zack, Pap has a little daughter less than a year senior of our oldest child Elsie May, named is Odessa." Mary J stood up and circled the floor. "But let's remember this Eunice, it's not the children's fault. We need to be very kind to them. Things that happen to us are not as important as the ways we respond to them. You and I are probably the most decent women in Harlowe; now, you need to stop flipping out just because Luke is looking at other women. Pap and Luke are among the best men to be found anywhere in North Carolina; we just need to encourage them to attend church on Sundays. Only the Lord can straighten out some of the stuff going on in this community. Girl! You better just quit worrying so much, unless you want your brother Walter, the undertaker, to bury you next."

Eunice stared hesitantly out of the front screen door. "These men today are something else! Looking back towards Mary J, "But regardless, trust is the key to a healthy marriage."

Mary J pounded on the wooden part of her chair with a firm fist. "You are right; trust is the glue that holds things together. Yet, the most dangerous emotions in this world are resentment and bitterness; like cancer, they gnaw away at a person's insides. These emotions are destructive because they color one's viewpoints. Luke is not an easy read, but nor is he a devious man."

Mary J and Eunice found themselves laughing until their sides ached. Eunice looked down at her hands, curled up on the sales counter. The tension had been relieved as Eunice's anger dissipated into mid-air—now she was able to think more reasonably with a cool head. Eunice admitted to Mary J that she had been quarreling with Luke about his overnight activities. She had to acknowledge that there was no real benefit from this type of discussion. In her mind, Luke only became more argumentative when his back was pushed against a wall.

"Well," Eunice said, "and well again. I owed it to my husband to believe in him and always give him the benefit of the doubt. If I am not capable of doing this, then our relationship will be threatened. Luke has always expressed to me a very relevant point, one that I cannot ignore. He has whispered into my ears, in many ways, that our marriage is forever until death separates us."

Eunice now refocused her attention towards Mary J. By the way, "I am going to give you some advice about nagging your husband. No man is perfect including Pap! There will be troubled times; so, don't nag him to death!"

Mary J laughed. "If you can recognize just how right you are, we might be able to do business together."

Eunice was careful not to smile. "I am willing to bargain with some more advice. Pap is a good man: he is not like my husband, who stays out all-night in New Bern, sometimes for several days. Luke's outside child, Walter Dennis, is the one that takes care of the farm when he is away from home. If it wasn't for him, our farm wouldn't yield a crop this year. Nevertheless, Luke needs to get back here and help with farming this week. I am afraid that he is going to work Walter Dennis to death. I got to give it to his son; he is a smart boy."

"Glory to God, you are right," said Mary J after noticing Eunice's perceptiveness. "Now, don't you worry about Luke, he will be on my special prayer list this Sunday at church. Luke has always been very kind to me. As you know, he loves my husband like a brother."

There were no customers in the store, so Mary J and Eunice went outside and sat in front of the store. People from the local community came walking by; several decided to rest awhile, they appreciated the power of community storytelling. Some of their stories were so sad that Mary J covered her face with both hands and sat frozen for several minutes. Slowly, she slid her hands down her face, swallowed back her tears, and then looked away in prayerful thoughts.

A lady name Rosanna was walking towards the store; she continuously came by several times a week for tobacco products. Rosanna was in her forties at the time, but she looked sixty. She was wearing a flour sack dress with a wrap-around scarf over her head. As Rosanna approached the store, you could see chewing tobacco dripping around her mouth, especially as she tried to talk with everybody. One could tell that she chews tobacco and dipped stuff regularly by looking at her teeth. She was always very loud. People could hear her shouting at Eunice, an eyeball distance down the road.

As Rosanna approached the store entrance, she said with a high pitch voice that could be heard nearly a mile away: "Eunice, I hope you got my stuff and tobacco!

Eunice hollered back, "yes, I have it, baby come on and get it!"

When she got close to the store, Eunice said, "Now, take a moment, Rosanna, and meet my good friend Mary J. She is Pap's wife."

Mary J stood up and said, "I am glad to meet you."

Rosanna turned her head to look directly at her. "Oh, my goodness, I heard that Pap got married. They said that he went over the Creek and got him a pretty little girl. I guess the women around here aren't good enough for him."

Everybody started laughing at the way Rosanna displayed her words like a comedian. They all said, "you right, Rosanna, tell her about it."

"Come on now, Rosanna, and tell the truth," said Eunice, "your husband John is not from around here either."

The bystanders began roaring with laughter; they thought Rosanna was the funniest woman in the whole community. They all said: "You're right Rosanna, go ahead… tell everybody the truth!"

"You got that right," said Rosanna, "my John is from heaven. There is no man anywhere like him. You know, he will be here to pick me up shortly. The man is crazy with jealousy over me; he can't stand for me to be out of his sight. You will see his old beat-up car coming around that corner to get me shortly. Anyone can tell my John's car because it smokes so bad that all the mosquitoes will disappear like magic."

Mary J laughed and laughed just like everybody else; she thought Rosanna was so funny. Rosanna's shiny reflection was sparkling with glittering wet eyes.

Eunice paused from laughter to consider her statement. "Rosanna, aren't you shame of yourself—telling all those lies? John is probably somewhere with a pint of liquor in his hand, right now."

Rosanna interrupted Eunice, "You don't know my John. We had to leave New York City because he shot two people for flirting with me."

Everybody giggled again because of Rosanna's crazy ways.

One of Eunice customers said, "Rosanna is not lying because when John gets drunk, he thinks she Mother Goose."

Everybody just continued to laugh with amusement because of her funny words and disposition. They thought Rossana was their community's most humorous character; she could make almost any topic intrinsically amusing. One thing for sure, they loved being entertained by her.

Pap returned to pick-up Mary J; they all said, "goodbye." Eunice walked into the store to serve her customers and to get Rosanna tobacco products. Mary J got into a vehicle with her husband. They quickly drove away towards Fisher-town.

The next morning around 10:00 a.m., Luke showed up at the Fishers' homestead. Pap was in the front of the house feeding his hogs with corn and soybean meal. The hog pen was located between the front yard and the Creek on the left side of the old hand water pump. Pap suddenly noticed the darting of a fish through the water in the middle of the Creek.

Luke, with a blushing face, said, "Good morning, my cousin."

When Pap turned back towards the house, Luke was standing in front of him. "Well! The man of adventure has returned from New Bern."

"Just for the past two days," Luke explained with a degree of tiredness. "Now Pap, you know I cannot run my businesses set-up under my wife. I have many times, sit down with her, and discussed our situation. When I stay away overnight without contacting her, she tends to look troubled with worries that stimulate unhappiness, just as if she was bearing the weight of the whole world on her shoulders. Pap, can you find a better description of depression? I have a difficult time dealing with her strange emotions and mood swings. I have done my best to make it up to her, she is just sensitive to my overnight travels... I wish I could drill a hole in the top of her head and then use a funnel to pour some happiness into her. But if necessary, I will apologize to her again. I wish that my wife could understand the business side of my life. I am beginning to dislike our frequent quarrels."

"Yeah, right," Pap said, "but here is the proposition. Although you may have a bag or two hidden in your closet, your solutions may be found in regulating your business activity. Eunice doesn't ask for the moon. Her parents were like the salt-of-the- earth. Except for one thing, they never showed much confidence in her. They would say, 'Eunice, I hope you will never be like Maggie down the road.' Years ago, Pap continued, I heard someone say: 'Children are the world's greatest sponges, soaking up a large amount of information from their environment.' One thing you have to remember; children are their worst interpreters. They usually absorb most of the inadequacies around them. Because of their parent's self-centeredness, children misinterpret much of what they take in; this dramatically affects children's sense of worth. When these types of children become adults, they mostly feel: 'You are acceptable, but I am not good enough.' Now, this attitude has been embedded in Eunice's personality. This causes her to paint a false picture of herself; just show Eunice that you care and believe in her. She needs to be the center of your world."

Luke laughed, embarrassed, and dropped his eyes as he butted his cigar. He then looked at the hog pen for several seconds. "Ok, Pap, I see your point. My wife continues to hear the voices of her Mom and Dad. You know, her dad could be very critical and then slowly turn kind within the same hour. Her Mom was one of those quiet and gentle people like a dormant volcano, but now, she could erupt at any time without notice. Don't get me wrong, they were good people, but at the same time, they were unpredictable."

Pap clapped his hands lightly. "Exactly! Exactly! Eunice's mother used to dress her up in the morning to play in a brand-new dress. And then she would say, 'Now, when you go out, don't get any dirt on your pretty dress. I have worked hard to iron all your ruffles.' Now you could well picture what her dress looked like by the afternoon. Her mother would scold her angrily: 'you naughty girl, you never obey me.' These demands were unrealistic to put on a little child, just going out to play. Additionally, her mother would measure out some type of punishment, leaving a cloud of guilt hanging over her. So, my cousin Luke, if you are going to be away overnight, let the crows watch over your home. Crows build their nests near the top of very tall trees, so they may-be watchful of their surroundings. This way crows can see their situation from an incredibly higher angle."

Luke now had an irritated look upon his face. He took out a new cigar, clipped the end off with a cigar-cutter from his waistcoat pocket, put it in his mouth, lit it slowly, and then let out several clouds of smoke. "Pap, you got that right! There is no doubt in my mind that my wife worries about me. On the other hand, there are times when she is toeing the line; it forces her to pay a heavy price that adds up to emotional dishonesty."

Pap looked at him strangely, "I know a woman can be puzzling like chemistry in a cake, but the term emotional dishonesty is something new to me."

Luke began clenching his fist, "I see emotional dishonesty when someone is communicating a particular feeling but in actuality experiencing a different one."

"I think," Pap said, "that I see what you mean. Like snow when feet have trampled it. It's still snow, only is it?"

Luke ran his right hand through his hair, stroke his cheek, pulled his right ear, and lick his lips. He then turned his attention back to Pap's hogs. "You're feeding those hogs too much food. You can't make a profit being that generous."

Pap said with a half-smile on his face. "Let me tell you the proposition that's surrounding these hogs. They are only for my family to eat, not making profits. My family is going to use these hog parts to make bacon, ham, pork scratching, and pig feet, along with hog head cheese, hog maw, and even the traditional crown dish of chitlins for the holidays. Now, those pigs and hogs over there, in that pen, are strictly for the market."

Luke said with a cigar in his mouth. "Now Pap, for those pigs and hogs over there. I have some hog feed at my store for sale. This feed costs a lot less than corn, plus it has a higher fiber content at a lower cost. The next time you are near the store, tell my wife to give you a bag to try out."

Pap knew that his cousin Luke had strongly ingrained respect for the value of a dollar. After thinking about Luke's life. Pap realized that Luke had learned from a very early age that it was important to be a contributor rather than just a taker. From living through the Great Depression years, Luke had seemed people putting their pride in their pocket, their hat in their hand—asking for help. Luke understood the hard work it took to get your hands on a dollar. According to Luke's point of view, if you have a penny, it's worth something. If a penny was lying out there on the street, he would go out there and pick it up.

Pap looked at him profoundly, considering his background. "Ok, cousin Luke, what is the real reason while you are here?"

Luke said with cigar smoke coming out of his mouth and nose. "I have a proposition for you and your wife,"

There was a silence, and then Pap said in a soft voice: "What's your proposition?"

Luke struck a match and lit his cigar again—releasing a cloud of smoke. With a small chuckle, "my wife thinks a lot of your wife. Mary J comes out to my store just about every week to sit with her. Mary J is interested in the store business. As you know, Pap, I have another general store with a juke joint in the rear. It is located within the Corner intersection as you enter our community. This prime location is the cornerstone of our community. Now, there is a piece of property I have just purchased across the street from it. I am going to build a little house for you and your family. We can work out a deal later; Mary J may start selling retail items right there in the house. I will purchase additional items for her little operation each week. You may pay me as you go alone; now, from time to time, when I am in a bind, your wife can help me at my store."

Pap always careful not to exaggerate, glared at him. "Sounds good, come-on let's go into the house, so that we can talk over this proposal with my family."

Luke and Pap walked toward the house. Just as they came close to the front porch, Luke immediately saw Pap's mother, Rachel, through the screen door. She was looking garden-fresh in her long dress covered by a beautiful cotton apron. In Rachel's opinion, her white apron symbolized generosity and hospitality.

Luke said while opening the screen door and entering the house: "Hey there! How are you folks during this morning? Oh my God, is this my cousin Rachel? Your beauty is an earthshaking revelation. Well, I tell you, sweetheart, time is doing you no harm!"

Rachel accepted his greeting pleasantly with an unusual smile; then she said: "Well, Luke, you just look at your mother for the perfect example of beauty in our family. She is my aunt, you know! There seems to be a circle of light surrounding your mother's beauty. Her kind of beauty can do no wrong."

Luke laughed and coughed a little bit, then blew out a cloud of blue-grey smoke from his cigar while having a proud look on his face. "You right, because beauty is as natural as water for our family."

Mary J abruptly barged into the room and then immediately began cracking little jokes. "Mr. Luke, you may be taken mother Rachel comments a little too personal. She was talking about her aunt and your mother, not you!"

This struck Rachel as being so funny that she began to laugh out loud along with Pap and others in the room. Everyone from this point on was laughing and playing around with each other.

Luke cocking his head to one side as he turned his attention towards Mary J. "Well here the prettiest and fusses of all, how are you doing Mary J—Pap, you better treat this little girl right!"

Rachel laughed again, thinking he was making a joke. "You don't have to worry about Mary J; she knows how to take care of herself."

At the heart of this excitement, Mary J believed that Luke had some intoxicating proposal. Her emotions began moving around like tiny vibrating strings. "Now, Luke, what do you have for us?"

Luke instantly feeling her different modes of vibration like sounds of music. "Well, I have a little house that I am building for you and Pap to stay in, so we can do a little business together."

Mary J now ready to express her G and F notes. "You got a plan—now you are talking, when is all this going to happen?"

Luke grappling with the opportunity of presenting a coherent picture. "The house should be ready in about thirty days. Its foundation has already been set. Although there is only one bedroom, you will have plenty of space throughout the house to set up extra beds. I will carve out a second bedroom before your family moves into the house."

Luke stood looking at her for a long moment, then dusted the ashes off his cigar into a matchbox—cleared his throat. "Mary J, this could be your gold mine, because you can start your own little business right in the living room. I can bring you some cakes, fruits, and peanuts each week to sell. There are a lot of people coming down here from the military base and to the beach. Now you can start a little retail business, and then move on from there, just let time progress in your favor."

Mary J realized that if she and her family were ever going to get off Pap's family homestead, now was the time. She looked at Pap and then said, "I am ready to move, if you are happy with this arrangement."

Pap looked at his mother and said directly to her. "Now Mama, don't you worry about a thing, we will be standing by your side. I will still take care of the farm and you. We will be back and forward, plus Alma Tucker and Fred will continue living here with you."

With a little teardrop in her right eye, Rachel nods her head. She had depended on her son Pap tremendously since the death of her husband. "I know, my son, go and build some dreams. As long as there are fish in the Creek, chicken in the coop, and beans in our garden, we will be alright."

Luke smiled reassuringly at everybody. "Well, this deal is closed, I will be expecting you all to start moving into your new place within 30 days."

Pap narrowed his eyes towards his wife, then got slowly to his feet. "Sounds good Luke, you can count on it."

Mary J was now grinning to herself. "I will be ready to start my little store business immediately upon arrival in my new living room. Luke, you better keep your side of this bargain."

Luke chuckled at her response, looking towards her with appreciative eyes. "You know I am straight with you and Pap—we are family."

"Sure!" Mary J said. Everyone started to laugh and poke fun with each other again, knowing just how much Luke loved a dollar bill. Some people said that Luke was so tight with a dollar that you could hear his shoes squeaking from old age.

Just about this time, Mary J's baby sister Lorraine ran down the stairs hopping and skipping towards the living room. All dressed up in a beautiful new dress made by her Grandma Mag.

Luke smiled at her. "Now! Who is this pretty young lady here?"

Lorraine raised her head and laughed with pleasure. "I am Mary J's sister."

Luke laughed a little, then became more serious. "You Know Pap. I guess beauty just runs in Mary J's family. I tell you one thing; you are a fine-looking young girl. Pap, you have found a nest full of gorgeous girls. You are blessed that those Godette boys let you get out of their narrow-minded neighborhood alive. Most of our boys usually have to fight their way out. You have taken some of their most valuable jewels."

Luke hugged everyone, then walked outside to his 1943 Chrysler New Yorker. He drove away, leaving a cloud of dust behind him; the inside of his car was blazing with a ton of cigar smoke. As he was driving, Luke kept thinking, how Pap was an exceptionally hard worker with an extremely ambitious wife. Luke smiled when he thought, *when a person has a dream deep down inside, like Mary J, it will usually happen. I must be there to nurture her single-minded devotion towards her goal for store ownership. Her untapped potential is like an oil well that's ready for a blowout. Of course,* abruptly putting his cigar into the car's ashtray, *I will make a little profit along the way."* Speedily, his car faded down Fisher-town's dirt road—around a deep curve until it was out of sight.

As Mary J went outside to think about Luke's offer under the pecan tree, her eyes became dangerously bright. She was moving her arms rapidly as if she was striking a snake. Mary J began stamping her feet—thinking: *Pap and I have been married a little over three years, with no store on the horizon. One thing for sure, I will never get a store living on my husband's homestead while he is taking care of two families. Although there are gambles with Luke's proposal, it does offer us new pathways. All signals are saying to me: Go forth, reap your destiny. You have a mission Mary J—put confidence in your goal—burn your ship!*

151

Chapter

17

THE CORNER INTERSECTION

L uke, according to his word, built a small house within the central business intersection known as the Corner. This intersection showcased the business community of North Harlowe. The road shaped like a T-junction, with three business sides, which included a minor road connecting to Main street. Luke's combined store and night club located strategically within the intersection. People came from all around, including the local military base, to pack his nightclub on weekends. His small new house was located diagonally across the intersection.

The well-known Della's restaurant positioned on the left side of Luke's house within the intersection. Della's café was a famous favorite of the community. It was opened six days a week with a rotating menu that changed seasonally. Local Customers knew the list when they came in for their favorite meals. When Della sold a bowl of large lima beans and cornbread, her customers could always count on a huge chunk of pork meat in their soup.

Pap and Mary J moved into Luke's house within two months after its completion. Mary J began her retail business right away in her kitchen and living room. She wanted to help her husband save up money to build a real store. As agreed, Luke started bringing her a small amount of merchandise on consignment. She sold items like apples, oranges, bananas, peanuts, snacks, and various beverages to drink. It was also customary for Pap to keep a gallon of whiskey on hand, somewhere in the kitchen pantry to share with his friends.

One Saturday evening, a group of people was sitting around Mary J's kitchen table when a man said: "Mary J, I know Pap got a drink of liquor around here... somewhere!"

Mary J's attitude towards money was a complex mixture of generosity and miserliness. She now had to guard every penny of her hard-earned income. She quickly began relegating her sensitivity towards the darkest corners of her heart. Mary J's woman instinct became her most excellent ally—she had to find the means to save money for her new store. She needed to find a way to maneuver this opportunity with unapproachable strength and warm charm.

Mary J laughed aloud. "He sure does, but it's going to cost you a quarter a shot."

Mary J quickly placed the gallon of whiskey on the kitchen table. She edged over to the table and pulled the gallon jar out of the brown paper sack; she placed it back on the table in clear view. Just over Mary J's sink was a small stack of Dixie cups, she took one from the pile. Mary J placed a cup on the table, gradually opened the gallon of whiskey, slowly poured out about an ounce of whiskey. Who would believe: Mary J had now sold her first shot of whiskey for only a quarter.

The man said. "Un-huh, this is alright!" He placed the cup back on the table. He reached into his pants pocket and pulled out a roll of money, secured with a rubber band around it. As he counted out his money, he said to Mary J: "Give everybody a shot of this good whiskey on me."

From that moment on, people started coming by not only to buy snack items but also to get shots of whiskey. In just a few weeks of selling shots of whiskey, Mary J was able to save several hundred dollars. For a new start-up business, this was a lot of money and a significant temptation. Mary J was getting only a little taste of the money made in the whiskey business. By comparison, her profit margins from Luke's retail items were significantly lower.

Privately the following Sunday morning, Mary J's fears crashed on her like a tidal wave. The pain in her eyes was suddenly desperate. She began thinking: *selling that man a shot of whiskey may not be the best idea; my faith calls upon me to undertake the arduous but thrilling task of building a better world.* On the other hand, she thought: *The Culture of our community can change fast. I need to look beyond the surface of my actions and focus on the social context. It's natural for us, as humans and individuals, to see the rest of the world more like us. Life is like seasons, always changing. What I do today, may seem strange years down the road. Nevertheless, I will always stay grounded in respectable principles. I will never be reckless when dealing with my community.*

As Mary J turned her mind towards getting ready for church, she clenched her teeth so hard that ridges stood out in her jaws. Mary J's head came up; eyes widened from a long night of rest. Sunday meant another morning of church service, where she could connect with God and her local community. Mary J began thinking: it's *a shame that my imagination haunts me like a child on some foggy night.* She looked at the pillow beside her, wondering if Pap needed to be on a Sunday morning business trip governing commercial transaction. She felt worried and then puzzled for a few minutes. *My God,* she thought, *I feel like I'm going to cry.*

Mary J remembered that Alma Tucker was coming to pick her up for church this morning. She quickly jumped out of bed and began dressing up in her white usher uniform; Lorraine had started dressing the children. In a short while, they were on their way to the church. Alma Tucker would always make sure Mary J's children were supervised correctly, so she could focus on ushering. Pap's mother, Rachel, would also help out during church service; especially, if the situation got desperate.

During most of her activities as an usher, she was warmly building relationships with her regular and future customers. While ushering, she would perform her responsibilities with an honorable glow that spread all over her face. In her mind, ushering was just like running a store. She was always during things: Greeting people, seating visitors, checking the restrooms, providing hymnbooks, making everybody feel welcome, and helping to make the offering time meaningful and worshipful.

Mary J would say to herself while ushering the people to their seats: *When I get to heaven, I certainly hope the Lord will make me an usher.*

After each service, Mary J always stood at the front doors; she would be greeting people as they left for home. Customers would whisper in her ear, "We're gonna come by your house later this evening—teasing with a smile; please get the shot glasses ready!"

Mary J answered quickly with a smile as though she had only been waiting for an opportunity. "Please come."

Alma Tucker would intentionally act like a customer, alleging in her ear some funny comment: "You just turn that charm on sister-in-law; just go ahead and do it. I know you got some new customers. You are planning on building that new store, aren't you? I am going home with you today; so, we can enjoy the fruits of your labor. Don't worry; I got your babies."

Alma Tucker went back to her seat, trying to hold back the laughter. She thought that Mary J's obsession with owning a store was somewhat weird. Although it was a hard bridge for her to cross, she had trouble ruling out the possibility. Alma Tucker tried to reason it out this way: *So, what, plenty of people do a great deal of things that are less than rational. They fall in love with outrageous people—believe in astrology, and some will even avoid the thirteenth floor.*

Immediately after the Church services ended, Mary J met up with Rachel and Alma tucker to help organize her children to go home. Alma Tucker said to her Mother: "Mama, I'm going home with Mary J—Pap will bring me back later tonight when he gets home."

"Alright now," said Rachel, "don't stay overnight because Fred is out somewhere, I don't want to be home all along, I guess, I'm getting old."

"You know Mama, I am 21 now, and Mary J is 24, we are women with hard-earned strength and dignity, along with an indestructible spirit. We are like two-notes of music forever yearning to be one-note again. Most of all, we are proud to be Fishers."

"That's right, children," said Rachel, "just count your blessings. You better eat dinner with Mary J because if Lester's children come by after church, there will be nothing left for you."

Alma Tucker looked around, not wanting to go home. "That's alright, Mama, let them eat all they can carry in their bellies."

Mary J shook her head and then laughed in response. "Mother Rachel, you got nothing to worry about, it looks like you and Pap gonna have a big garden this year."

Now Mary J, you must bring my grandchildren to see me this week. You and Pap need a break; we'll watch out for them. If you like," said Rachel, "when you come, we can stand on the point and catch a few fish."

Mary J said with thoughtful eyes. "Thank you so much—that will be fun and relaxing, like a vacation."

Rachel picked up her big handbag off the extended bench seat. She went outside of the church to catch her ride home. Mary J and Alma Tucker departed as well. When they arrived at Mary J's house, there was no one around anywhere. Suddenly, mid-afternoon, the door to Mary J little house flew open. Her porch filled up quickly with people.

Holding Elsie May by her hand, Alma Tucker stood at the front door entrance. She began chuckling as her shawl fell over one arm. Alma Tucker was a model of contemporary styles, with absolute confidence that was uniquely her own. Her dark eyes lit up with strange amusement as she gazed at the crowd. "Good Lord, come in the house. Mary J got plenty of refreshments for sale."

The people were scattered all over the place talking to each other; bystanders traveled throughout the Corner's intersection to various businesses. A large group walked over to Luke's nightclub and then onto Della's café, later on back over to George Boone's pool hall. Eventually, people trafficked back to Mary J's front yard and porch. The music from Luke's nightclub could be heard throughout the Corner's intersection. The celebratory atmosphere was happy from the moment a person walked into the midst of the intersection.

People just wanted to chatter and socialize in a spirit of community. They mostly communicate about various people throughout the community. Sometimes, what the preacher talked about in church. Although they smiled companionably at one another, their communication often failed because of sharing too much information. Some of them could never decide what to leave out. They would try to explain something without adequate background information or recommend actions without justification. Therefore, somebody always got upset about an incomplete message that provoked an emotional response.

Now for some strange reasons, these difficulties seemed to disappear when Alma Tucker invited them to sit on the front porch or inside Mary J's living room. She would tell them in her warm and gentle voice: "Nobody coasts through this life without any problems. There is no need to stir up emotional conflicts with people that have difficulties in expressing their ideas. Everybody can talk, eat, and drink right here—now buy something from Mary J in the kitchen. This way, she can make a small profit."

Mary J was in the kitchen trying to sell everything that she could get people to buy. The time had come for her house business to experience testability. Mary J had a standard sales pitch for every potential customer: "How might I be of service to you? Would you like something to drank or eat?" Mary J's church friends would sit around the kitchen, laughing, talking, eating, drinking, and sharing experiences.

Shadows of the late afternoon were deepening as a long-slanted ray of sunlight passed over the front yard. After dark, Pap returned to the house. Alma Tucker was ready to get home so her mother wouldn't have to be alone during the night hours. She hugged Mary J and the children.

"The time has come for me to depart, said Alma Tucker. "You know, Mama doesn't want to be home along during the night." Just before going out of the front door, she smiled and teased with the visitors. "You all spend some money so Mary J can get her store." They all laughed in a community spirit of friendship. Alma tucker jumped in her brother Pap's vehicle; they drove away towards Fisher-town.

Mid-day the next day, Mary J's first cousin James Miller stopped in to see Pap, as he often did throughout the week. "Hey, Mary J, where is my buddy Pap?"

"Oh James, come on in the house and find yourself a chair." said Mary J, "He is out-there on the farm working somewhere in Fisher-town."

"One thing I can say," slowly sitting down in a chair, "God has surely touched Pap with a deep and beautiful purpose to take care of his family. He is led by some stirring unrest that prevails upon him to rise above his circumstances. He has an industrious restlessness that urges him to make things better. One thing I like about Pap, he doesn't merely complain but always seeking to pull himself up by his bootstraps. I swear the kingdom; I got to give it to him!"

"I feel the same way," said Mary J. "Pap certainly isn't an imitator or somebody's echo. He is no mere puppet whose strings can be pulled this way or that way by others. Pap will not pursue any course that not of his choosing. He's an exceptional and spirited man, always working on some kind of business transaction."

"Well, I need to see your exceptional man!" said James Miller. "I will go down to Fisher-town in a few minutes."

Mary J quickly changed the subject: "How is the rest of my family over the Creek during this beautiful day?"

"The same old thing," said James Miller, "our Grandma Mag is as strong as a bear. She won't let you do anything for her."

"Oh, my Lord, that's the truth," said Mary J, "its Grandma Mag's nature of stubbornness that keeps all of us off balance. As you know, she is the very conscience of our family. Her law of life tends to evolve as she learns from history."

"But now," said James Miller, "the rest of the family is not faring so well. My sister, your first cousin Annie May, is still trying to deal with her husband Rudolph. The situation is just like your sister Lucy Gray, who married Rudolph's brother, Menace. They are dealing with brothers that love to fight and control their wives. Now I tell you something else; I went over to Assisi Line this morning. Her husband, Will, was trying to fight her. He pulled a section of her hair completely out from its roots. She had to call the sheriff. I clear the kingdom Mary J; it is difficult being married to one of those Godette men. I have done some thinking about this on my way here. I truly believe that you got the best husband out of the whole bunch. You can't beat Pap. He is as good of a man that you are going to find around here."

Mary J looked up at her cousin James Miller with a carefully concealed curiosity. She snickered. "It's true; the Godette brothers don't care about what others think of them. Their attitude toward money and women are a complex mixture of greediness and meanness. The Fishers' men don't fight their wives like some of our nutty men over the Creek."

James Miller looked as if he didn't know what to say about these men's insensitivity. "I clear the kingdom Mary J, you right. The men over the Creek just not trained to respect women, that's the whole thing in a nutshell." He took in a deep breath and blew it out in a moment of frustration; he then continued, "Now! I tell you one other thing, sooner or later, I will find a way to make a permanent break from any association with those godless men. Don't get me wrong, the Godette's men are very hardworking business people, but they scare the devil out of their wives and friends."

Mary J showed no signs of madness, but only a gloomy look of regret upon her face. "Look here, Cousin James," said Mary J in a somewhat hesitating voice. "I am trying now to be entirely honest. At times the Godette men seem heartless, although we know them as quiet, honest, and hardworking men. The devil must be mighty since there are so many miserable people. There must be terrible tormentors working within those men as they seek to punish themselves and their wives for no reason. They are suffering from an inner guilt of their past struggles, perhaps some type of child's abuse. How beautiful it would be for them to receive forgiveness from God and their wives. They truly need to pardon themselves of this curse."

During the conversation, James Miller was puzzling his head as to why—suddenly, he looked out of the window. "I clear the Kingdom; you're right—well, I got to go now before Pap leaves Fisher-town."

James Miller mustered up enough energy to get out of a low seated chair. He hollered back to Mary J on his way through the living room—towards the front porch. "Let's leave it alone for now… maybe it will get better over time. It's difficult for even the nicest, most patient people to understand them."

James Miller then took a deep breath and exhaled the air out very loudly. He walked out of the front door, across the front porch and down the steps in a tranquil spirit. James Miller continued towards his old Ford pickup truck, which he kept looking brand new. He opened the truck door and dusted off his seat. He then drove off towards Fisher-town.

Mary J sighed silently with relief after her cousin James miller walked out of the front door. Her eyes rushed rapidly as she began assessing the value of his friendship and closeness over the years. She smiled, thinking of it: *James Miller has always kept an eye on me since childhood. If I did something he thought was wrong, well, without a doubt, Grandma Mag would be notified of it. Even after I got married to Pap, he would still check up on me several times a week. If my husband needed someone to carry his crops to the market, James Miller would make time to help him. If I had a doctor's appointment, he would always take me. Pap, my husband, still enjoys eating with him, whether morning, noon, or late in the night.*

Mary J laughed out loud—thinking how her cousin James Miller could be a mediator of peace in her home. *If my husband got in an argument with me, he would say privately to him: 'I clear the kingdom, you right Pap.' If it was me, then he would say confidentially to me the same thing. Shortly afterward, everybody was happy again.* Mary J kept thinking that although she lost both of her parents during childhood, yet God had given her a few loving protectors to help secure her surroundings. She concluded, *maybe in some strange way, the Lord has sent them to help me get my store.*

CITOLE AND CINDY

The weather had improved slightly by the following morning. The sun even going so far as to put on a half-hearted appearance. The wind and rain had swept across the night before; Mary J's community now lay bathed in yellow sunlight. The grassy areas had soaked up the rain. Mary J stared resolutely out the window at the other businesses surrounding her, sensitive that only the future matters these days. Although supported by her trust in divine protection, yet weighty issues were playing games upon her mind. She strolled through her living room onto the front porch. She looked around with some evidence of reluctance but enjoyed feeling the fresh air blowing lightly across her body.

Mary J was reflecting on how little Elsie May had another lousy night of sickness. She kept thinking that her medical expenses would most likely eat up their small savings. Mary J troubled heart reflected her helpless eyes—both nature and fate seemed to be working against her dreams. She gradually sat down in her favorite porch rocking chair, trying to allow her body to relax the tension in her face—permitting a single tear to dribble.

Unexpectedly, Mary J saw Citole and Cindy painstakingly walking down the road toward her house. Her face changed from a frown of worry to a smile of delight; her fate didn't seem so desperate now with God-directed assistance. She thought they were indeed angels—propelled to nurture her family with motherly love. Mary J slowly stood up from her chair, then strolled towards the front steps as they approached the yard. Her head snapped up like a wild animal in the woods scenting water. A new mysterious strength of will seemed to flow warmly through her.

Mary J said out loud with a smile and uplifted hands. *"Well, now, here come two ladies who will help answer a motherless child's prayer."*

As Citole approached the front steps, she breathed a small sigh of relief. "Good morning Mary J! There is nothing wrong; I am stuck with these negative and destructive feelings again. But things aren't as bad as my mind trying to tell me—I just need to do a little scientific thinking. The real problem is that I have nothing to look forward to in this life except more years of fixed routines and sleep. My ordinary life doesn't annoy me; people do a lot of things that are not sensible. Just remember one thing, my little sweetheart; as a human being, we are only repeating our past in the present. You must come to terms with your childish hurts and wishes; stop being controlled by your unconscious desires and thoughts. If you keep this up, my shrink will be out here to give you some emotional treatment."

Cindy said sweetly, "Mary J, without sunlight, the Earth would turn cold, the stars wouldn't shine, and life in our world would be impossible. Your family is our sunlight; we are family. So now, you need to stop thinking like a little motherless orphan. I don't have any money to help you, but you are going to get your store someday, believe me!"

Mary J looked startled, then pleased, wondering how they could know so much about her inner thinking. After more careful consideration, she kept thinking that these intimate relationships provided her a sense of attachments, friendships, and community. Her heart was now stunned after hearing their incredible support for her dreams. She could only nod dumbly, thinking: *What did these women know about me? And how? They have put everything into perspective very quickly for me. I believe their ideas are the best way to survive and enjoy life.*

In a rapid series of insights, Citole eyed Mary J speechlessly for a moment. "If you need to wash today, just let us know. My niece Cindy can take care of the cooking, washing, and ironing, while I look after your children. So now, you just get your little store set-up. So what If you have to sell a few shots of whiskey to make it, the Lord will forgive you."

Mary J said politely. "Thank you… Citole and Cindy," She then looked away towards the kitchen: "Cindy, please make some good tasting biscuits with those dry beans. James Miller and Pap will be back in a few hours, ready to eat."

"Okay, Mary J," said Cindy, "but please don't give all the food away to Tennessee and Mark Washington. They are always looking for a bit to eat, especially dinner time. They are just taking advantage of your good nature. My goodness, here comes Gala Hawk, the man eats till he sweats. God knows, he is always hungry. Mary J, you need to stop feeding all these people. You and Pap are going to go broke messing around with these people. You can't take care of the whole community."

Mary J's face lost some of its glow. "Well, you know Cindy, these are hard times. We can't let people go hungry! I was born at the end of World War One; the year after the 1918 influenza pandemic. My Mother told me this flu pandemic virus killed more people than the World War. The economy suffered as businesses were force to close due to sickness. I experienced my childhood during the Great Depression. I can recall being parentless, in my youth, while my siblings were waiting to share my few bits and pieces of food. I have lived through many dark periods—dark as any before or since. We are now living through another global war; they call it World War Two. These kinds of events have devastating effects on the lives of people. But now, on the other hand, when Pap and I get our store, we will already have loyal customers. Remember, Cindy, we are investing in people, not just giving them a hand-out."

Citole words were clear, "Now Cindy, stop it. You need to listen with both ears. Mary J and Pap got one chance; they are going to take it. So be calm, please don't let me get started on your situation. You know, your son Big Jim will be in the same line with Gala Hawk after he had a few whiskey shots."

Cindy's hands flew to her belly. "Of course, we can spare a little bit, but don't forget; I got to take a plate home. My man, John Thomas, has to eat too."

"Citole looked from the corner of her eyes at Cindy as she moved slowly towards the kitchen. "John Thomas is working with John Carter today, maybe his wife Reba will give him supper."

163

Unexpectedly, there were loud voices in the front yard. Citole went to see who was out there. "Mary J, guess who is coming?"

Mary J said quite emotionally, "Who?"

Cindy speedily looked around, then dashed to peek out through the living room window. "Looks like your Uncle Charlie, with his son Monroe and your brother James Westley."

"Is my Uncle Charlie drinking?"

Citole answered speedily, as though she was waiting for a chance to speak. "No—thank God, they all look sober to me."

Cindy made a vague gesture. "Well, your Uncle Charlie certainly looks like he had a few to me. I better make two pans of biscuits."

Citole patience cracked. "Cindy, why are you complaining about Mary J's people? It won't do any good. Now look, my girls are crying. I know Elsie May wants her hair fixed, and Dora Lee is hungry."

Cindy raised her eyebrows with quizzical mockery. "Oh, my goodness, now here come Walter Dennis… bring you some supplies."

Mary J shouted: "Nice! Please open the door for him."

Walter Dennis burst through the front door with several boxes filled with various products. He was feeling wonderful—drinking his daddy Luke's ways—with a cigar in his mouth. "Hey, ladies… now Mary J—daddy said this is all he has for you this week. If you run out of anything, just come over to the store, and we will try to put something together for you." Now listen, he said, placing both hands on her shoulders—teasingly with a loud chuckle. "I got to go open up the Beer Garden shortly; you can just send your little crowd over to see me."

"Thank you," said Mary J with thoughtful eyes. "Just remember one thing, you are too young to be smoking a cigar like your daddy. You need to stop trying to act like a big shot."

Walter Dennis studied Mary J's face. He felt a legitimate interest in his welfare, then laughed explosively. "You're right; I got to go now before you start fussing at me."

Mary J's uncle Charlie walked in as Walter Dennis was leaving: "Hey there… Mr. Beer Garden, when are you going to open up? My boys are thirsty for something that will help tame their minds."

Walter Dennis hesitated before replying—he drew on his cigar. He watched the bright end of it cool, gradually turning to ashes. He started acting as if he was considering the question, while walking out of the front door. "Boys, in just a few minutes."

James Westley and Monroe were standing on the front porch, talking to the ladies. They hollered inside at Mary J and then told Charlie, "We are going to take these beautiful ladies off Mary J's porch—right over to the Beer Garden."

James Westley's eyes lit up, and his mouth opened wide from the smell of large lima beans coming out of the kitchen. "Cindy, those beans smell good—tell my sister, we'll be back later."

Cindy shook her head, vigorously. "I don't care what you all say about me; nobody is going to eat up all this food. I got to take my John Thomas something to eat!"

Monroe said teasingly, "Come on now, Cindy, you can spare a little bit for us."

Cindy shook her head but kept her temper with treacherous bright eyes. "Hum, you need to let those lazy women—you got out there, fix your food; they are going to drink up all your money anyway."

Abruptly, everybody on the front porch left for the Beer Garden. All of them laughing with a high spirit as they crossed over the intersection. Mary J quickly displayed all the merchandise that Walter Dennis just delivered to her. She starts selling things right away.

Plunt drove around the back of the house. He got out of the car with a gallon of liquor under his arm; peaches were mixed in for a smooth taste. "Hey Mary J," said Plunt coming through the door, "I am going to put this in your pantry for Pap. I got to run now and pick-up my girlfriend Willie, maybe we will stop back later."

Plunt walked back outside to his car. As he started the engine, it quickly roared to life. The car loud cherry bomb mufflers puffed out a sigh of relief. Suddenly, the engine idles down from its boastful start. Plunt drove out of the yard very fast—even spun the back tires. A friendly stray dog was in the backyard. The dog barked and ran down the road behind his car.

Cindy smiled silently at the dog through the kitchen window—thinking as she looked up at the sky: Thank the Lord—one less mouth to feed!

Mary J opened up the gallon of whiskey and started selling shots to some of her customers. She felt good about having several irons in the fire at one time. Her goals were costly, yet she felt that the price was worth it. Throughout her childhood, she knew that to get something, she had to give up something else. There weren't enough hours in her day to work, keep house, look after the children, and have time left over for anything else. Being a working mother, this meant giving up her social life. As an alternative, she just began socializing with her customers, treating them like family. She tried to maintain mutually supportive relationships with all the people living in her community. It didn't matter if he or she was a drunk on the street or a preacher from the pulpit.

The poor, old, struggling George Moore knocked on the front door. He was now aging with many aches and pains. The pain in his eyes revealed a stunning portrait of quiet desperation. Although he couldn't read or write, he loved to quote inspiring Bible verses. George Moore's private life foreshadowed his lifelong conflict over his faith.

Mary J opened the door and stood there, smiling, hands on her hips: "Brother George Moore, how are you doing this morning? Please, just come on in the house.

George Moore said somewhat tearfully. "The only thing I have that no one can take away from me is my salvation. I have one constellation, my relationship with a living God."

Mary J studied his face until he looked away. "Although you can't read or write, yet somehow, you certainly know the Bible."

"You see that bible over there on the shelf?"

Mary J said. "Yes, I do; it's our family Bible."

Well continued George Moore, "We are subject to the laws of God just like a machine. Our brain is nothing but an information processing device; the human soul is nothing but a program run by the brain. Inside the covers of that old and worn Bible, sixty-six books have been written by many different men under the Holy Spirit inspiration. You see, the Holy Spirit guided those men as they wrote the Bible. Now you see, that same Holy Spirit shows me what's in the Bible the same way. He just processes this knowledge on my mind and heart. You know, praise God, the Holy Spirit can even teach an uneducated fool like me!"

Mary J laughed: "The reason is simple; you had Godly parents that implanted Bible verses within your unconscious mind."

After searching his memory, there was a long silence. "My God, you are right! But now Mary J, I got to go—so now, please pour me a small shot of Pap's whiskey. You know, that's the only thing that eases my arthritis."

Mary J poured him a shot glass full of whiskey. George Moore drank the entire shot of liquor in one swallow. "Mary J, please give me another shot to get rid of my morning stiffness." Afterward, he gradually took out two quarters from his right pocket for payment. He departed quietly out of the front door after drinking the second shot glass of whiskey—he never said another word to anybody.

After George Moore departed, Mary J began reflecting on her current situation—living in a small overcrowded house—selling whiskey by the shots. She wanted to cry. Panic touched the edge of her mind, but Mary J pushed it away. Things seemed awful all around her; she could hardly bear, making herself draw the next breath. She couldn't understand what was making her feel so miserable. Believing that successes were always more important than losses, it was like being at the crossroad of life. She had made a momentous choice of security through uncertainty.

Mary J roamed restlessly around her living room and kitchen. She was hoping vigorously to someday set up a legitimate business. Her load was weighty to bear; she was drifting over treacherous waters. It was hard for her instinct to figure out what was right or wrong. She thought, it's crazy right now—little Elsie May sickly, my husband investing his little money in moonshining and farming. How long is this going to continue? I can't stand it any longer; if only my God would open a way for us.

Mary J went to bed that night, struggling to understand what was happening all around her. She soon found an escape in daydreaming through several modes of thinking that was so real. Her mind circled back to her Aunt Loretta's store and childhood. During those times, the Great Depression chilled the nation to the marrow. There were many poor struggling workers: people freezing overnight in doorways, soup kitchens, malnutrition, and starvation was a threat even on the farms. Mary J could still hear the radio announcer describing events at the bottom of the Great Depression: 'Millions struggle to survive and look for ways to forget their problems.' She went over this again and again until her head ached. Her sleep, when it came, was brief and restless.

BIRTH OF A SON

Mary J was lying in bed, unable to fall asleep while Pap was out moonshining. She was somewhat depressed and adrift; her thoughts cluttered by worries of self-protection. After much thinking, she yawned and stretched—then slipped back into a deeper sleep. She began dreaming about her drive for success and its cost. She kept seeing a hanging neon sign with lights blinking on and off: The American dream—start your business—be your own boss—make money. She awoke at the dawn of daylight, fighting passionately to be in charge of her destiny. She was confused and afraid, thinking—what did this dream mean?

Mary J suddenly jumped out of bed and ran with frantic awkwardness into the kitchen. There she fell on her knees and began vomiting into a paper bag used for trash. She couldn't imagine what was wrong with her. She felt somewhat seasick for some reason—slowly, her head rose from its sagging weakness—her eyes and mouth opened wide with discovery. She thought hesitantly: Oh my God, I'm pregnant. I am pregnant! Her hands flew down to cover her middle in a protective cradling for the new life growing within her body.

Mary J wasn't even aware that she had been missing her time of the month. It had been so undependable for so long. There was an inevitable resignation in her expression as she wiped away her tears, then squeezed her eyes shut. She shook her head and sighed, thinking softly: Nature is never wrong; God is the ultimate authority of life. Now I really must have a family's plan. My children will work in my store throughout their school years. In return, they will have free things to eat. This way, the store can stay open sixteen hours a day—seven days a week! We may not get rich, but my family won't have to suffer as we did during the Great Depression years. Of course, most of all, we will have heaps of food!

Months and months went by before the baby was born. Finally, after nearly ten months, Mary J gave birth to a baby boy. Talk about baby-loving! Cindy and Citole pop their badges with pride. They told everybody—even the bent-up older man who swept out the trash around the Corner's businesses. The baby boy was the talk of the Corner before he had drawn his first breath. Even the local drunks, including Mark Washington, toasted a drink of celebration with their friends.

One day during mid-morning while her baby boy was sleeping, Mary J was saturated internally with dividing conflicts and emotions. Her new baby boy would begin his years of life in a business environment that included Luke's night club, Della restaurant, and George Boone pool hall. An atmosphere where drinking was a cultural fixture. On the other hand, Elsie May and Dora lee had been born on Pap's homestead under the influence of his family. A safe environment that was free from bad influences—except for Fred's weekend drinking.

Mary J walked over to the backdoor and looked across the open field. With eyes turning toward the sky, she seemed to be trying to find answers in the white, fluffy clouds riding over the invisible wind. My God, she thought, I hope my son doesn't become a drunkard. If so, our luxurious family beauty and happiness will undoubtedly turn into a scorched wilderness.

As Mary J was thinking, James Miller came by to take her new baby boy around the house, part of a long-time family tradition. As soon as she saw him approaching her front door, she thought, maybe he is the answer to my prayer.

Mary J shouted: "Cousin James, come on in—tell me the good news."

James Miller grinned. "Well, I'm here." How's my little boy."

169

"Well, let me tell you, that little boy woke up sharply when the first red streak of dawn was on the horizon. It's hard to get anything done until Cindy or Citole get here. Lorraine went over the Creek early this morning. So, you see, all my helpers have left me."

James Miller went directly to the bedroom and picked up her baby boy. Taking a deep breath and several chuckles, he said: "I am going to take your little fellow and walk him around the house. This supposed to create happy pathways for him."

On his way out of the front door, James Miller smiled and chuckled quietly again as he rocked the baby in his arms. He was singing a spirited little song: Rock-a-Bye baby, repeatedly as he carried the baby around the house. People passing by stopped to see this special event; they just stood around, grinning and shaking their heads.

Cindy and Citole also arrived during this special event. They were cheering with their support even before entering the front yard. Being named after his dad, Citole started calling the baby boy, at that very moment, by the nickname: Buddy. For some reason, the name stuck with him.

After the ending of this fabulous event, James Miller carried the baby back to his crib. He drank a shot glass full of liquor to complete the celebration. He then just picked up his hat and eased out of the back door.

Mary J went outside to the clothesline to hang out her diapers. All of a sudden, little Buddy started an extremely fussy cry in the bedroom.

"Citole," said Cindy, "please take care of little buddy while I go out on the back and clean some fish."

"Oh sure," said Citole, "little Buddy will be just fine."

Citole dropped back, being exhausted from all the earlier activities. "Now Elsie May, you and Dora Lee, please just let me handle the baby. Every time little Buddy's start hollering, both of you are right there trying to grab him. Why don't you all go outside with Cindy and your mother?"

"Yes, ma'am," said both of them together. They flew out of the back door, slamming the screen door with a bang as if a human evolution was taking place."

"Lord have mercy," said Citole. "What's wrong with these children slamming that back door like somebody going crazy?" She then peeps out of the back door to check on the girls, and discover a cloud of dust behind them.

Cindy hollered out in a panic towards Mary J while she was cleaning fish. "Hey Mary J, those old revenue agents just passed by looking for moonshiners."

"What did you say, Cindy? I can't hear one thing with these children making so much noise."

Cindy laid down the fish in her hand and walked a little closer to her. "I heard a loud noise. It sounds like somebody blowing-up a liquor still. I sure hope Pap and Levy are okay. A carload of revenue agents just went down the road."

"Okay, Cindy," said Mary J, "just pray a little prayer for them."

Two hours later, Levy and Pap drove up behind the house. Pap says to Levy, "It looks like our little moonshine operation is over."

"You think so, Pap," said levy with tears in his eyes. "Well, if so, I'm broke."

"Well," said Pap, "we will find a way. The issue at stake is not failure itself, but a question of attitude. Our attitude can either strengthen or destroy us. This loss is only a small setback in our struggle to make a living for our families. We must look upon our business loss today as building blocks instead of stumbling blocks."

"You make an excellent point, Pap," said Levy. "I guess the secret is to thrust a defiant chin at our loss."

"Now-here is the proposition," said Pap, "no one enjoys defeat. No one delights in failure or making a loss. So, remember Levy, mistakes mark the progress of humanity. Without friction, there is no heat. Our attitudes toward bad experiences can cause us to build a castle or a pig-sty."

Levy started laughing; and then said to Pap: "If I were you, I wouldn't go in there telling Mary J that we just lost all of our money. She is trying so hard to start a retail business in that little house. I don't see how your wife can do it. There is only one bedroom in the whole house. Along with that, she fusses like a madwoman, but she is truly trying to help you get ahead."

"Well, Levy," said Pap, "let's go inside and hear my wife start fussing about our business lost. Mary J may even blow up the house when she realizes that there is no money to rebuild our operation." Pap was shaking his head, "we were trying to save up a little money to buy a piece of land."

Pap and Levy slowly got out of the car and proceeded towards the back door of the house. Mary J's met them as she was returning to the house from the clothesline. She quickly noticed a struggle of shame on their faces. "Why are you hard-working men looking so sad? Stop and think about it for a minute. What makes men successful? Hard work and long hours."

Pap frowned as if the world's weight was upon his shoulders. "Mary J," he said slowly, as his words were groping for guidance. "We got bad news, sweetheart; revenue agents just put us out of business."

The stunned look on Levy's face told Mary J how devastating this situation was for them. With a troubled heart within—fumbling with his buttons, Levy turned with a sick look. His eyes wouldn't come up: "Pap and I don't have the money to rebuild because we lost our money today. We put all our money into the final run last night. Before the mash could reach the boiling point of alcohol, our little business was gone. We had a good plan wherein everything was all sold out for a large profit. But now, how are we going to find the money to rebuild? We could have made big profits this week if only everything went according to our plans."

Pap looked down again, nodding his head, concentrating: "He's right. We will need several hundred dollars to get started again. We are just coming out the Great Depression years, who's got that kind of money to burn?"

Levy was feeling as low as he had ever felt in his life. His eyes were somewhat misty as he looked up again and said directly to Mary J. "I know you are working very hard to get your store—it's also hard-times now. Our farm isn't making any money. So, what else can we do but make whiskey?"

Mary J gazed intently into her husband's eyes. "Those little jugs of whiskey that you and Plunt have been leaving in the pantry. Well, I have been selling drinks by the shots. Come on into the house, let us see how much I have saved from my labor."

Levy and Pap followed Mary J into the house to the kitchen table. Mary J said: "you talented businessmen sit down, while I get the money out of the bedroom."

Pap said. "Okay, I will sit right here with Levy. We might need a shot ourselves."

Levy's said, frowning, "I might need double shots."

172

There was a moment of silence while Mary J went into her bedroom. Pap and Levy looked up, surprised, as she returned with a brown paper bag in her hand. She had saved several hundred dollars from her home-based business. Levy was holding a ragged cap in his rough, dirty hands, in front of his patched jacket. He began shedding tears as she counted out the money. Pap raised his head and laughed with pleasure. At the same time, he hugged his wife—straightaway, Pap and Levy went back to buy the material necessary to restore their business operation.

Several hours later, Mary J found herself staring outside of her window through dry eyes. She thought, I just gave up all the money my family has in this world. We can't afford to lose. What if their little moonshine operation gets blown up again? We have no money in saving—we now have three small children—not counting my sister Lorraine—all of us living in this crowded little house. This is foolish! I have reacted emotionally rather than reasonably. How will I ever get my store this way?

Chapter 20

MARY J NEW HOUSE

Within six months of Pap and Levy rebuilding their moonshining business, a mysterious strength of new vitality seemed to be flowing through their operation. They sold cases by the truckloads, even shipped some up and down the eastern seaboard. Their full circle of influence included workers, customers, and legal authorities that politely looked the other way. Pap was a moonshine Robin Hoods that gave back to his community, through Mary J, by helping the common man, old folks, and local churches.

Mary J once again had her brown paper bag partially filled with cash. She was now singing and striding confidently around her small dwelling place. She had an iron-willed determination to follow through on her plans—refusing to wallow in the backlash of mediocrity. As sudden tears of happiness poured down her cheeks, Mary J leaned back against the wall and threw her arms wide in a luxurious stretch. She kept thinking that from a logical perspective: *Life isn't a spectator sport; the only way to derive any satisfaction is to keep getting your feet wet.*

Pap came home earlier than usual, trying to escape the rain, wind, and mist crowding the atmosphere. There was no reason for him to be concern about anything other than a rainy and windy afternoon. When he got out of his truck, a flight of birds dropped to the ground, began scrabbling for bits of food; they quickly flew off into nearby trees. Pap just kept walking through the yard towards the porch.

Mary J met Pap at the front door with dancing eyes, a beautiful smile, and with her heart-opened as vast as the sky. "Arthur Becton was by here today. He owns some land on the other side of Charlie Reed's house. It's less than a quarter of a mile away—right on this main road."

Pap eyed her speechlessly for a moment. "So, what's the proposition, did he say anything about selling the land?"

Mary J was resting one hand on her hip. "Without a doubt... trust me, Arthur has no problem selling us sufficient land to build a house, maybe even enough to build a store. He has ten acres right across from Clift and Harry's houses."

Pap, expressionless, hunched his shoulders. "Don't take this the wrong way, Levy told me that old man Levi has five acres on the waterfront for sale. It's located just around the belt from here, across from Hazel Carter's house."

Mary J swallowed down a sudden dryness in her throat; her head turned slowly from side to side. She had a goal—all her thinking poured into achieving it. She believed that Arthur's land was in the perfect location to add a store right beside the house. She began thinking: *the main road goes directly pass Arthur's land—all of the Corner's traffic would be just footsteps away. Our new store and house would only be a short walking distance from this very Corner intersection of various businesses.*

After Mary J had thought it all out, she replied in her usual fussy style, "Who in their right mind would put up a store that far away from the main road?"

Mary J began laughing as she walked into the kitchen to start supper. She just began stacking the dishes, peeling potatoes and washing the string beans. Next, she started preparing the meat—smearing it with lots of butter—adding pepper and salt. As Mary J finished one thing, she quickly started on something else. She mixed up some flour, eggs, and milk into a batter for the pudding. Being truly impressed with her incredible recipes; Mary J began humming positively to herself.

As Mary J was working in the kitchen, Cindy poked her head around the door several times—volunteering to help. Mary J declined her offer;

she told Cindy just to finish ironing the children's clothes and later make her mysterious biscuits. Mary J was now thinking about important things, so she began ignoring Cindy's questions.

Cindy, with her wild and exploring mind, thought at first, what a mountain of food! However, after reconsidering how quickly and continuously food vanishes from Mary J's kitchen, Cindy only hoped to get a plate to take home. She knew that an entire plate of food could disappear without a trace.

Even though timeworn adequate to be Mary J's mother, Cindy enjoyed cooking and ironing clothes. She was capable of skillfully pressing out the deepest wrinkles. Although Cindy's biscuit recipe was always one of Mary J's household favorite; she had a strange way of sharing her recipes. Cindy would intentionally give people an altered recipe to keep someone from repeating her results. It was always something simple, like changing a quantity from teaspoons to tablespoons, or leaving out a crucial but distinct ingredient.

Cindy shook her head and then took a deep breath. She couldn't forget so easily that Mary J lived in her own little biosphere—seeing the world differently than most people. *Somehow*, thought Cindy: *things keep happening in Mary J's head nearly every waking moment.* For a minute, Cindy couldn't speak, but somehow, she managed to find her voice. She said, "Mary J, I'm not trying to be difficult; please stop rushing and thinking so much. You can't do everything around here—just leave the cooking and ironing for me."

Staring at Cindy's face, Mary J saw the shining love behind her sunken eyes. "My dearest Cindy, you and Citole will never know how grateful my heart is for two loyal friends."

Cindy smiled and nodded politely; her eyes were softly luminous. She spoke slowly, in a serious tone: "I understand how you feel. Your family has certainly been a big piece of my life. If the Lord permits, they always will be—hopefully for many years to come."

As Mary J went about her household task, she began using mental images and positive affirmations to restart her childhood dreams. She could see herself washing dishes in her new home as well as a brand-new store next door. A store full of merchandise to sell with overflowing customers, as she warmly parades around them. She could see herself fussing at salespeople, proudly letting them know who owns the business.

Pap gently walked into the Kitchen. He pried several worried fingers down his arm. "That's all right, Mary J," he said awkwardly. "You've done a mighty good job talking to Arthur about his land. Go ahead and see if we can get the whole ten acres. But remember, you are daydreaming unless we can come up with the money. We are proceeding ahead into the unknown with a real savvy businessman. It is no telling what he wants for his land. We need more than just confidence to sustain us, baby we need money! That's what we need to close this deal, lots of money!"

Mary J made a fussy reply, "Daydreamers don't believe in what they dream. Their dreams are only a whim, a wish, a fantasy. Our dreams for land, a house, and a store are not only possible but also will become a reality. Pap, just look around at our current living condition. How can we be content living in a one-bedroom house with five bodies squeezed together in this little ramshackle house? Everybody breathing down each other's sweat, air, and misery, day in and day out. We have bigger plans in mind for our family. We need our own house and land for these children to enjoy their childlike hearts and souls as human beings."

Pap looked around their neat and tidy overcrowded one-bedroom house. "I see what you mean; even when problems and obstacles threaten us like a mountain, we must hold firmly onto our dreams. It's like making a sweet, mouthwatering dessert out of vinegar. You know, the Depression years have choked mountains; just maybe, Arthur might be in a tight squeeze himself."

Mary J saw Arthur Becton walking towards the front porch. She simply stood there, trying to breathe as her stomach rolled over and over. Mary J sighed in a moment of reprieve—her spirit sagged as he approached the front porch steps. She began to visualize the pain of rejection, especially if Arthur wouldn't accept or suggest a reasonable deal.

When Mary J turned her head slowly towards Pap, something inside her jump-started like an old car battery that got a boost. "Oh my God, Pap! Here is Arthur knocking at our front door; this is the Lord's work."

Pap confidently made his way towards the front door while shaking his head with laughter. "Hey Arthur, just come on in here and take a seat.

Mary J has been determined to build a house and store. As a matter of fact, right now, she is dreaming about your land. But here's the proposition, I can't convince her that there may be a gulf between our money and your price. My wife has a mindset that refuses to give up on her ideas."

"Well, Pap," said Arthur, "I have ten acres of land right down the road. If you need enough land for a house, that's not a problem."

"Now here's the second part of this proposition," said Pap, "we need enough for a house, store, and some farmland."

Arthur looked surprised, then please, "well now, you need the whole ten acres, don't you?"

Pap drew a deep breath of delight and leaned back against the chair. "You are exactly right, Arthur, but in truth, we don't have all the money to buy your land." Pap commenced shaking his head with a little laughter. "It wouldn't cross my mind to ask for any kind of special consideration."

Holding a cigarette in his hand, Arthur took a slow, deep drag, analyzing the situation. Inhaling the smoke into his lungs, he stared at Pap for several moments and then exhaled several gray clouds into the air. It produced a split-second cloud in front of his face. "You got that right! I have worked extremely hard to get what I got; I just can't give it up on a whim."

Pap leaned back, his eyebrows rising in agreement, "Arthur, please don't be ridiculous—you know me better than that... there is no free lunch, but some lunches are cheaper than others."

Arthur's eyes narrowed a little as he scratched his head—looking at them thoughtfully. "There is nobody I respect more than you, and Mary J. You and your wife are highly respected in this community as hard workers. There are several ways in which simple math may accommodate us." Handing Pap a piece of paper, "here's the cost in writing, just pay me a third today and the rest when you get it."

There was an uncomfortable silence; Pap made no response. Mary J jumped up and went into the bedroom. She returned within a few minutes, then said to Arthur in her fussy manner. "This may sound silly, but all of our saving is in this brown paper bag."

Mary J placed the brown paper bag on a small table in front of him. Her eyes were focused directly upon Arthur's facial expressions as he began opening it. She thought for a moment that perhaps her play-acting was slightly insignificant. Mary J closed her eyes very tightly in anticipation of Arthur's objection. By some means, her habits of thought projected an emotional response of determination.

Arthur began thinking: *Mary J got one devil of a nerve. Her proposition pierced with holes.* All of a sudden, he shook his head with laughter. He then said to both of them: "Just give me a whiskey shot and this bag of money. You and Pap may pay me when you get the rest; your word is good enough. I will be back next week with the property deed for the entire ten acres of land." Arthur quickly swallowed down one-shot glass of whiskey; then he began to depart with a warm goodbye, "I will see you, folks, next week," laughing as he went out of the front door.

Mary J now filled with an unbelievable mood of happiness beyond her imagination. A feeling of warmth began to spread throughout her entire body. Her face brightened like the sun dawning on a beautiful new day. She was again like a child, playing store owner in the backyard. Once again, She has before her an ocean with endless possibilities, Mary J could finally see a pathway toward her childhood's dream.

There was a dazzling light of delight in Pap's eyes as he smiled at her. He said, laughing. "You amaze me, every time we are in trouble—you bring out that old wrinkled brown paper bag. Even so, I am impressed with how you handled this land deal with your sugar-coated tongue. You can force a dose of liquid aspirins down a person's throat... disguised in a flow of sugary sweetness. The person is thinking about how the sugar tastes—not how bitter the medicine. Your appeal is cable of melting the hardest of hearts."

Mary J threw her arms around Pap, burning with happiness. "To be quite truthful, it's a nice example of how to turn something bitter into something surprisingly sweet. The gravity of this, I realize too well. We are now only a few steps away from our house and store."

"Well, now Mary J," Pap spoke slowly, trying to get the words just as they were within his mind. "I know this is a big decision for us. It may mean tremendous sacrifice."

Mary J laughed with delight, "the ability to survive comes naturally to us, just like the honeysuckle vines that grow naturally in the wild. We don't allow ourselves to be caught up in our world, unmindful of other people—even if they are strangers. We show warmth and openness to our community. In return, people are more willing to help us.

Pap stood up on his feet and began walking. "When a person is an entrepreneur, he usually rushes around like an animal; but there comes a time when a person must settle down and make one dream a reality. A person just needs one powerful idea to hold onto with all their strength. One solid vision with self-determination and persistence can create a pathway to success. You have had one solid dream since childhood, which is to own and build a new store. There is only one problem with us—

Finally, Mary J blurted out, "What could that be?"

Pap hugged and kissed his wife tenderly as though he was going to shelter her. "I love you, sweetheart, but you need to know this: We are trying to create something valuable out of nothing."

Pap and Mary J started working doubly hard to pay Arthur for his land. Pap and Levy were now finally running a profitable moonshining operation while expanding more into farming. Pap felt the fresh earth under his bare feet as he cultivated it on his mother's small farm, along with his newly purchased land—many times from sunrise to sunset. Mary J's home-based business was growing with new customers. They soon paid off the balance owed for the property. Immediately, they started saving for new construction.

Mary J was not aware, but Pap had already started laying the foundation for their new house. He took command of all the new home construction, including the house plan. The problem was that Mary J wanted an upstairs like her Grandma Mag first house before it was destroyed by fire. Yet, Pap stood his ground by demanding a long hotel-type hallway instead of stairs.

Pap designed the house with a large wrap-around front porch and an attached garage on the right side of the house. Starting from the front porch as a person entered the house, there were two living rooms; one enclosed for special occasions and another opposite it for everyday family, friends, and visitors. Walking the hallway, people would notice a piano near the living room; several large beautiful pictures on the walls; four huge bedrooms, a bathroom with a walk-in closet; a large family kitchen area, and an executive type dining room divided by a bar counter.

As one walked outside the back door, eight acres of farmland prepared for planting with a tractor and plow. Pap commenced planting a garden to raise enough food to sustain his family throughout the entire year. The whole family participated in cultivating, planting, and managing the Garden. What a different experience for this family, going from Luke's one-bedroom house to a large beautiful personal home; now, Mary J and Pap owned one of the largest family homes in their community. On the right side of the house, there was one acre for a potential store.

Immediately after moving into her new house, Mary J sensed a power of faith that allowed her emotions to work in harmony with her intellect. Mary J's logic began dealing with the probabilities of a store, while her feelings dealt with her dreams of owning a store. She started stretching her imagination beyond what was probable to what was possible. She immediately resumed selling merchandise not only from her kitchen table but also expanded into using her dining room area. Of course, the most profitable beverage sold from Mary J's kitchen table was Pap and Levy's fireball whiskey filled with peaches. Mary J kept selling it one shot at a time while visualizing a new store across from her kitchen window. She kept saving her money in the wrinkled brown paper bag.

Cindy and Citole sent Mary J word that they would be coming, as usual, to help keep the family together. For these two, finding something to do around Mary J's house wasn't hard. There were always dishes and clothes to wash, food to prepare, sweeping, dusting, and children to watch. This way, Mary J could spend most of her time running her home-based business—from morning until late in the night—seven days a week, except for church times.

As anyone could guess, Cindy and Citole eventually came to scrutinize Mary J's new home with exploring minds. As they walked through the front door without knocking, the depth of their emotions produced a warm and delightful spirit that tried to savor the sweetness of the hour. They wanted so much to nurture May J's sensitive passions with clouds of love.

Cindy tossed her head back and started laughing after seeing the long hallway. She could hear her voice echoing throughout the house: "Where is Mary J? I love her new house?"

Citole turned her head slowly towards Cindy with a soft smile tugging the curves of her mouth. Citole had the pride of a grandmother. She said, "Someone is out on that back porch—at the end of this long hallway."

They walked down the long hallway, wandering about the rambling noise coming from the back porch. Cindy looked at Citole for a moment, almost as if she was going to say something, but then changed her mind. Suddenly as they came closer to the end of the hallway, Cindy hollered out with a shout, "Where is everybody?"

Mary J's oldest sister Ella came out with her million-dollar smile and infectious laughter. She shouted back with her uniquely cheerful voice: "How are you folks doing this morning?" Then, Ella laughed so hard that it hurt her stomach muscles. Like her sister Mary J, Ella was less than 5-feet tall and weighed only 100 pounds. When she smiled, one could see that her top front teeth were missing. She was so simple in personality, yet lovable in style and grace. Her presence could turn a negative environment positive. She filled Mary J's home with a breeze of fresh air.

Cindy joyfully replied to Ella, "Look at your sister's new house... isn't this something? It is the largest house in our community."

"Now listen," Citole said. "How in the world will Mary J keep this big house clean?"

Cindy looked surprised for only a moment. "What makes you ask that? "I will help with the washing, ironing, and cooking."

Ella gave Cindy and Citole her warmest smile, enthusiastically said to them, "you have a painter! I will be painting the back porch today."

"I'm happy for Pap and Mary J," said Citole, "especially for their three little children and her baby sister Lorraine. They needed to get out of Luke's little house on the Corner."

Cindy nodded, then cleared her throat. "Mary J and Pap will share whatever they have with others. All their families and friends will be staying and eating here. Her brother James Westley and Cousin Monroe will be here whenever they come back from fishing in Louisiana. Pap's family will also be coming and going."

Citole tugged in her breath. "Just look at you and me. We will also stay right here, like family. Who else is going to look after us in our old age with decency and respect? It is as if God put this family here to help us form a sense of community and a network of friendships. I will tell you this; more people are sick from isolation and loneliness than love. A strong sense of community will help us live more productive lives. That's precisely why, I am going to stay right here and help Mary J build her dream store business."

"You are right," said Ella, "Pap and Mary J never marginalize other people. My family taught me to make my way through this world, by helping others along the way. The pitting of mind against mind is one of our most effective ways to educate each other."

"That's precisely right," said Citole. "It seems that God chooses people with shortcomings, give them work to do, then supplies them with sufficient grace to do it."

"Believe me," said Ella, "all of us have problems that we must face every day, but nothing love can't heal. For example, my husband, Earl, sometimes is the meanest man in this whole world. Just the other day, when it was raining, thundering and lightning, he throws us outdoor. My little children and I crawl under the house to keep from getting wet. Do you know why? It was because his supper was not ready when he got home. We just came over to stay with my sister Mary J for a few days; God bless her heart. It took all the strength that God gave me to forgive him. Down to this day, I must force myself to keep on trusting, hoping, and enduring these hardships."

Citole whole body began to shake with anger, just thinking that someone could hurt such a kind little woman like Ella, then she said, "You are surely a better woman than me, if that was my husband, I would surely be in jail."

Ella looked uncomfortable for a moment. "What kind of future can you have with no education, no skills, no regular job, and no experience with life? My husband Earl is a hard man, hardened by the life he has lived, the pain and suffering he has seen. Life has taken out of him the good spirit he had. Nevertheless, this is his life; he must make the best of it. Somehow, God has tied up my destiny with Earl, at least throughout this lifetime. Sometimes, I can hear a cheerful voice within me saying: "Don't worry, Ella. That isn't your fault. You will be ok."

"Well, Ella," said Cindy, "I am with you. The only person I plan to murder is the woman trying to take my man: John Thomas. I would take a butcher knife and cut her head off."

"Well, I tell you, my sweet little niece," said Citole "you got nothing to worry about because nobody wants that drunken fool but you. John Thomas lives with you in your family house and only works occasionally. Now Ella, your husband, just got a lot of devil in him." Citole began shaking her head in disgust as she spoke, "we can easily deceive ourselves, especially when we take a powerless approach to difficult situations. In most cases, we are usually just engaged in the form of pain dodging. The kind of men you ladies got; I am sure glad as the devil to be single."

Cindy immediately responded, cutting Citole off, "I don't care what nobody says about my man, so many times he has been there for me, just like I've been there for him. I can't just let go of my man and watch him sink. My man, John Thomas, means too much to me."

Ella's ingrained hurt had been part of her everyday existence for many years. She had built an invisible glass wall of immunity around her life at home, which created an aloofness in her personal life. If she couldn't be touched, she couldn't be hurt. Ella only wanted to make her pain go away, smooth her road, and protect her children from the ugliness of a mean husband. She knew that came with a high price tag. From Ella's point of view, her vows of marriage to Earl had never changed in all their years together. For now, Earl and her children were her whole world.

Ella rubbed her tearful eyes. She lived in a world of symbols, but yet, somehow, a smile lit up over her face. She said, "I got to start painting this room. We can talk later."

"You Right," said Cindy, "otherwise Mary J will be fussing with somebody, especially if these children mess up this house. I am getting a migraine headache just thinking about how that woman loves to fuss. By the way, do you have a BC powder? I'm already feeling the pain.

"Oh yes," said Citole, "right here in my apron; there is one for you and one for me." They both strolled down the hallway in a fit of laughter. After seeing the house, they departed for home.

Shortly after Cindy and Citole departed, Mary J returned from the outside Garden. She found herself sitting and resting on the front porch.

Although happy about her new home, Mary J was slightly depressed about her plan of action to own a store. She thought that nothing could be more horrifying than missing that opportunity. As Mary J drew back into her chair, her answers were still somewhat incomplete. She wanted to cry out her deep-thinking thoughts: Why am I? Who am I? And to what purpose? I am not satisfied merely to live, eat, and have children.

Mary J now with trembling thoughts of mental anguish. Her fingers kept wobbling their way up and down her right jaw. She kept saying with a quiet voice to herself. I believe in miracles, but yet, I feel a little insecure about getting my store. God knows I can't stand this kind of pain. My goals must not be confused with daydreaming; I am not engaging in fantasy. I need a legal business so that my family can be proud of our accomplishments in this community. I know that Pap is paying an appalling price for my dreams to own a store, but he knew this before our marriage. I will guard every penny with a fuss, until I see that store beside this house."

Chapter 21

THE STRANGE HOUSE GIFT

E arly the next morning, Citole arose with the sun shining and its heat just beginning. She got up because it was too hot to sleep. Her sheets felt like wet burlap, so she washed up and went into her sparkling and neat kitchen. Unexpectedly rain-spattered, then lashed down against the windows. At the same time, sunlight began sloping through the rain. Citole thought that there was something unnatural about rain one minute—sun the next—then suddenly, rain again.

Citole was moping around like a chicken with dropsy. She felt fantastic about her special house gift lying on the kitchen table. She wanted to give Mary J something extraordinary for her new home. Citole dressed quickly, hoping that the break from the rain would last a while longer. She walked hastily out of the front door with her unique gift, tightly held under her arm.

The sun was shining again as Citole walked along the dusty road. She took notice of the various people that passed by her. Some were walking while others were riding. There were older adults as well as young people, even little children. They all seemed to be traveling somewhere special. Citole felt proud that She also had somewhere special to go, with an unusual gift. When she arrived at Mary J's house with her distinctive gift, Cindy met her at the door.

Cindy smiled at Citole as if the gift was for her. "Good morning, I am sure that gift is for me!"

Citole leaned against the door to catch her breath after walking for twenty minutes at a brisk pace to get there before the rain. "You are wrong. It's Mary J's housewarming Gift." She swallowed down the lump in her throat, and then began walking down the long hallway. She was finally starting to feel her age.

"Ah," said Cindy after closing the door. "At least tell me what it is, for heaven's sake! I just can't wait to know." Cindy emotionally waved her hands in the air and chuckled.

"I will," said Citole, "this gift will help make Mary J's home more prosperous. This way, she can stay wrapped up into her hopes, dreams, and fantasies—where is Mary J this morning?"

"She just went out of the back door to the garden with the children."

"Come on in the kitchen with me," said Citole, "so we can find a place to hang it. As you know, hanging things can get a bit tricky." She set the box on the Kitchen table, opened it, and pulled out a wind chime unit that came down through her family tree."

Cindy stood silently with her arms crossed tightly over her chest. She began laughing at Citole's strange looking housewarming gift. "Tell me, what in the devil is that?"

Citole smiled at her. "This is a special and beautiful angelic wind chime from China. It stimulates energy that entices blessings. This wind chime will repel evil spirits and attract compassionate ones. Don't you see, each home has a spirit guardian that brings special powers, inclination, and abilities? Now, this will be a prosperous home. You'll see, Mary J will get her store, believe me."

Cindy eyed the gift judgmentally, especially based on Citole's senseless statement that something from China could bring blessings, through some guardian spirit. Cindy knew that Citole was a person who had inspiring wisdom from the past that frequently puzzled her. A woman who knew a lot about things passed down through the sea of time. Cindy often noticed that Citole mostly kept her eyes on the children, continually sitting near doorways, watching people as they entered and left the house—always trying to play the role of Mary J's chief advisor.

As Cindy respectfully stared at Citole, she began thinking that she was a very mysterious and shrew woman, who was ancient sufficient enough to be Mary J's grandmother. For this reason, she definitely wouldn't disrespect her. She knew that Citole wouldn't intentionally do anything to harm Mary J. It was primarily through her that Cindy became one of Mary J's helpers.

Cindy looked and looked and looked at the unusual gift on the table. There was something curious about Cindy's eyes, something unpleasant as if an outraged animal descended upon the house. "Tell me, where are you going to place it? It ain't no wind in this here kitchen!"

Citole shook her head. "Let me think. I'll think of something. Let's put it right in this kitchen, so that it can be in contact with the whole family. We can hang it right above this half wall, over this split-level countertop, between the kitchen and the dining room. Let's make sure it's facing the kitchen table."

With great care, Citole decided the wind chime unit should be placed in a central position. The other decorations on the wall were immediately organized around the wind chime display. Citole's lips quivered into the tiniest smile. "This position is crucial since there is a need to understand your surroundings. A person's feelings need some control over his or her space in time."

From Cindy's point of view, Citole's words sounded like an echo of darkness from the past. Cindy was shocked because of her audacity to do this without Mary J's permission. Her behavior made Cindy speechless at first, but she soon mended her thoughts. She would not dare challenge her, especially since she could be easily upset.

Cindy wiped her eyes on her sleeve. "Now, please explain what it does again. So, I can have a choice of fighting or fleeing from this house!"

Citole felt a thrill of pride while giving Cindy more details about its history. "The energy around us is called Chi by the Chinese. Chi energy may influence our thoughts and surroundings to attract blessings. These chimes must be placed in special areas to attract good energy that will create the most positive influences. We live a life of feelings and emotions, moods, and thoughts. It all comes to life around the family table. Now, do you see why I picked the kitchen?"

Cindy suddenly laughed with just a hint of mischief, thinking: *my God! Citole knows how to get her wishes without causing problems. She must be using some type of psychological manipulation; because, one of her most common tactics is pretending to serve a higher calling. But in her heart, I know that Citole wouldn't hurt a fly. Citole has her ways but has always been a true friend. On the other hand, I know she will tell a lie about the places she has traveled, but maybe that's more natural than this kind of stuff.*

Ella overheard Cindy and Citole's conversation as she was painting the pantry shelves. Ella kept thinking: *it could be that Citole has gone off her rocker because she knows nothing about China. But now—perhaps, she just came up with this crazy scheme to impress Mary J with a memorable gift.*

As they were talking, Ella walked into the kitchen to see what was going on. She started laughing: "What in the world are you ladies doing in here?"

Cindy closed her eyes on Ella's question, then reopened them again, very slowly, as though her eyelids had lead weights. She then spoke suspiciously, "Citole knows how to bring special blessings to Mary J's new house. She got a gift from China, and now she has rearranged all the wall displays in the kitchen."

"This is outrageous without Mary J's consent," said Ella. "Under these circumstances, I would prefer going out for a walk then hearing a great deal of fussing in here. Of course, maybe I'm wrong, but I thought that wind chimes are outdoor decorations. As far as I am concern, the devil can stay outside. I have heard a lot of bad things about wind chimes, believe me! Some people believe chimes can change the laws of nature, through some murky veil of mystery filled with superstition."

Cindy said fervently. "So what? You know Mary J loves gifts."

"For one thing," said Ella, "wind chimes supposed to attract evil spirits."

"Oh, my goodness, Ella," said Citole. Wind chimes are popular decorations all over this world for over 3,000 years. They are like musical instruments creating sounds that give a calming effect on people's feelings. It's a great conversation symbol, a special kind of wind chime for my friend's home. It has a special blessing upon it. Now, you small thinking women just need to stop acting so crazy."

"If you say so," said Ella. "I don't want anything to do with the devil. This sounds like trickery and bewitchment to me."

Suddenly, the wind blew through an open window on the chimes that created several musical sounds. Silence fell upon everyone in the kitchen for a moment or two, a silence that brought something of a discomfort to Ella's religious consciousness. Unexpectedly, everybody was afraid.

Cindy hesitated, being frightened for herself; she then said with a nervous voice that was somewhat ill at ease. "What's that sound? I sure hope it's not an evil spirit."

"Oh, please, for heaven's sake," said Citole. "Beautiful sounds bring gaiety!" This wind chime is only a reminder of the good spirits blessing this home. These musical sounds are good spirits, like angels, trying to communicate with us. Communication is how all kinds of influences reach us from the awesome powers of the cosmos. As you already know, People will determine their blessings or curses by the way they synchronize their energy through others—not utilizing these wind chimes."

Cindy said, somewhat uneasy. "I sure hope you are right; otherwise, I am getting the devil out of here."

Ella interrupted; her forehead beaded with sweat. "I want my sister to be prosperous through God's blessings—not demons."

Citole hastily intervened to correct their devastating opposition. "Let's think about this right now. Wind chimes have been used in the past to scare away evil spirits and to discourage bad breaks. Those who practice such behavior; put them in doorways and windows. We have a mind that always tries to be right about everything, so that we might use it to our advantage. Let's become a seeker of blessings, actively looking for them in our daily experiences. Use these wind chimes, only as a reminder to attract positive energy from others that harmonize with our energy. Then, and only then, we can all pray and thank God for his goodness!"

"Well, ok," said Ella, "let me get back to painting. Mary J probably won't pay much attention to it anyway."

Mary J suddenly walked through the back door, headed towards the bathroom. She hollered out, "Someone looks after the children while I wash up."

Ella shouted out: "Sure, they will be alright. I can see Elise May and Dora Lee while painting this room. Little buddy is still sleeping."

"Mary J," said Cindy, "Look at your beautiful housewarming gift from Citole. It came from China."

Mary J watched the big smile that lit up Citole's face. She winked her left eye at Cindy. "Well, it is beautiful! I sure hope it wasn't too expensive, especially coming from China."

Citole looked up, and up, and up. She seemed to stretch towards the ceiling—slowly turning in the direction of Mary J: "You and Pap have been good to me. I wanted to get you something that would be a permanent reminder of my appreciation. This wind chime is part of my family's heritage, something past down to me through several generations. Mary J, I am getting old, and my days are few."

Cindy's eyes glanced vaguely towards the wind chimes. "These wind chimes will bring you blessings."

As Mary J walked towards the bathroom to clean up a little, she turned and said: "Well, Cindy, just remember Pap's favorite quote. 'A lazy person is almost never lucky.' If we work hard, anything can happen, Citole's gift is just decorations. Now I got to wash up."

Citole shook her head towards Cindy. "I don't care what you say about my chimes. Don't try to kid yourself; no one ever accomplishes anything of consequence without a goal. So, you see, Mary J has a goal, you know why? She wants a store. You and Ella are filled with confusion because neither one of you knows where you are going. These wind chimes are a reminder that we can choose to create either positive or negative energy around our circumstances every day. So! You and Ella need to stop being so negative! Mary J wants a store—our energy must synchronize with hers. Just think, If Mary J owns a big grocery store, we will never go hungry."

Cindy stepped out of the kitchen and went down the hallway, laughing. She began thinking that Citole is one strange woman. Her wind chime gift to Mary J, even more unusual.

Mary J came out of the bathroom and went into the kitchen to see the wind chimes again. She decided to let them stay there so Citole would be happy. Mary J's tears overflowed and ran down her cheeks to her chin. She didn't move her hand to wipe them away but began thinking: *My good friend Citole has a good heart, and she is my faithful helper. She comes to help me during the sunshine, rain, thunderstorms, even hurricanes. These wind chimes will be a memorial to her, so that we won't forget her faithfulness, goodwill, and companionship.*

Mary J called Citole over and said, "Let's go sit on the front porch for a few minutes."

Mary J was extremely sympathetic towards Citole's loving intentions. She respected her sensitive independence as well as the way she shared the secrets of her heart. Mary J wouldn't allow any more negative conversation concerning her housewarming gift. Mary J and Citole just sat in the porch swing together—rocking back and forward together—entertaining each other with smiles and laughter of times long ago.

"Mary J," said Citole very thoughtfully, "I may not be here to see, but you will get your store. A brand new one, right beside your house. Now I got to go home; if God is willing, I will be here tomorrow morning."

Citole hugged Mary J, then hollered down the hall to say goodbye to those in the house. She walked slowly off the porch and down the road. She faded away as she made a left turn at the Corner intersection.

After arriving at home, Citole felt a little tired, so she began preparing for bed. She sat down in her favorite chair near the window and watched the light of day fade away. Her imagination drifted as though she was a child again, moving in her mind between the past and present. Now for some reason, she had no fear of dying. She had long contemplated what she may face on the other side of the grave. She found her prospect bright once she put all her troubles in the Lord's hand.

Citole began thinking about meeting old friends and family, especially those she still loves and hopes to see again. She thought of her beloved Dad and Mom that had died many years ago. She gradually went to sleep with a steady pace of rocking, as the last pang of life departed from her. Finally, when Citole's end came, she was carried to the church cemetery in a traditional wooden coffin. Pastor Michael Moore gave her final eulogy. Although Citole wasn't a conventional Christian, she said her final farewells in a beautiful Christian ceremony, in a manner dictated by her faithful friend: Mary J.

Chapter
22

MARY J'S DREAM STORE

One year after Citole's death, Pap and his partner Levy had hired three additional workers to help turn cornmeal and sugar into a substantial profit. They steadily saved money—expanded their moonshining operation as well as built a loyal customer base. Within a few short years, they had made quite a name for themselves. People liked their smooth, pure and, clean-tasting whiskey; customers came from miles around to buy it.

Levy and Pap were as objective-minded and coolheaded as scientists. They wanted to own the means of their livelihood. Although money and good jobs were hard to come by, Pap and Levy believed that money was the medium for exchanging hard work for food, and other life necessities. In their opinion, a man who didn't spend his time working was a disgrace, and money wasn't working, even more disgraceful.

Pap was sitting at the kitchen table, counting money that came in from his moonshine operation. He began to realize that survival in the business world was touch, full of risk, and backbreaking. He had learned not to worry continuously about things that he couldn't control or change. He knew that a good business person must be able to see the rose while it was in the seed, the spark while it was still in the flint, and the rain while it was a mist rising from the seas—at the same time, mentally seeing the water drawn by the rays of the sun.

With sparkling expectations before him, *Pap* was now ready to plunge ahead into a new opportunity. He thought: *what an excellent thing to be a real man—knowing what to do at the right time—seeing the unusual in the usual—never throwing good money after bad or reloading cash into a losing proposition.* In the rings of his thoughts and emotions, Pap was ready to start legalizing all of his business activities by being open to new ideas—even Mary J's dream store.

Mary J entered the kitchen to start breakfast. She walked past Pap—cherishing her feelings. She needed to smooth her hair, but the wisps that had escaped the elastic stubbornly refused to be tamed, so she gave up. Depressed and somewhat adrift, she had a hard time sleeping during the night. Mary J kept saying to herself, "where do we go from here? How do we get there?

Pap raised his eyebrows and blew out a breath. "Here is the proposition Mary J, we are beginning a new phase in our lives by opening a brand-new store right beside this house. I think we have saved enough money from your home-based business and my operations to start building right away. Luke has already put me in contact with some people who will be able to start on Monday. The retail merchandise that you have scattered all over our house should be out of here in a few months."

Mary J's head lifted—her eyes widened with lips curved into a smile for him along. Unexpectedly, the mild morning breeze drifted into the kitchen from two open windows over the kitchen sink. The breeze caused Citole's wind chimes, on the split wall over the countertop, to gently tinkle sweet musical sounds. They both thought of Citole's crazy hypothesis that her wind chimes will bring them special blessings, from some power mystical world.

Mary J's knees were like water; her heart was racing. She continued thinking about her old friend, who had died a year ago on this exact day. Mary J said to Pap: "Citole must be smiling in her grave. She always knew that I dislike being hemmed in, held down, and trampled upon as a mere number in a sea of faces. She wiped her eyes with the back of her wrists:

"Now I know that the Lord will answer prayer, I have been longing for my own store since the age of eleven."

They smiled companionably at one another. Then Pap resumed, "Perhaps, our family may enjoy a crest of the hill lifestyle. A place, where the air will be so much cleaner: no smoke, no foul odors, no smog, and a lot less bootlegging!

After raising one of her shoulders slightly in a universal manner, keeping her eyes lowered, Mary J wiped her eyes. She then looked up and stared into her husband's eyes. A deep groove appeared in her forehead as her mind and eyes searched for words to express her feelings. "When I was a youth, I lived my life in a state of great expectation. After my parent's death, it was like being the sole survivor of a bombed building. More specifically, I was like a child that had just narrowly escaped great misfortune. My whole family became a catastrophic event. It was liking rushing forward in the fading glow of late afternoon. The idea of owning a new store became the basis of my life's composition. The dream of a new store became the theme of life that produced melodic tunes in my heart for living. I had no second thoughts as I dreamed dreams and saw visions of a new store. I have spent so many nights feeling sorry for myself. But now, I can hold my head up high again, because God didn't let my dream crumble. There is no stopping us now—the grass will be greener and smell sweeter than honey."

Pap answered quickly, as though he had only been waiting for this opportunity. "You are right; we cannot be like a child with a hammer because everything looks like a nail. Here is the proposition, my little Sugar Dumpling! Let's seize this opportunity to benefit from the newly built military base, just a few miles down the roads. This means that a lot of soldiers and jobs will be coming here. But remember, we have no wealthy relatives to bail us out of a deep hole if we fall into it. We need a birdcage before we buy a bird. Our family must work hard, day and night, to come out of this with skin on our backs."

Mary J stared at Pap for a long moment and then said to him: "At least our tireless struggle of hard work has helped us develop an iron-will determination to achieve our goals. We can't fight shadows, let's recognize our roadblocks; so, we can determine our circumstances. Now the ladder is up, the flags are waving, and even our internal instincts tell us to go!"

Pap could see that Mary J's determination overflowed with emotions. He smiled, then he continues pushing the accelerator, "We are going to open up a full pledge grocery store because this community needs one. I have already contacted the gas people so we can sell gasoline for automobiles. I am even investigating the opportunity of building an oil change facility on the right side of the store. The way I figure it, by expanding into a variety of undertakings, maybe we can reduce some risk and prove the pundits wrong. Now, I am still going to invoke my basic financial principle: A safe dollar is worth more than a risky one."

Mary J's face brightened like the sun dawning on a beautiful new day. "Day in and day out, we have been working like a dog at building our little business—saving every dime we can scrape together—taking on enormous risk—striving to make every day count. It has been difficult, for sure, but this is why God has put us on this earth. Our children must not fall into the category of laziness, even if they don't need to work from dawn until midnight like us. I hope they will feel duty-bound to do something useful with their lives. Our Christian upbringing has taught us that work is a good thing."

Pap leaned forward so Mary J would have to look at him. "By our children working with us, they will acquire good principles and become mentally mature. I hope that somehow our belief system will be passed down to them. Our principles support hard work, honesty, and love for helping people through difficult times. Of course, the chief trouble lies in the fact that the young people of today, never see themselves as the old people of tomorrow."

At this moment, Pap was everything that Mary J could desire him to be. "You're a brilliant man; we are going to make it right here in this community, even if we have to work daily from dawn to midnight. Our children and my sister Lorraine can help us with the store. There is no doubt that Cindy will help take care of the housework. My sister Ella is a good interior painter. She is ready and eager to help us."

Mary J then gave her husband a big smile, squeezing his hand— realizing that working together turns dreams into reality. She wanted to throw a shield of protection around his soft heart; so, she could forever seal this moment within a steel trapdoor.

"There's another general point here," said Pap. "We have painted a rosy picture that our bank account can't match; over-optimism seems to be a common thread when concentrating only on the bright side of things."

Mary J felt her eyes spilling uncontrollable tears. She pressed her head back against the wall and closed her eyes as if calling for strength. "Our faith must be stronger than any fear. Even when things don't seem probable, we must remind ourselves that all things are possible. We have to step out of this box of comfort and security while we strive towards our dreams. No one enjoys failure in the human's experience when attempting to achieve a goal. Real security lies within our heart and soul as we travel towards our destiny; advancements is continuously made by those who dared to fail time and time again."

Pap paused for a brief moment before answering. "You're right, mistakes are neither black marks on a person's record nor indications of weakness. They are only an important part of the learning process."

Mary J promptly responded with a slow smile that crossed her face. Her eyes were misty as she looked at her husband. "Let's stick to our old formula, don't ever look backward unless we are going that way."

Pap laughed with delight. "Now it's time to put on our selling shoes. It's time to start building your new store. For far too long, so many people want to have their cake and eat it, too. People want the pleasures of one choice and the consequences of the other. They are constantly looking for opportunities in hindsight. They cannot hope to get the roof on if they haven't constructed the foundation."

Unable to resist smiling, Mary J stared at Pap as if the sky cheered above their heads. "No matter what people say, if we don't try at all, we will never know. I believe that the person who finds the opportunity is the person who develops his or her ability to see it. The problem is that many people spend their lives trying to figure out a way to beat the system. When it doesn't work their way, they often blame luck, fate, or someone else for their failure."

That's right, said Pap, "God has provided an abundance of opportunities all around us. All the waters run into the sea, yet the seas are not full. The earth's oceans are alive with marine creatures of every description—."

Mary J shouted. "And who can number the grains of sand on the beach?"

"—that's right," said Pap, "We must see the rose while it's still a seed."

Mary J stood facing Pap, jumping up and down. "Yes, Pap, we must see the spark while it is still in the flint, so that we will do it." She put her hand in his, "thank you!" Mary J felt as if she had scored the triumph of her life.

Pap tasted the air and thought of finally fulfilling his wife's childhood dream of being a store owner. Sitting still at the kitchen table, he foresaw real challenges and sacrifices ahead of them. Pap said thoughtfully to Mary J, "our little businesses need to make a lot of profit to build a new store." Scratching his head, "we have the money to start the foundation right here on the table, but what about the rest?

Mary J felt as if she had scored the triumph of her life; her spirit began to rise. She then put her hand in his. "Thank you; we must turn our disadvantages into advantages—our stumbling blocks into steppingstones."

On his way out of the front door, Pap, looking back, said quietly: "But now, here's the simple, straightforward confession. One thing is for certain; we don't have all the money. We have one chance—we are going to take it. There is only one way for us to avoid shipwreck—we must become one team. If we go underwater with this deal—drowning is a real possibility."

Everything in Mary J's soul cried out. She looked at Pap with a stonily determined face as he opened the door. "Pap, don't panic. We must rejoice, mourn, labor, and suffer together. We shall find out that the God of Israel is among us as the Good Book tell us: We will be like a small town upon a hill; the eyes of all the people in our community will be upon us. We will deal justly with them, show mercy toward the poor, be a friend to the fatherless, and care for the elderly. This is the true spirit of living in community with our neighbors and friends. We must be linked together into one destiny as a single garment. Just like a tree, we must all grow together in a spirit of harmony."

Pap laughed as he shut the door behind him. He was now bombarded from all sides by demands on his time. His attention could quickly become unclear in the urgency of tomorrow's affairs. The potential for failure was his continuous companion. The eye of reason was hovering over his mind. His traditional matrimonial views called for the husband to work, but like his cousin Luke, he wasn't going to fight about his wife going to work as an entrepreneur.

The commitment to building a new store was a great business decision that caused Mary J to wrestle with her fears. She realized that fighting shadows wouldn't help overcome obstacles and roadblocks that stand in achievement. Suddenly she felt weakly—her mind forcing panic away—her movements were so slow that she made no sounds. She looked eagerly out of the window towards the store site. She kept thinking; *my family has every right to participate in the American dream. We must make the most of our nation's opportunities.*

GRAND OPENING CELEBRATION

Mary J understood how hard it was for a woman to control anything outside of her home. She could readily admit that the two most important roles for women were housewives and mothers. She had to protect her mind from negative overkill by not finding ways to push unpleasant thoughts into her mind. She could neither accept the idea that her husband was the only breadwinner nor any role only designed to contribute unpaid work and services. She believed that a store was her single pathway towards greater participation in the business world. She refused to dwell on emotional conflicts that divided labor along gender lines.

As time passed by, Mary J felt the pain of building a new store from the ground up. She wanted to move faster than the slow pace they were crawling with cash payments. She kept thinking that her dream for a new store must be indestructible, just like an atom. Pap and his workers could change things, modify them, or alter them, but they could never destroy the heart of the matter. In Mary J's mind, she had the right to dream; Mary J knew what she truly wanted—she was willing to pay the price.

The children came along as regularly as the years. Bearing two more children, Susan Lennie and Lee Thomas didn't hold her back too much;

she allowed four weeks of downtime between births. Cindy always helped with the cooking, cleaning, and washing the clothes. All around her house were flowers and plants turning their faces to follow the sun inside and out.

Mary J would frequently stare at the wind chimes hanging on her kitchen wall. The idea of building a new store sometimes produced many motivation blocks, especially when negative thinking and attitudes showed up. This prompted her many times to recall Citole's forecasting message—'your store will be built right beside this house.' So, whenever Mary J looked at the wind chimes, it was a powerful reminder of Citole's words and expressions. Days and months after Citole's death, Mary J could still mentally hear and feel her chilling message, mainly, when she walked past her picture on the living room mantel, staring into eyes that seemed to stare back.

Mary J regularly witnessed the new store construction progress from her kitchen window. She enjoyed watching the various stages of the building process, especially as walls began to close up with insulation. She looked forward to the day when the store drywall would be sanded and primed for paint. Her imagination drifting—struggling to be reassured—hoping for the best possible outcome.

When Pap was away from the building site, Mary J would be out there fussing with the workers, mostly regarding the rubbish tossed in her front yard. In her mind, the real problem wasn't managing the resources but the people. The workers never got mad because at noontime, alone with Cindy, she always brought them a hot lunch. During lunch, the workers would be making little jokes about Mary J's fussing; at same time, wringing out the last bit of fun.

The grand opening day for the new store was indeed a special event—bursting with excitement for the entire family. There was a storefront banner with gallant gold leaf letters: Pap and Mary J's Community Store—stretching across the front entrance. Directly under it, a white banner with black letters. It was hard-pressed across with the reason: Grand Opening.

The store was three times the size of Mary J's Aunt Loretta's store during her childhood. The stock was fresher and more diverse with lots of variety; neatly labeled wooden shelves filled with product choices from the walls to the center floor, not far from the big potbellied stove in the center. A fresh meat butcher center—grinding and cutting raw meat as ordered—right in front of the customer's eyes. There were large boxes and glass jars that stood temptingly on the front counters—packed with candy and cookies. All the signs of a well-run store were there, including the smell of fresh paint.

Mary J's heart leaped with joy as she spoke like a rushing river— longing to accept the gratification of Citole's words as she greeted each customer individually. She couldn't help but think at the end of her first day: My Lord! Citole was so right about my family's store being built beside the house. God has used his angels to help work out my destiny according to His perfect will—and in that, I will rejoice! My childhood's dream store is now a reality. The Lord has made it happen for me by lighting an unquenchable flame.

All the next day, Mary J still had a smile on her face. Her private life laced throughout with her new business. She felt inside a compelling urge and ambition to make her way in this world positively, with a strong desire to help others along the way. Mary J danced around the store as if she was a little girl again; yet, all she owned in this world was now her family store. At the same time, she could hardly believe her new reality. Even her friends and relatives had no idea that she would become the luster of her small business community.

Mary J shook her head, while deep excitement lurched within her. She kept seeing her business Motto in the light of her mind: Friendliness creates miracles.

When customers came into Mary J's store, she was there to greet them. "Good Morning…would you like a tour of our store?"

"I sure would," said the first customer of the morning.

Mary J was standing at the sales counter, facing the front entrance. She began the tour by showing the customer how reasonable her prices were on various items. When a customer arrived at the meat counter, Willie was there to help out. "Would you like to taste some of our fresh-cut rag bologna?"

"Oh sure," said the customer as she reached out her hand.

Willie responded quickly, as though she had only been waiting for an opportunity. "Here you go!"

"Oh, that is so delicious," said the customer. "Please give me a pound; I just want to taste another little bite, thank you."

There were two other men behind the meat counter huddled over a piece of equipment. They said to each other, "Here comes the boss: Mary J."

One of the men said, "She is prone to be fussy, touchy, and stubborn when things aren't to her liking."

The other man put things into a proper perspective. "When a person puts all their money into a business, terror is their constant companion. If you don't believe me, the next time you meet a new entrepreneur, big or small, young or old, female or male, ask: So, how are you coping with terror? You will probably get a look of surprise or even shock."

Suddenly a shadow filled the meat counter entrance. There stood Mary J watching the men tinkering with the meat slicer. "What's the Matter?"

After a moment, one of the men muttered: "we were just adjusting the thickness on the meat slicer blade. This way, your customers will be happy with their service."

Mary J looked at the equipment, cleared her throat: "Good idea, keep up the good work!"

The men breathed a sigh of relief, knowing how much she loved to fuss at various times. They began to smile companionably at one another— each of them thanking God that nothing went wrong. There were even sounds of laughter, followed by soft singing.

As Mary J led one of her customers back towards the sales counter, the customer commented: "You have a well-run store... with reasonable prices, competent workers, and warm and friendly service. It's so clean and fresh in here! I am delighted to have your business in our community."

Mary J didn't laugh or joke about this weighty subject. She explained: "This is a community business—set-up to address the challenges we face together. My family is held responsible for this community, with our profits reinvested right back here. Just think of us, as a friend of the family. Thank you so much for coming to support our grand opening this week!"

Out of the blue, Lorraine burst through the side door, almost out of breath, "Mary J, let me handle these customers so you can take a break and talk to your friends."

Mary J smiled, then introduced Lorraine as her sister. She then added: "You see, we believe that our community is an exceptional place. This store has a lounge area near the front corner windows, so that we can exchange ideas. Great communities can't exist successfully without a means of communication. We must have ways of connecting to produce a beloved community."

"Well, good luck with your new store," said one of the customers. "I will be getting my grocery right here from you and your husband. I think that I have learned a great deal about your store. You are certainly right; a community should be a place where people live, work, and have fun together. Every improvement in communication makes it possible for a more effective way of living with each other. You and Pap are definitely during a double share, increasing mutual understanding and goodwill."

Lorraine said to Mary J, after the customers left the store. "You have been here working so hard; you are tired, so sit down and have yourself a Coca-Cola."

For a new business, there was a steady flow of customers. Mary J had no chance to analyze her practical assessment of things. *There were successes,* she thought, *but unfortunately, there were failures that could have been successes.* All the time, Mary J was planning her next move. Like a snake, charming a chicken, she felt her customers' feelings, apprehensions, and annoyances.

Mary J's eyes widened as she stared at her sister for a long moment. Then to Lorraine's surprise after clearing her throat, she said, "You're probably right."

Lorraine shook her head, "Lord, if it ain't your brother-in-law: Fred Fisher."

Mary J grabbed Lorraine's arm as he got closer to the store entrance. "Do you think he has been drinking?"

Lorraine's eyes flickered, "wait, and let me see."

Before Lorraine could answer the question, Fred walked through the front door. "Where is my sister-in-law?"

Mary J was almost shaking with anxiety. A million thoughts rushed through her mind, but several seemed to flash urgently in red colors—demanding an instant answer. Has Fred been drinking, and if so—how much?

Mary J quickly pulled herself together. "Fred, please come over here and sit down; so, I can keep my eyes on you."

Fred walks in with a smile on his face: "Do you know who my favorite Sister-in-law is?"

Mary J said: "My brother in law, Why don't you tell me?"

"The lady's name is Mary J. Do you know her?"

The stunned look on Mary J's face told Lorraine that she was getting the picture. Mary J shifted her body, cleared her throat, and commenced rubbing one side of her nose. "Ok, now Fred, you just sit over here and be nice why I take care of my customers."

"Well," Fred said. "I am a customer too. Today's first order is that your sweet little sister gets anything she wants in your new store."

Lorraine hesitated for a moment. "Alright, Fred, I will get it later."

Larraine recalling her Grandma Mag's golden words of wisdom: 'Treat everyone with equal kindness and respect.' Mag's wise words caused Lorraine to begin thinking about Fred's psychological health. She felt that if it had not been for Fred's weekend drinking, he would socially be a shy fellow. She kept thinking that his mother Rachel, allowed him to overindulge in a way that she had never permitted her other children. Lorraine believed that Rachel had molded him into being an avoider, by always shielding him from personal risk and responsibilities. She thought that Fred was probably intimidated by his mother's silent signals of fear and pessimism.

Fred, now feeling exceptionally cheerful, looks towards Lorraine: "I haven't the slightest idea of how much I drank—but I tell you what Sis, please bring me a can of corn beef, some crackers, and a Pepsi- Cola. I may be somewhat tipsy but not drunk."

Lorraine brought Fred all the items he requested; then, she started helping Mary J and Willie with the other customers. The store stayed busy for the rest of the day. Fred talked to everybody that came into the front doors, showing all the children how to pick up a Pepsi-Coca bottle between his thumb and middle finger.

By the time Pap returned home, Fred's reasoning was now tingling; he had been sipping whiskey out of a bottle behind the store. His helplessness was coming on so rapidly that his reeling thoughts began changing quickly, jumping from one issue to another. He gave such confusing information about his preferences to customers that they couldn't pin down a complete thought.

All of a sudden, it was now only friendship that was important to him. He wanted to share something with everybody that passed through the store. As Fred's eyes searched the store,, Pap walked through the backdoor. He said out loud, "My brother, get anything you want, I am buying tonight. Also, now, if you want—we can go on the back of the store for something a little stronger."

With her puzzling blend of many emotions, Mary J said to her husband with warmth and coolness. "Please give my wonderful brother-in-law a ride home. He has done enough exploring and tinkering for one day."

Pap appreciated the extra sensitivity that his wife had for his baby brother. Mary J always recognized Fred's bitter soul that had crippled him emotionally from accepting positive feedback, which was still clouded by pessimism.

Pap began laughing in agreement with Mary J's conclusion. "Come on, my brother, let's go home."

Fred smiled companionably at him. "I believe that you are a scientist that needs to get your feet wet. But this time, your observation and prediction are right on with the exact conclusion. It's time for me to go home. I have completed my ultimate experiment for today."

Pap grabbed Fred's hands in a desperate grip. "You are a true example of a time competent person—living fully in the present—free from any rigid inner values that need to conform to social prescriptions. Come on, let me take you home."

The pain in Fred's eyes was suddenly anxious as the shadow of whiskey commenced overwhelming him. "Fine, fine, you are receiving the right message. I need to go home."

Fred and Pap locked arms going out of the front door. They both got into the truck and went smoothly out of sight. Mary J and Lorraine laughed at them, knowing Pap was doing all he could, not to attack his brother's character.

In a few seconds, Lorraine had thought it all out. "Well, I guess that one of the great rules of life is not to judge others' conduct. You know, it's nice to live in a community where people have a caring attitude towards each other."

Mary J agreed. "We must give the other fellow a chance, and they must give us a chance."

Mary J's community business started to prosper because of several factors. One primary reason was the new military base that had just opened its doors. It created many new job opportunities as well as added a considerable number of military customers. Because of the military base, Mary J's community and surrounding areas went from a few hundred people to several thousands .

The newly formed International Longshoremen's Association also created many full and part-time jobs for the community. The Longshoremen's Association was a local union of maritime workers. They loaded cargo from the dock onto and from incoming ships. Because they only worked when ships came into the port to load or unload, Pap was able to join and become a member. Sometimes, members would regularly work; other times, a few weeks would pass by before the next ship. Some of Mary J's best customers were longshoremen. They were always in and out of her store.

Shady View Beach was five miles pass Mary J's store; busloads of people came to Shady View Beach throughout the summer. They would always stop at Mary J's store on their way to and from the beach. The store would be pack with people from the beach traffic. There were also several nightclubs surrounding Mary J's store and home: Luke's Corner night club, Blue Bird Inn, Boone pool Hall and Dallas night club. If you wanted good food, one could count on Della's café right in the middle of all the entertainment. All of these businesses, except the Blue Bird Inn, were across from each other at the Corner intersection. On Friday and Saturday nights, these places would be packed with people. Cars were parked not only in their parking lots but also overflowed alongside the highway almost to Mary J's store. These surrounding businesses were significant traffic generators for Pap and Mary J's community store.

Moonshine was also a booming business in these parts for many years. It continued throughout World War II and beyond... well into the 50s and 60s. Moonshine production was a way for small farmers to help take care of their families by manufacturing excess yields of their crops into corn whiskey. It required a two-step process of fermentation and distillation; corn and sugar were crucial ingredients for its production. Large shipments of sugar were sold regularly through Mary J's store, supplying dozens of moonshine operations scattered among the nearby woods, and on the banks of creeks.

Mary J's store also profited from keeping moonshiners' money in her large iron safe. She would just give them a cigar box with their name on it. They could come and audit their cigar box of money anytime. At their request, Mary J would take their cigar box out of her safe; so, they may complete their withdrawal or deposit. Banking accommodation was a real benefit considering that many moonshiners buried their money in mason jars, in heavily wooded areas. Many times, their buried money was never found after the moonshiner's death or a severe sickness. They also feared being robbed when away from their buried money.

THE COMMUNITY STORE

People came to Mary J's community store for retail goods, charity, friendship, longshoremen's work schedules, socialization, and entertainment. They were always in and out until closing time. People love to discuss the issues of the day while children played in her front yard, older people sat on the porch. As people came and went, Mary J always watched the motions of the muscles in their faces. She believed that facial expressions were a rich source of communication.

Despite overflowing love for her community, Mary J kept personal dreams close to her chest when dealing with negative people. She often wonders if they were allowing their minds to be programed with destructive thoughts. She would often walk up and down her store repeating to herself: *Negative thinking people are chasing away their dreams; only if my little words could help them. Why can't they evaluate and face up to their problems?*

There was no fog this particular morning. The weather turned out to be a bright and sunny day with high wisps of clouds in the sky. The trees behind the store and house were motionless; silence was dominating the moment. Sitting along in her store, Mary J began muttering busily to herself. The silence was more profound than she had ever heard it—no chattering voices of customers or family, not even a dog barking.

Mary J had been engaging herself in a nonstop whirlwind of activities—long hours—rushing around like a crazy animal—yet, working quietly—letting success do the talking. She was feeling somewhat overwhelmed and a little scattered with a lot on her mind. Without much effort, she began carving out time to reflect on her journey as a store owner. She felt just as shrewd, hard-headed, calculating, and adventuresome as any other business owner. But in Mary J's mind, there was one main difference, she saw failures as learning something new—signs of taking a risk—moving towards the goal. This attitude allowed her to remove the failure and success labels that seemed to attract negative emotions.

Mary J began thinking about some of her family's most disturbing moments. The kind of moments that most people would rather forget. She could see picture Pap telling her, 'The quickest way to derail a dream is to quit when things look bleak: nothing in this world can take the place of persistence—not even being a genius with talent and education can energize a person's life without determination.' Mary J could see her husband shaking his head: 'Persistence and determination along are unstoppable.' She quickly understood the message: without struggles and hard work, there's no genuine progress.

Mary J continued to sit quietly without touching the back of her chair, hands in her lap. She thought about family routines from earlier times. She could feel her family working tirelessly in the trenches together. Each member of her family going individually to eat what she had fixed for breakfast, lunch, and dinner. After their meals, they would return to the store so others could enjoy a bite to eat. As her children grew older, they would many times take their friends inside to eat with them. If there was nothing in the house they liked to eat, they could pick out other choices from the grocery shelves.

Mary J hesitated in her thoughts; there was compassion in her eyes. Next, she began reflecting on how Pap usually opened the store early in the morning between 6 and 7:00 a.m. After breakfast, she would manage the store until Pap returned around 6 p.m. After dinner, the entire family would stay in the store together, working, and entertaining friends. As one family member came into the store, another person could take a break or go to the house for a few minutes. The whole family would share in working the store together until closing time, 10 or 11p.m.

On Sunday, Pap would stay in the store while she went to church until 2 p.m. Mary J always went to church regularly. After her Sunday services, she would go to an evening church service or just visit her friends and relatives for a short while. Nevertheless, after her church services and visitations,, she always joined her family in the store till closing time.

Mary J looked up, and up, and up as she felt her way through various parts of her life's journey. Shebegan thinking about how television first came to North Carolina during the late 1940s and early 50s. Shaking her head—thinking, smiling faintly: *Of course, as one may guess, many folks came several times weekly from the local community to watch their favorite TV shows with my family. They would sit in the store lounge—near the sales counter—enjoying their ideal refreshments.* Now laughing at the thought, *she had no television in her home for many years,, only in the store to share with the entire community. The poor, as well as self-sustaining members of our community, were all able to socialize together.* Tears flowed down her cheeks—thinking about how her store played a role in unifying the community.

Mary paused in the shadow of her thinking again. She smiled, knowing that, her community went from a vertical to mostly a horizontal social structure that produced an unbreakable bond, which strengthened and empowered the people into a single family. *A community*, she thought, *with high social integration that accentuated people as social beings rather than just individuals—anchored by local businesses and churches that help shape people's behavior, attitudes, and life chances. Crime almost unheard of—doors of homes left unlocked during the day—private troubles frequently becoming community news—the well to do and the poor habitually mingling together.*

In Mary J's community, there were two poor little boys—Henry James and the other known as Scale-Lee Bread. They came to play, work and, eat with Pap and Mary J's firstborn son: nicknamed Buddy. As one could imagine, Buddy having parents that owned a large community business during the 1950s, made him extremely popular. Henry James and Scale-Lee Bread admired Buddy's parents and strived to have a relationship with

211

his family. People in the community could hear them brag about how wonderful they were treated by the Fishers: "just like family."

When Pap took his children to work on his farm or to a movie theater, Henry James and Scale-Lee Bread would always jump on the back of the truck. Pap would just shake his head, then said, "Let them go."

Henry James, along with his Mother Havana, half-brother Theodore and his stepdad Current, lived next store in a one-bed-room house. Henry James could just jump across the ditch and be standing in the store parking lot. He had lost his left eye because his Stepfather Current hit him with some type of metal object across his head. Because of this, he always resented his Step-dad. In Henry James' mind, Buddy was his brother, Mary J, and Pap were his adopted parents. All the Fisher's children had work to do on the farm and the store, so Buddy could count on Henry James and Scale-Lee Bread to help out.

Scale-Lee Bread lived with his single mother, Khalily and grandmother Mathilda, along with several other brothers and sisters in a small one-bedroom house. Everybody called him Scale-Lee Bread because he was always begging for food. At home, he simply couldn't count on getting enough to eat. By Scale-Lee Bread coming to play with Buddy, he was guaranteed several tasty meals throughout the day.

Pap and Mary J had a passion for the poor as long as they didn't steal. They felt like everybody should share their food with poor struggling people. In their opinion, poor didn't mean forever stuck in poverty. Pap would regularly tell Mary J, jokingly, that even the nimble rabbit hops noiselessly into a vegetable garden, and then helps himself to the carrots.

During this particular Saturday morning, there was a wonderfully refreshing breeze blowing softly through the store's front door. Scale-Lee Bread's grandma, Mathilda, showed up while Mary J was cleaning up her store. She always had a big smile on her face, even if she didn't have a quarter to her name. With a long vowel sound, she called everybody: Sugar.

Mathilda said slowly, "Hey Sugar, have you seen my little grandson Scale-Lee Bread this Morning?"

Mary J's eyes became alert. "Let me think about it for a moment; I believe he jumped on the back of Pap's truck with Buddy. Most likely, they went down Fisher-Town to work on the farm."

"Oh, Sugar, I know you all must get tired of that boy. He loves coming up here so much."

"That's alright, Mathilda," said Mary J, "he's alright with my family."

"Lord, Sugar! We don't have a thing to eat this morning. Could I get a few things on credit?"

Mary J continued sweeping the floor. "You sure can get yourself a cart. If you need some fresh-cut meat—just let me know."

"Sugar," said Mathilda scratching her head, "you and Pap are like angels from heaven. We have been out of food now for three days. My other two grandsons, Charles Earl and Stink, got caught stealing from John Carter, but he let them go with a warning."

Mary J looked intently into her bright dark eyes; she could see that Mathilda was slightly desperate: "You just get enough food so they won't have to steal."

Mathilda wiping tears from her eyes: "Please cut me some ham, bacon, pork chops and, fatback." She steered her shopping cart down one aisle and up another until it was overflowing with food. Afterward, she took her cart to the sales counter so Mary J could add up all the items and charge her account.

Mary J grinned cheerfully at her. "Anything else!"

"Oh no, Sugar," Mathilda said. "When I get my little check next week. I will be here to pay you and your husband. You all are so good; may the Lord bless and keep both of you. Luke wouldn't trust me with a piece of bubble gum."

Mary J smiled as if she was reading Mathilda's thoughts and agreeing with them. "The Lord will make a way for us, especially if we trust in him. I know when I was just a child, I lost both of my parents. Just keep the faith, you'll make it."

Mathilda held up her arms with pride, displaying her slim silver chain through a single hole of a sand dollar pendant. "Sugar, this was my Mother's necklace. I wear it to remember her. She passed away many years ago, but I still miss her every day. We had the same eyes, you see. So, whenever I look into the mirror, I'm reminded of her. Losing a mother is always hard, especially when leaving behind little children."

Mary J was embarrassed to find tears flowing from her eyes, with a voice now filled with sadness, reminded of her parents' early deaths. Somehow, Mathilda's eyes were warm with understanding, inviting Mary J's confidence.

Mary J nodded, "We have a lot in common, it seems—"

"Oh, my goodness, Sugar! There goes Down Award with his mule and Cart. He will give me a ride home. I hope a car won't hit us before we get there. Lord, he probably can't see the road for his cigar smoke."

Mathilda's face quiet beneath the overshadowing brim of her elderly hat, went quickly to the front door, hollering for him to stop. "Hey... Down-A-ward, please stop, I need a ride."

Mary Sparrow, as usual, was sitting on her front porch. She hollered out to him, pointing towards the store. The side of the road had some ruts from recent rains, Down Award's wagon wheels pressed against a soft texture. He hurriedly paused for a moment, pulling over into the store's parking lot and went inside.

As Down Award was coming towards the store entrance, Mathilda walked quickly towards the sales counter. Hastily stepping over a small corrugated box, she paused and said as he entered: "Sugar, please take these groceries home for me in your mule and cart. Lord knows I am too old to be carrying all this stuff around."

"No problem," said Down Award, "Mary J, please give me a cigar. Just put it on the books till I come back for my groceries."

As Mary J gave him the cigar, Mathilda went to put her food inside of his cart. Down Award rushed back to his mule and cart—off they went—cars were passing at high speed. They almost got pushed into a ditch before leaving the store parking lot. Down Award just kept blowing out smoke from his cigar.

While showing signs of distress, Mathilda's face looked worried with pain; "Sugar, can you see through all that smoke?"

Down Award responded with a half-hearted smile, "I got this, Sugar!"

Mathilda swallowed, searching for her voice, she held up her hands, and said, "My Lord! Please help Sugar make it to my house."

STORE'S CREDIT

W hile standing behind her sales counter, Mary J pulled out a thick charge account book. People bought and bought; they paid and paid, from month to month and from time to time. Mary J's store credit accounts provided her customers with a unique title statement: Charge it, please! There were no fees or interest on these accounts. She gave out credit to anyone with a sad story. She shared her business resources with whoever needed food, drink, friendship, or clothing.

Mary J's compassionate actions were always in demand within her community. Being a child of the Great Depression, she saw the people of her community as an extension of her own family. Not surprisingly, sometimes, charge accounts produced hard feelings. There were times when Mary J wouldn't get paid and became stuck with the bill. Still, she saw credit like some of her houseplants that grew in the direction of darkness, then suddenly swapped strategies toward the light. In her opinion, they will come around at some point.

Pap had warned Mary J that credit was a losing proposition. He had no problem constructively helping the poor. If poor children were around his family during the day, he would put them to work on his farm. Sometimes, he would urge Mary J to let them help clean-up the store. The exception was the credit issue, which became a significant divide between them. Pap believed that a system built upon credit was an evil system. He felt charging interest on credit accounts was highway robbery.

On the other hand, extending credit as a whole was mostly a loss in profit. Pap's famous saying about credit: "You can't 'Squeeze Blood' out of a Turnip." The delicate question in his mind: "How Can I ever help my wife understand these matters?"

Mary J had been working in the store since the early morning. Lorraine came to give her a hand just as she put the charge account book back under the counter. As she looked up, Lorraine was coming through the side door.

They smiled companionably at one another. Then Mary said to her. "It is about time someone comes out to help me."

Lorraine looked at her sympathetically, then leaned over to whisper: "Oh, my sister! Pap is going to be mad about you charging all that merchandise."

Without waiting for Lorraine to question her further, Mary J spoke to her in a fussy voice. "Children and old folks are the heart of our community. I can't stand to see them hungry. You know how tough it was for our family. These people are not alcoholics or thieves but mostly church folks. We are just providing them a support system."

Laughing with a smile, Lorraine gave Mary J a light slap on her hand. "Oh, quit fussing at me, save it for Pap when he gets home. You know, these people must accept some type of responsibility for their own lives. You can't give people store credit on any terms. When they come in on Saturday morning, just start totaling up their account. You must demand these people pay their bills on time, from week to week. If they were lucky enough to get credit at Luke's store, he would surely demand his money each week. In some cases, Luke would ask for some collateral arrangements, like land. He had an old man, Elijah, put up his land against his loan when he couldn't pay; he just took his land away from him."

Mary J raised her eyebrows with a sidelong glance. "You are right, but I can't demand every Saturday morning that these people, who go to church with me, pay their whole bill. Just remember, some of this earth's smallest living creatures support their communities by helping and sharing."

216

Lorraine cleared her throat. "A wise flower gives as little nectar as necessary to attract a pollinator, but now, some of your customers are worse than bees. They are hummingbird pollinators—your store is their flower."

Mary J surprised her sister by smiling. "A pollinator moves around pollen to accomplish fertilization, so that plants can make fruit and seeds. As children of the Great Depression, our family moved pollen around to uplift their community. During those times, no-one called a repairman or a plumber. Our parents exchanged favors for their needs, made clothes out of flour sacks for each other, baked bread, and raised a garden for vegetables to share with friends and neighbors. When a person gives correctly, it comes back in a thousand ways."

Lorraine tasted salt on her lips. She suddenly realized that tears were flowing from her eyes. "Look at me; you and Pap raised me from a child. The only parents I have ever known. Just look at little Scale-Lee Bread and Henry James; you feed them like family—plus give their parents credit until they are able to pay. Maybe that why Pap is so lucky; look at how careless he goes about making whiskey in the woods. He will ride down the street with half of his ingredients uncovered on the back of his truck, but nobody bothers him. Just look at the farm, his rows of crops are usually crooked, but somehow, he reaps an abundant harvest. As you say, it comes back in a thousand ways."

Mary J watched her baby sister shed tears of appreciation over their journey together. She paused for a brief moment before answering her. "Perhaps most importantly, our Christian's faith provides us a sense of purpose—a feeling that life is in the end, meaningful. There should be no need for special projects to feed the hungry in our midst. Sharing with the poor should be as natural as drinking water."

Lorraine stared at her, "without a doubt; you have a sympathetic heart that requires a response to reaching people desperately in need. Somehow, this works like a charm for you—even the meanest people in this community respects your generosity." She paused and added in a falling tone: "It doesn't matter how much you fuss, there is never a sassy word in return from anybody—even the local drunks respect you. Little Henry James will walk right into this store—with a crowd of people standing around—he will look directly at you and then said to the crowd:

'This's my Mama, right here!' Scale-Lee Bread will brag to this whole community how you and Pap treat him just like family."

Mary J chuckled and lowered her voice. "Trust is essential for a community to grow and develop. If we create a climate of trust, we can reduce our own and other people's fears of betrayal and rejection. Of course, trust involves risk, but without it, trying to live together in a community would be unimaginable. My sweetheart, trust in a community, is like sunlight; without it—our hearts would be cold—happiness together would eventually die. I am in a situation where a choice to trust on credit can lead to harmful consequences for my family. Nevertheless, it still makes chills run up and down my spine to see hungry families with small children. Especially when I know there are continuous economic hardships threatening them."

Lorraine paused to consider her statement. "I see when you trust others; most of the time, you will gain more than you will suffer. But I tell you the truth, my sister, some of the people in this community aren't trustworthy. When Pap says no, you still feel compelled to help them. Even though some of these people are like birds that disappear every fall, reappear in the spring. In the meantime, their credit issues cause you and your husband a lot of sleepless nights."

Mary J's eyes widened somewhat curiously. She then tried desperately to ignore her credit failures. "I have enough work discussion for one evening. I can't make predictions. I am going into the house for a while to help Cindy start dinner."

Mary J began to move indecisively towards the side door. Her steps dragged as she walked towards the house. It was as if the heaviness of her heart had traveled to her feet. She felt very much alone. She dreaded telling Pap about her customer's debt levels. Mary J wasn't expecting any understanding or compassion from him; but she was always hoping that Pap might shine a larger light on her chosen path.

The next morning, Mary J awakened from an edgy sleep; she went into the kitchen to prepare breakfast. Her eyes were understanding but somehow wounded from Pap's denunciation on the store's charge account activities. From Pap's point of view, Mary J's kind-heartedness had created a loss in working capital. This meant that profits from his whiskey and farm operations were now needed to keep the store profitable.

Pap hid his smile while sitting at the kitchen table without raising his eyes. "Our profit margins are getting a little bit thin from the store's charge account activities."

As Mary J continued walking towards the cookstove, she responded sarcastically in a quarrelsome mood. "Why don't you ask your buddy Luke to help feed some of these poor folks in our community?"

"The devil with Luke," said Pap, "we just need to run our businesses. I know Luke is not going to help people that cannot pay him. He believes in the adage that 'It takes money to make money.' The idea of needing money to make money is especially true for folks like us who started with little or no money. I understand your compassion to help the poor in our community, but your approach is my problem. We must select customers that are most likely to pay their bills. Most importantly, we must decide how much credit to extend each customer. For most people, our terms are from week to week. Now I will admit, people like John Thomas are the exception. He regularly pumps gas for our customers."

Mary J felt a yank somewhere near her heart as if she was pulling the ocean. She smiled at him warmly, her eyes misty. "Pap, these people are the working poor. Their earnings are not high enough to lift themselves out of poverty. These poor workers have extremely little space for slipups, misfortunes, or financial changes. Understanding the working poor is simple; they neither have the family advantages nor the resources. Balance sheets only reveal the past, not the future."

"Yes," said Pap, "that's true, but these people are not homeless or without vegetable gardens. They also have family, relatives, and other social networks to provide support. I know, some of these hardworking people are struggling with alcoholism, depression, and family problems."

Mary J was fighting mad about Pap questioning her credit choices; she began going off into one of her fussing panache. "We cannot set outright conditions upon helping the poor in our community. People who are kind to the poor makes loans to the Lord."

"Those who have nothing may be just as greedy for things as the well-to-do," explained Pap. "If someone tells you that you eat like a bird, the implication is that you don't eat much. Yet, for their body weight, birds eat a lot. Let's get down to the heart of this matter. I think that some of these people want a share of our profit, without any capital investment."

Mary J gave a wary glance over the kitchen table towards her husband. "Pap, like other creatures of the earth, we are made to live in the community. Animals feed on the energy stored up into plant parts. Zebras tap into that energy when nibbling on grass, and lions tap into it when they're nibbling on zebras. All creatures living in the same area normally make up a community. We need to help others to help ourselves. It is part of living in a community."

"Human nature doesn't change that much, Mary J," said Pap. "People feel happier when the sun is shining than when it's raining. People want peace and sometimes fight wars. They even create delicate works of art and then commit violent acts." Suddenly, Pap raises his hands in the air as he was walking out of the front door. He looked back at Mary J, then said, "I'm through with it."

As Pap was walking out of his house's front door, James Miller drove up in Harry Taylor's Grain Truck. "Hey Pap," said James Miller, "I'm getting ready to go down your mother's place to take your farm crop to the market."

Pap walks over to the truck, "have you had breakfast yet? If not, Mary J is in the kitchen. I will go down and get everything ready for the market while you eat something."

"Well," said James Miller, "is Mary J in a good mood?"

"Maybe not," said Pap, "I am bring money in the front door as she gives it out through the backdoor."

"Now! I clear the kingdom; you are right, Pap!" said James Miller with a mouth filled with laughter. "I know some of our people over the Creek, even right here in this community—ain't going to pay you and your wife."

"Ok," said Pap. "Just go on-in there and eat breakfast, maybe you can talk some sense into your first cousin."

"Alright, Pap, I will be down there within the hour."

James got out of the truck, knock on the back door, and then hollered, "hey in here."

Mary J insisted with one hand on her hip as she held the other one towards him: "just come on in." She then gave him a sunny smile.

"Pap said you got some good breakfast ready."

"I sure do; come on in here and take a seat at the table."

As James was sitting down, he said, "What's wrong with Pap this morning?"

"He thinks I'm giving away too much credit to my community, but if we don't help these poor folks, who will?"

Mary J passed James Miller a plate so he could serve himself from the food on the table. He was really quiet for a minute or so while he drank in her words. James Miller began gobbling up the bacon, grits, and eggs. As he grabbed for another one of Cindy's buttermilk biscuit, he said, "I clear the kingdom, I know you're right, whatever the situation."

Mary J fixed James Miller another cup of coffee with some fruit pie. She continued her conversation. "Look at all the help we got from Grandma Mag and others along the way, especially after my parent's death."

James Miller being highly sensitive towards her feelings. He completed his breakfast, and grabbed his hat, and then said with a long stretch: "Now, I clear the kingdom Mary J... you're right this morning! I got to meet your husband. We should be back from the market by dinner time. By the way, the food was good!" He then rushed out of the back door to his truck, jumped in, and drove away.

Mary J picked up her untouched coffee, only to find it had grown cold. She couldn't help thinking how disappointed her husband continued to be over her previous credit decisions. She felt Lorraine had made a valid point, but she didn't have the heart to demand total weekly payments or else. Although naturally fussy, Mary J had a way of establishing warm, personal, and trustworthy relationships. She knew how to interact with other people by reflecting a caring and compassionate attitude, especially during difficult times. She assumed that if she refused to give credit, there would be neither profit nor loss. In Mary J's mind, it would be better to get paid eventually—rather than not at all.

Mary J's business had given her wings. She didn't want to create any unnecessary walls with her husband. She tried to stay free to follow her heart. She began re-thinking how Pap had been working so hard to make up the store's financial losses. She started tasting salt on her lips as tears flowed around her eyes. No one could see her heart pounding; she forced herself to breathe slowly. Her medicine was bitter; she kept thinking that there is a need to seek a light within the human heart.

The sun was reflecting off the kitchen window, sparkling like uncovered treasures. Mary J's heart had been elevated from the ground, casting its dust in the atmosphere. Out of the blue, an idea came into her mind. She knew what to do to lift her husband's spirit. She would fix Pap's favorite meal of raccoon, sweet potatoes, and cornbread to share with his friends.

Chapter 26

THE BIG DINNER

E arly the next morning, after cleaning and restocking her store shelves, Mary J left Lorraine to run the store. She went to get fresh vegetables out of the family's garden. While walking outside the side door, she bitterly asked herself if customers would ever learn to pay their bills on time. She wanted desperately to believe in the purity of a person's word, but somehow, fate seemed to be working against her. With a smile and uplifted hands, she stood prayerfully in front of the garden for several minutes—grappling with the problem of organizing a brand of community that could produce a network of friendships—developing a real sense of community.

Cindy started making preparations for cooking the garden vegetables by cleaning the kitchen utensils, chopping boards, and countertops. She couldn't help noticing Mary J through the kitchen window. Cindy had a natural gift of intuition, yet she couldn't understand what made Mary J somewhat miserable on such a lovely day. She kept roaming restlessly around the kitchen table—thinking that Mary J's earthy vigor and robust attitude spoke to the deepest and best part of her nature.

Mary J unexpectedly walked through the back door, loaded with all types of fresh garden vegetables. She was eager to start cooking her husband's big dinner. Without a word—together, they began selecting recipes, dicing up garlic, cutting onions into thin slices, and chopping veggies. They also started boiling the raccoon in lightly salted water until tender—afterward, placing bite-size pieces into a large baking pan. Now ready for the oven, they put sweet potatoes around the meat and then season it to Pap's favorite flavor.

As time went by, Cindy said sweetly: "Mary J, you are my wonderful friend—life is too short to worry needlessly. Sometimes it's best to sit back a little; let the situation work out its kinks. When life isn't fair, please don't dwell on it. Move on. Ask yourself, will this matter tomorrow?"

Mary J was looking like a poor little lamb profoundly hurt. She smiled up at Cindy and said, somewhat absently: "Yes, of course, I'll think about that another time."

Cindy waited a minute in the silence of the kitchen, trying to get her words straight before bring them out. "The best way to survive and enjoy life is to put things in proper perspective. Your faith must be stronger than your fears."

With burning eyes, Cindy gazed for a long moment at the pots on the stove. Because Mary J appeared unconcern about the subject, Cindy thrust her shoulders back and started cooking vegetables.

Mary J stopped abruptly and stared in amazement at her: "what in the world are you doing?"

Cindy laughed while picking up another Pot: "I am getting ready for your husband's party. Now, you stop biting the hand that feeds you."

Mary J laughed this time with her: "If that's the case, I don't think I need that little bit of food."

"Well," said Cindy, "I think Pap is spoiling his family. All of you got to learn how things are sometimes."

"Maybe so," said Mary J, "but that doesn't mean we have to accept them, maybe we won't either. You need to be worrying about your John Thomas, where ever he is."

Cindy, finding nothing else to say, turned imperiously and headed for the pantry. She was thrilled that Mary J was back to her old self again—fussing everybody out.

Pap returned home shortly after dark from a long day on his farm. He had planned to work in the store till closing time. As he toiled in the store, Pap enjoyed mingling with the hard-working, salt-of-the-earth type people. After all, he'd grown up dirt poor and earned every penny he ever made. He was known as a man you could trust; when he gave his word, it was as good as gold.

All of Pap's friends had been gathering within the store for his big dinner. They were smiling companionably, thrilled, socializing, and talking about business, farming, and politics. After Mary J announced that dinner was ready, Pap would escort small groups from the store to the house, sharing his special meal. Luke, James miller, Cleveland, and Oscar were among the first group of arrivals. Of course, there was a bottle of Pap's whiskey in the pantry to share with a select few.

After dinner, everybody returned to the store. Luke lit one of his cigars and blew out a little smoke from the side of his mouth. The smoke particles came off the end of the cigar as white smoke came out of his mouth. Suddenly, he gave Pap a fiery look, banged both fists down hard on a side table. "Pap, you need to let my son Walter Dennis bring you two pool tables and a jukebox. This way, you will have a grocery business, gas, games, music, and dancing. In a small community, well, you need to have it all to be prosperous."

James Miller was holding a soft drink in his right hand. He appeared to be very much amused by Luke's money-making schemes. His eyes were heavy and motionless like his hands, then he spoke abruptly, "I Clear the kingdom Pap, he sounds right to me. But, of course, as they say, 'the proof is in the pudding.'"

Cleveland grinned at the group sociably, shook his head, and then moved his chin several times through the opened air. "You surely have space on the other side of this store to grow your business. People want more than just food, clothing, and shelter, which are the conditions of mere existence. As Luke suggested, the general public wants a whole host of things: companionship, music, and, plenty of activity. If you can supply this, you got to make money."

Oscar lit a cigarette and strolled idly towards the storefront window that overlooked the gas tanks. Everything around him was still for a moment, except the subsonic suggestions of Pap's friends and honorary board members. They were sitting in a circle to see and hear each other fully. Oscar owned a funeral home; therefore, his association with the business community was a critical part of his marketing strategy. Oscars wiped his lips again, and then looked at his handkerchief as if he expected to find blood. He drew his thick black eyebrows close together, fingered the right side of his weather-beaten nose, and re-approached the group again.

"Well Pap," said Oscar, "my brother Willie runs a beach several miles down the road from here. His buses, with loads of people, pass-by your store just about every day during the summer. A business needs new products and services to attract new customers. As an entrepreneur, there should be only one consuming obsession: to grow your business. From my point of view, Luke probably got a good idea."

Luke burst into laughter, being very much amused by their support. "It's all fixed; we will work together. This way, we can keep all the businesses in Harlowe between Pap's family, Della Café, and my businesses. Of course, Willie has the beach during the summer months; Oscar will get all the funeral business. We should keep in mind that the opinions of others have a great deal to do with determining what we do—most people like to follow the crowd."

James Miller's hands flew to his belly. "I clear the kingdom Pap; this sounds good to me. We all know that Mary J can handle it—without any extra help. The men can play music and games while their wives and children shop for groceries."

"Pap, if you don't mind me saying so." Cleveland went on, "I think you need to do something with that open space. The key to the whole thing is management. Now James said that Mary J could handle it—this way, you can spend most of your time doing other things. Who would know better than him? Mary J and James Miller grew up together with the same grandmother."

Pap stared at them with substantial optimism. "My friends, I heard your voices deep down in the chamber of my soul. A fair judgement must fit the facts, as determine by someone observation. I am willing to test the accuracy of your conclusions. Mary J and I will add a jukebox section with top musical selections and pool tables. This way, people will be able to socialize and dance while other family members are buying groceries.

Day in and day out, my little family works at building our store business. Even though it's physically exhausting to us, we truly want to serve our community."

Cleveland shook his head sharply. His cigarette jerked as he dropped ashes on his shirt. He looked back at Pap, then began pinching his cigarette between his fingers, with a sort of twitch. His hand seemed to be shaking a little, but his face was still smooth. He nodded. "Oh well, I agree, you will never know unless you try. Life is like seasons always changing; our community must grow so we can make opportunities easier for others."

James Miller's mouth twisted into a smile. A person must never, never give up on ideas for improvements. A business person must take advantage of their opportunities; it's the only true mark of birth pangs. Each of us knows the bitterness of a missed opportunity; it has the thorniest taste. I think Luke has a good point."

Oscar shook his head slowly, methodically, rigidly unemotional—then he shook it again as if clearing it of sleep. He rubbed his eyes and a smile broke across his face. "I believe that passionate workers strive in the context of a calling, which includes unbelievably risk. We must ride on these ocean currents when they come our way. Our fears tell us, there is danger, be alert to it, examine it, evaluate it, and act upon it. In other words, do something about it!"

Pap snapped his teeth and waved a brown paper bag while his confidence was oozing in his spirit. He had a friendly smile. "What a person does today may seem strange years down the road, but my family needs to spread their wings. My deepest appreciation to all of you who have generously contributed your time and expertise. Mary J and I have been extremely fortunate to share true friendships with our community leaders."

"That sounds mighty nice," Cleveland said. "Many times, if we listen, we will hear a lot of useful things from others. Before us lies the ocean of endless possibilities. But now, people have to work sensibly together if they truly want to contribute something of value."

Oscar gave a hard look as his voice lowered. "New minds can bring fresh air and light into a business previously shut off from a wider horizon. There must be some rays of light to inspire an entrepreneurial journey."

"Now… we are talking," said Luke. "Something of value—something useful. There undoubtedly will be some dumbfounding surprises, winds of fates, and embarrassing cracks in profit. But I tell you another thing, the best ways to know whether the fruit of one's labor has value is to try selling it on the marketplace."

James Miller stared at Luke coldly, listening to every word. "Now, I clear the kingdom—you're right. The whole key is to provide the customer with what they want. Now you take Mary J, helping others is woven into the very fabric of her soul."

"Generally speaking," said Cleveland, "a business person has to consider risk when engaging in a new idea. However, the things we typically risk our lives for are seldom worth the chances."

Pap spoke quickly, as though he had only been waiting for an opportunity. "Only if Mary J would lighten up a little bit in extending credit."

Luke turned and then looked Pap straight in his eyes. His voice became an icy drawl as he proceeded to speak. "You and Mary J lack the imagination to use the great strength of credit. Instead of defining the world, use your imagination for goodness sake."

Cleveland turned suddenly towards Luke, and said, "What in the devil does imagination have to do with credit decisions?"

Proud of himself, Luke said slowly and calmly—stamping his right foot: "There you go—so now, let's face the elephant in the room. Here's what I mean—compassionate actions are out of place for those in the credit business. When it comes to credit, I haven't any feelings or scruples in this world. All I have is the itch to make money. I will allow a person to miss three payments; then, someone may lose their land. I do not play being a Good Samaritan with crooks trying to steal my products. Because I am against crooks, this doesn't mean that I will not help a stranger. In my business, I use the principles of imaginative credit." Luke laughed sarcastically; then, he said: "You can't lose with an imaginative mind and common sense!"

James Miller looked at Luke in shock, immediately pulled out a handkerchief and blew his nose. "But Luke… my first cousin Mary J is a good Christian. The Bible teaches us to practice basic generosity within our community"

Luke became so emotional that he stood up. "Now listen to me," he roared, "that's the problem! Credit has always been a corrupt system. People during biblical times voluntarily sold themselves to creditors to work off their debts. Now, your preachers teach all of you to be Good Samaritans. But now, I do rational thinking, what there is of it; especially, before I give my store products away to thieves and liars. Like they say: 'Never trust a hungry dog to guard your smokehouse.'"

James Miller laughed out loud as if Luke had said something, especially humorous. "Now... I clear the kingdom; the devil will not get a free lunch from Luke's store."

Oscar's voice rose to a point between hoarse whisper and shout. "My man Luke, let me get this straight: what is the connection between a credit system and a slavery system."

Turning, Luke looked directly at him. "That's right Oscars, as long as the credit system flourishes as the basis of our economy, slavery will be the keystone of social progress—

Pap jumped in, waving both hands up and down. "Here is the proposition. The practice of making immoral loans that unfairly enrich the lender needs a re-examination as unchristian. A loan for food that take people's land is too excessive. Luke's type of credit is like a mosquito feeding on your blood. But I do grant him one thing, people intentions aren't always clear. Sometimes the answer needs to be, not only No, but heck, no."

An excited stimulation ran through the group as if horses were coming onto the track. They stared at each other with open-mouths, shining eyes—roaring with laughter. This group continuously mixed fun, pleasure and business together. There was always a spirit of entertainment in their midst. A burst of childish laughter would begin over and over again from nearly every opposing statement.

"But Now Pap," said Luke, "Mary J has been too kind with all of her friends and neighbors. I give it to James miller; she has tremendous popularity with all groups of people, the old, young, sinner, and even the so-called holy people. My wife and I love her to death. But when it comes to credit, Mary J should only grant credit if there is an expected profit, the devil with popularity. Before I let people rob me of my hard-earned dollar, they can burn in hell with the devil."

"In other words, Luke," said Oscar, "Mary J isn't running the community welfare center."

The group again overflowed with laughter.

"I clear the kingdom," said James Miller, "I am with Pap because it's funny to think that a person could lose their land for a few bags of groceries."

"Well, now," said Cleveland, "Luke and the slave-traders aren't too far apart."

Everyone picked up laughter again.

"Now Pap!" Luke said. "You and Mary J can go broke messing around with credit. You can't be listening to these knuckleheads!"

Cleveland hanged his head down, shaking it as he stared at the floor for a quick moment—then lifted his head again. "So, Mary J is in a dilemma because if she refuses credit, she makes neither profit nor loss. If she offers credit, there is a probability that the customer will default. She then will lose the cost and profit on her merchandise."

Pap's face darkened righteously. "Charging interest is a sophisticated way of enslaving people. Using collateral to secure loans is a way of stealing people's land. My wife and I will not do these things to our friends and neighbors."

Luke stared at all of them with wide eyes. "Well then, get the devil out of the credit business. If you get credit from me, you are going to give me interest or collateral. I will do both if I can get away with it. Some people are just plain stupid. I have acquired a lot of properties using this method. You need to get them before they get you, that's my philosophy."

"So, I see now," said Cleveland. "The evil genius of the credit system becomes evident when one considers that a poor man may work twice as hard to buy something... in which a rich man may easily afford—despite his idleness, by taking advantage of someone else's toil."

"The rich man is not simply putting money to work," said Oscars, "he is putting his slaves to work. People need to understand the danger of becoming additive to credit. When a person starts running their life through credit, it becomes the devil's quicksand. A hole that keeps getting deeper until it kills a person financially."

Pap chuckled, then expanded Oscar's point of view. "A coyote is good at tricking other animals, but he is always getting fooled himself. Credit may express signs of pleasure for a season but it also shows how easy it's to be fooled."

Cleveland nodded his head. "Believe me; I have been there!"

Luke suddenly recognized the time. "It's almost ten o'clock; I need to get out of here."

James Miller and Cleveland had to go as well. Everyone gave thanks to Pap for sharing his special meal. They left cheerfully and full of spirit. Just another day that these men came together to discuss community issues. These types of discussions were common practice throughout the week.

Pap began thinking of a way to deal with his wife and the store credit issues. He started reasoning along these lines; perhaps we should examine our credit records to determine which customers are most likely to default. For example, if ninety percent of our customers have been prompt payers, we need to get rid of the ten percent that are slow payers. There is nothing wrong with the prosperity that Luke was talking about, especially when rightfully gain.

As Pap walked towards the store's front windows, he stopped to stare at several birds roosting together on his gas pumps. Suddenly, a bright streak of light shot across the sky. The birds on the gas pump just quickly flew away into the great beyond, speedily towards the clouds. Pap began connecting the idea that people were like birds—intensely emotional—bound together by a common destiny. Nevertheless, one conclusion was final for him. His wife must stop clinging onto dark clouds with credit terms too generous for any business.

Chapter

27

BELOVED COMMUNITY

E arlier the next morning, Mary J heard from Cindy about Pap and his friends' degrading comments on handling the store's uncollectible accounts. She wasn't only restless this bright morning after her husband's big dinner party but now experiencing an unfamiliar melancholy mood—harboring a dark forecast. Regardless of pride or stupidity, this tore her up inside. She felt abandoned in a pit without loyal friends.

Refusing to crawl around with her tail between her legs, Mary J began mentally to rationalize the situation concerning credit terms. *Some accounts will almost certainly never be collected—how in this world can those fools think that my store uncollectable should be zero. They need to perceive things differently. If we deny them credit, they will certainly take their business elsewhere. The folks in our community have a high probability of paying their bills, but if you want to know the truth about it, they just got bad luck. Most of them lose everything they try to do. What should I do—let our relatives, neighbors, and friends starve to death?*

As usual, Mary J's light steps came along the invisible pathway between the house and the store. As she approached the side entrance to the store, Pap was preparing to switch from the store to the farm. There was dead silence between them for a minute. Regret and grief and guilt merged into a hard, hot lump in her gut. In her mind, she could hear Pap already telling her: '*You have to learn how to determine the probability of outcome when giving out credit.*

Pap felt that something was wrong—even more problematic than it had appeared from a distance. He looked towards Mary J with an air that gave a sudden strength to his face. He waved his hands around in the air, then gave a dry chuckle. "When the road of life takes those crooked turns. We must find ways to push unpleasant thoughts from our minds. By working together to understand our store credit problems, we can find new ways to help our community."

Mary J stood still for a moment, listening—then, she resumed moving towards the side door entrance; her breathing had begun to make noticeable rasping sound, like a small file on softwood. She yells out to him: "Do I look like a fool?"

As Pap opened his mouth and spoke, his voice was as peaceful as winter rain dripping past a bedroom window. He took several steps towards her—caught her arm—pulled her inside the door. Pap then reached for her with a beautiful smile: "No, I am."

As Mary J entered through the side door, she reached for a broom to sweep the floor. "Pap, I got work to do. Nobody cares about all the foolishness that you; Luke, Cleveland, and Oscar were chitchatting about yesterday. Cindy overheard you and your friends talking about me."

Pap smiled with an easy laugh, reassuring Mary J that sometimes things may get mixed-up. He paused to give himself time to think, then replied, "You are wonderful, but the pathway to goodness lies in searching for everything. We must seek truth to determine reality. Only in this way we can see the big picture."

A dark look flashed over Pap's face for a moment. His stricken soul poured forth a lamentation. He felt utterly unsure as to what was coming—thinking that Mary J's behavior was as mysterious as land plants found flowering in a pond. He quickly walked out of the side door along the path behind the store. He got inside his truck, then drove-off towards Fisher town.

Right after Pap took-off, James Miller drove up in front of the store. He got out of his truck and walked towards the front entrance. As he entered the store, he saw Mary J cleaning up. He said in a teasing voice: "Snap it up; I need some service this morning."

As she concentrated on her work, there was a somewhat strained laugh that came from her without looking up. Mary J turned towards him, lifted her head: "Strange how people will rush head-on into evil and then try to think up ways to escape after the crime. Cindy told me how you all were talking about me in here yesterday."

James Miller hated seeing the pain in her eyes. He couldn't understand what was making her so miserable. Now his instincts were at war. After walking quickly to the counter, he tapped his fingertips together—trying to think of some comforting words. "Now you know Luke will not help these people around here unless they sign over their land. You got to extend credit unless you want people to go hungry."

A look of annoyance flitted across Mary J's face before she returned a reply. "Now, for you all information, Luke's words are the real dust in the wind. He is talking like a blind man fumbling in the darkness. Tell me, how can you take people's land for a bag of grocery?"

James Miller nodded as if her words were very logical. "Yes, he said judicially, I can see your point. Luke certainly is a blasphemer against loving your neighbor as yourself. I swear the kingdom, now that's the truth!"

After smiling companionably at one another, Mary J chirped. "In the old days, our parents and grandparents had enough food so that no one in their community went hungry. I intend to make sure no one goes hungry in my community. This store is my little vineyard, where I carry out the Lord's work."

After thinking about it, James Miller smiled again: "I clear the kingdom, you're right! Our parents had a big garden, along with all types of berries in the backyard. We also had fruit trees such as cherry, apple, pear, and even peach. Your Mother Ada loved to cook and feed the hungry, especially little children wandering around hungry. She even fed hoboes drifting through the community."

"You know," said Mary J, "my mother would be singing the vineyard song, especially as she was cooking and feeding desperate souls during the Great Depression."

James Miller shook his head. "God Knows, Your Mother Ada could sing that song. Please sing it for me, right now; you know you can do it!"

Mary J stiffened her spine and stepped forward with a refreshed heart. She began singing the vineyard song so beautiful that a little tear came into James Miller's right eye. A song that not only characterized Mary J's Mother Ada but also symbolized her spiritual journey. Mary J voice sounded like an angel from heaven to him, particularly as she was singing the chorus line lyrics:

"O' Lord, I'm your child, I will go into thy vineyard, and I will work there until you come. "Stand by me, Lord, stand by me, I will go into thy vineyard and wait there until you come."

James Miller started getting happy right along with her—just like the old days. Mary J was waving both hands with a steady voice. James Miller said silently to himself: "This is what Pap needs to understand about his wife, the reason why she extends credit to desperate and poor people. There is only one conclusion; she sees herself working in the Lord's vineyard."

Silence suddenly fell upon them—a stillness that brought something special into their memory from the past. Singing the vineyard song for Mary J's was like therapy. Just like her mother, she loved serving and caring for her community. Singing and serving her community was all she had to hold onto from past memories of her mother's disposition.

Mary J fixed her eyes on James Miller, "our parents worked together to make our community a better place. It's only through suffering together as a community that we all grow stronger. Our actions in the present will always determine our future. We must counteract the shameless intrigue to conform to our merciless social remedies."

"Now," said James Miller, "I swear the kingdom you right! A community should unite through a bond of love. The most important characteristic of angels is not that they have the power to exercise control over our lives, or that they are beautiful, but they work on our behalf, just like you and your husband."

Mary J frowned slightly, then said, "Listen! I think it's no accident that Jesus had the same kind of difficulty talking about his kingdom that we have speaking about our community. His kingdom is the closest equivalent there is of a true and beloved community. If church folks don't love their community, they need to get out of the religious business."

James Miller looked thoughtful., "Well, I'm like you. Jesus told us that his kingdom was in the midst of us. I believe the best way to find God is through a loving community. People must play a role in their economy, even if it's just raising their children with good manners."

"Now that's the point," said Mary J. "Everyone who works contributes something to a community and its economy. Believe it or not, we should begin teaching our children good manners starting at birth to guarantee acceptance within the community."

"You right," chuckled James Miller. "Children with gracious manners produce loving personalities. On top of that, our business community is like living near an ocean; it provides us with many resources. If the people of our community have loving manners, we can all enjoy those benefits together."

Mary J said teasingly, "now hear me clearly—that includes credit so poor folks can eat a decent meal!"

Mary J and James Miller just laughed and laughed, knowing this credit business was driving Pap mad. They looked at each other through some childhood flashbacks. Suddenly James Miller jumped up, "I'm getting the devil out of here before Pap gets home!" He buttoned his coat, cocked his hat jauntily, laughed again, and then strolled out the front door to his truck. He then just drove away.

Mary J began thinking that maybe Pap was right about their slow-paying customers. She could still hear his voice: *'therein lies our problem... payment my dear—we need some money!'* She couldn't help considering how Pap had given them the benefit of the doubt, yet their unreliability always caused him a great deal of anxiety. Thinking about her own experiences, she knew that Pap had struggled in every way to help his family stand tall. So, when the store didn't make a profit, his other businesses made up the difference. The reasons for Mary J were now bright as sunshine. The store aging uncollected credit accounts were affecting not only profits but also their family team spirit. She began thinking, *we have to play as a team, there's not much room for prima donnas.*

Unexpectedly a cat passed by, Mary J's mind instantly snapped out of her preoccupation. It dawned upon her that a black cat had crossed over her store-front. She began thinking that no matter how depressing things are now, *could things get worse? The world couldn't be so bleak. My goodness,* she thought, *life is just like a chick pecking slowly within its egg, slowly cracking it.* She couldn't help thinking what her husband always told her. *'There is no need to put a live chick under a dead hen.'*

Chapter

28

A COMMUNITY
FADING AWAY

The next morning somewhere around 5:45 a.m., Pap and Mary J were roaming throughout the house. Pap was stretching as he walked over to the window. He pushed aside the strong coarse curtain and began gazing over his ten acres of land, including the store. Bright drops of endless pelting rain flashed into view, pounding upon the unbreakable glass. Abruptly, the rain stopped for a breathing spell. The torrential downpour had somehow quickly overwhelmed the ditches and fields. The low areas had built up substantial water around the house and store.

Pap looked out of the back-porch windows only to notice that the backbreaking Earth seemed to be lying there in puddles of water. Thinking how its soil was so crucial to life, he couldn't help rationalizing that as the world becomes more urbanized, fewer people will have intimate contact with the land for their survival and prosperity. Pap thought that the Earth's soil would continue to supply people with nearly all of their food, except for what comes from the oceans. He just thanked God for the Earth's open-handed resources, hoping that societies learn to love it. *For in the end*, Pap kept thinking, *people will safeguard what they love.*

Suddenly, there was an intensely emotional man that kept knocking on the front door. He raised an enormous cry and kept shouting something unclear about his brother. Pap hurried down the hallway somewhat bamboozled over the continued banging sounds. Mary J abruptly walked out of her bedroom into the hall. She and Pap bumped into each other; they stood there in silence for several minutes staring with puzzled eyes. Mary J stepped back, discerning, breathing rapidly. She looked startled while her brain was reeling: *What's the devil Pap so furious about this early in the morning.?*

"Okay," Pap began hollering as he continued down the long hallway—assuming some bad news.

As Pap gradually half-opened the door, the man cries out—breathing rapidly: "Pap! My brother Ike had an accident this morning. I need gas to get him to the doctor. Please open your store for me."

Pap quickly opened his store after realizing that the man was apparently in fear of losing his brother. He detected the man's broken heart through his helpless eyes; his load seemed almost too heavy to bear. The man had startled briefly out of self-absorption. A painful moment for him—he was nearly reaching a breaking point. He was experiencing the ultimate fear—death of a loved one. After pumping his gas, Pap kept his voice quiet, but his eyes were warm and compassionate. He tried to fill the gaps in his thoughts with a few questions. He breathed a deep breath of humble admiration.

Pap spoke soft and gentle in a caring manner: "Nature is always active in our affairs. We'll never get away from her influence, for she is ever about us. I have found that when people let go and put themselves in God's hands, everything will be alright. When people try to do everything alone and rely on themselves, they will begin to make major miscalculations."

The man-made no answer but looked up into Pap's face with a twisted mouth, trying to hold back his tears. He shook his head several times—tears running down his cheeks. Slowly, he said in a soft voice. "I am hoping my brother's life will be spared from death."

The man quickly departed the store without giving any more information, except that a tractor had turned over on him. He stumbled back into his car. His emotions so battered the man that getting out the parking lot appeared impossible for several minutes.

Mary J rushed out to the store for more information. She had the jittery like Mexican jumping beans. "Dear me!" She gasped, "what's going on?"

Pap hesitated, then took her hand. "Ike's tractor turned over on him; it's most likely fatal considering that the brain is the control center. Death surely cuts the cord that holds us in this world."

Mary J lifted her hands; then, she let them fall on the sales counter. As Mary J took a seat, she noticed that her hands were beginning to shake with a pounding heart. "I hope it's not true."

Pap said wearily, "as the chicken grows, it develops feathers, but with humanity time will bring pain. Life isn't necessarily fair."

Mary J brooded until she reached her omega point, then her emotions exploded like a gunpowder concussion. She kept looking at her husband; the atmosphere was becoming somewhat strained. She said, "Pap! We live in this community; its happiness must gladden us; its sorrows must bring us grief."

"Oh dear," said Pap, searching for words to comfort her. "In our living world, the attempt to find order and reason is sometimes hard. A person is born, grows up, becomes mature, declines in old age, and eventually dies. I have always been strong, but now what does it matter? I am also growing old, one day, I shall die as well. Don't worry; we shall help them as we get more information."

Mary J was somewhat surprised, laughed lightly, and squeezed Pap's arm. "That's true; we are all link together. In our community, people are so closely related to one another that an evil to a single person, affects many others."

"Oh, yeah," Pap said. "It's hard to realize how much money it takes to keep alive in our community. There is generally much suffering when there is little money or when money is idle. Even our social and political activities would be impossible without money flowing through our economy."

"By the way, Pap," said Mary J, "you are right to keep telling me that every business should maintain an orderly bookkeeping system. Nevertheless, I still want to do things my way."

"Sure, you do," said Pap. "But never forget, we need good bookkeeping to maintain solid accounting information. This information will help us understand where we spent the money."

Mary J quickly dropped her gaze towards the floor; she shook her head and then smiled up at him. "I respect your cleverness. I am lucky to have found someone who works smartly with their head, but most importantly, someone who works hard with a heart. We are a winning team because we work hard with righteous hearts."

Pap looked at her, then beyond her, his eyes slowly filled with hope. He perceived her surplus of life, impatience, strength, and heart devotion through a will of her own. He just wanted Mary J to keep away from taking crooked turns. Pap was now in a state of bliss, just like a river flowing downstream.

"Well," Pap said with a short laugh, "Remember my little sweetheart, the best way to survive and enjoy life is to put things into proper perspective. You are like an apple that grows in a big orchard. In the spring, little buds form on the tree branches. Soon the buds open into beautiful flowers. Honeybees carry pollen on their bodies from one tree's flowers to another. This pollination makes the flowers produced new seeds. A small green apple grows around one of the seeds, like a protective package. The apple gets bigger, and as it ripens, turns red."

Mary J looked at Pap warmly, "If that's true, you are the honeybee of my life that gives me the pollen!"

"Under the circumstances," Pap said. "I would prefer you becoming an apple that ripen and turns red."

"Sometimes I wonder," Mary J said, after she shrugged her shoulders: "Oh, well…never mind. Let me take care of my customers."

Mary J proceeded speedily behind the sales counter. As usual, most of the customers wanted their goods on credit. The icing on the cake for Pap was when Mark Washington, the local community drunk, without a steady job, stumbled to the sales counter—looked Mary J directly in her eyes. He asked for two cigars, then said to her: "Charge it please!" He immediately took the cigars off the sales counter and slowly walked out the front door.

Pap stared at Mary J, then walked towards the side door with his hands up in the air, muttering under his breath. "I'm through with it. Mark Washington will never pay us for those cigars." He gradually disappeared out of her sight.

Mary J stood there for several more minutes after hearing her husband's words. She started fussing out loud to herself after feeling the painful hurts of repressed memory. "Pap, you got no business mixed up with my customers. Your actions are all crazy. Since civilization began, people use credit to improve their standard of living. We must stand at the forefront of change in our community—give the people what they want, even if that's credit. You are thinking like a philosopher—who is always questioning the value of knowledge—trying to draw boundary lines and issue strict warnings. But I think like a scientist, whose primary concern is with the discovery of knowledge—this means more opportunities, to make even more money."

That same night, Mary J and Pap went to bed shortly after closing the store together. Who would believe this would be their final night together? Early the next morning, Pap earthly life came to a peaceful end. Mary J heard the birds singing outside her window. She reached over for her husband Pap to only discover that the angels came and took him away. Her face hardened as sparkles went out of her eyes.

Mary J began crying weakly, tears streaming unchecked down her cheeks. She felt abandoned as if she was in a mysterious pit—struggling along in darkness and silence—wrestling within herself. Swallowing her tears, Mary J could no longer hide her grief from a shallow spirit. For her, the finality of death was fearsome, frightening, and unnatural. Death had taken her parents away when she was only a young girl; now, it has taken away her beloved husband much too soon.

Alma Tucker, her faithful friend, and sister-in-law rushed over to comfort her. She put her arms around Mary J, trying to ease her tremendous pain. Alma Tucker began shaking her head. "This whole community is already in shock by Pap's death. His departure is like an empty stage that has left a large hole within our community's very heart. There isn't a family in this community that he has not done them a favor. This community overflows with sorrow, a community that vows never to forget him. A community that realizes that this man was the factor behind your kindness to them. You and Pap's shadows will forever be cast over our community."

Mary J still weeping, "Pap was the one that fueled my dreams to become a store owner. Now, all I have left are the memories of our time together. Pap was like a glittering light reaching across an ocean that has now turned dark."

Alma Tucker drew a deep breath and said: "Well, Mary J, it's unquestionably mysterious. Your memories of Pap will forever be tangle up inside your imagination. You may even find yourself waking-up throughout the night—calling his name. You may occasionally still feel the breeze of his presence. All the same, your physical life with Pap has now passed into darkness."

The pain in Mary J's eyes was desperate. Unconsciously, Mary J's throat began tightening as she pressed her hand against her cheek. Suddenly, she felt a chill of darkness after realizing that her husband's life was now lost in the wind of time. She kept thinking how Pap had worked so hard to replace her bad debts in the store with his cash—just so, she could maintain her dreams; now, there was no other human's light to shade away her darkness.

Mary J gave a long shivering sigh, and then laid her head back despairingly upon her chair's cushion. "Only my Lord knows," she said, looking up at Alma Tucker, "the chances we took with our money to help this community. Our profits went back to our community in credit terms for the poor, feeding the hungry and uplifting widows and orphans. God's hands touched us with a beautiful purpose to serve our community. There is no doubt, Pap and I wanted to rise in this world by bringing our beloved community with us. We stood together in our community during a period of critical expansion. It was difficult—sometimes impossible—for the store, farm, and even Pap's whiskey business."

Alma Tucker turned a suffering face towards the window in deepening twilight. It wasn't easy to know what to say; she rubbed her face, thinking and searching for words of encouragement. "Certainly, you and Pap's drive for success had its cost with numerous potential failures. Yet, you and Pap offered a more balanced view of our community because of the willingness to take risks. You and Pap were visionaries and opportunists, using money purely as a tool—to express generosity, cement family's togetherness. You cannot separate Pap, the man from the courageous myths that surround his unique character. Everybody loves imitating his personality, by constantly mimicking his gestures, especially during business engagements and general conversations.

"It isn't going to matter now," said Mary J as she folded a towel and placed it upon her lap. "With the death of Pap and men like him, our beloved community will begin to fade away—so will the businesses, and our community cohesiveness. This up and coming generations of young men and women have no desire to maintain a business community or independence. They only want a good job wherein someone lay out the work for them. All of us know why entrepreneurial opportunities are usually nourished by working tirelessly to overcome obstacles, where risk is a way of life. The chain and branch stores will begin gobbling up our entire economy, in the name of cheap prices. Our community will become so weak; there will be no demand for them to reinvest their profits. They will take it all away from us: our businesses, farms, and even our land in general. Without community businesses, there is no communal economy. As you know, we have no real men left—who will defend and fight for our shared principles.

"Honey," said Alma Tucker, "you sure are right in your thinking. These chain and branch store owners won't even live in our community. They won't care if we live or die. You and Pap cared about the people that lived here. Your store out there is the last of the old businesses standing—when you close your door, it will suck the real love out of this community. Everybody doesn't go to church, but everybody came to your store to talk with one another. You and Pap gave the community a way to respond, in helpful ways, to each other's problems and concerns: a way of communicating acceptance and support, a way of modeling for our young folks."

"This is only the first glimpse of our community future," said Mary J. "There are things our young people need to learn about in this world. These young folks have no vision for our community. Believed me, the day is coming when there will be no more local businesses in our community. There will be no more Della's cafes, Luke's Beer gardens, Willie beaches, Walter farms, or the Godette businessmen; even the gardens, fruit, and pecan trees will begin to fade away. It's a real possibility that our young folks may be faced with ending relationships with old neighbors. The world outside will steal our community away, while the next-generation watch in dismay."

"You right, Mary J," said Alma Tucker. "This new generation of young people have a job mentality and not an entrepreneurial spirit. They are missing the American dream: start your own business and make your own money. Over the next few years, all of our local community businesses will cease to exist. I mean…. there won't even be any farmers."

Mary J said with a shaky voice and hands. "With the deaths of our community business leaders and unsung heroes, so goes our beloved community. They were role models for our youth to seek their advice and guidance. Their philosophy governed their actions even with a crushed hope. They were deeply concerned with important economic challenges, willingly accepting the heightened risk in front of them. They were small entrepreneurs who dreamed up ways to help their families and communities survive out of nothingness.

Leaders who have represented the voice of our community now stand in the shadows of darkness—dying off like flies."

"Mary J," said Alma Tucker, "think about your situation. You and my brother have worked hard together for many years. But for what, your children won't appreciate it. None of them will work your farmland—your store under them will someday set idle and fall apart. The people of our generation will only be able to drown themselves in tears for their lost beloved community. They will only be able to talk of memories, often repeating how fortunate they were to participate in such a dynamic and shining community. Parents regretting not being able to pass their beloved community on to their children. I surely hope one of our children write a book, so the world can see how we lived in community—on our own land—running our businesses!"

Mary J had to chuckle as she drew a deep breath of delight. "Our generation surely has been a beacon of light within this community. Our business community has survived the tough times in strides during the 40s, 50s and 60s. We had a golden age of a growing community—where one could keep track of who's who—wherein the interactions felt personal and meaningful. A community that is slowly fading into the wind of time with the deaths of its leaders. A community that perhaps will never rise again—a way of life that's now being blown away into the unknown space of time.